TRANSFERENCE

by

Jan McPeake

Dedication

I would like to thank my good friend, Sarah-Jane McLaughlin.

Without your continued support, encouragement, tears and laughter, this book may never have left my head.

Forever grateful to you.

In memory of, James Ferguson, my gentle giant and comedian.
I had your support and friendship for seventeen years, but you will be in my heart forever.

Until we meet again, my freen.

Thank you to all my family and friends that put up with me over the years and never gave up on me.

Love and kindness to you all.

transference

/"transf(e)r(e)ns, "tra:nsf(e)r(e)ns, "tranzf(e)r(e)ns,
"tra:nzf(e)r(e)ns/

Noun

The action of transferring something or the process of
being transferred.

"Education involves the transference of knowledge."

Chapter 1

I remember the first time I heard the heart wrenching, blood curling wails in the still of the night. Human desperation tearing at the injustice of life and the finality of death. I remember that first time. I didn't know it was to be far from the last.

The day had been warm and sticky, the night more so. I, like most, had the windows wide open, trying to catch the faintest of breezes. Instead, I caught the sounds coming from the McNeil's house opposite.

At first it was barely audible. Just the discord of a raised voice in the dark, but with each shout of "Wake up! Get up!" Mrs McNeil's voice grew louder and more despairing. Finally, she screamed with a single note of terror that shot me out of my bed.

Her husband's deeper tones, choked, strangled by fear, heralded a heartbreak the like of which I had never known.

I felt tears in my eyes and a lump in my throat, but God alone knew why. I had no understanding of the disaster that was tearing the McNeil's apart. I was crying in sympathy and even though the fog of sleep had been well and truly swept from me by Mrs McNeil's scream, I still felt disorientated and confused.

Moving to the window, I looked across the shadowed street. Three of the five streetlamps weren't working, their plastic lamps smashed by well-aimed catapults almost a year before. No chance of a council repair crew coming to our aid. Not in our estate. The dim circles of light cast by the surviving two lamps shimmered across a gathering knot of neighbours, pyjama and dressing gown clad, gripping each other and hesitantly making their way to Mr & Mrs McNeil's home. Slipper feet making no noise on the pavement. A group of teenagers looked on warily from beside a hedgerow. Their phones out, I hoped calling for help, but more likely recording the drama for use on some crass social media site later. A little further on, barely picked out by the farthest lamp, a man, unsteady on his feet, trying to light his cigarette but swaying and missing. He finally managed it and looked up. Our eyes met.

He'd not broken his stare when everyone and everything in the street stopped at the sound of Mr McNeil's sobbed yell.

"She's dead."

The echoes of his words seemed to bounce around the street. Growing louder instead of diminishing. The drunk, still gazing at me from across the street finally regained his momentum, raised his middle finger and lurched off. His gesture seemed to break a spell and everyone became animated again. I watched my friend Sonya, the McNeil's closest neighbour, use her spare key to let herself into the house. I heard her calling out, "Mary, it's me, where are you?" I reached for my phone and called her.

No answer. I waited a few more minutes, my tears drying, but my whole body slick with sweat. The knot of people in the street growing ever larger. The teens

2

slouching away from the adults' stares. I tried Sonya's phone again. This time she picked up.

"She's dead," whispered Sonya.

"Who's dead," I gulped. "What the hell is going on over there?" My voice so tight I choked and coughed.

"Michelle, she's dead."

I saw the bright shining face of the McNeil's four-year-old little girl. She was a gorgeous wee kid. Like all children are meant to be at that age. Cute as a button, smiling, clumsy, inquisitive. Beaming and blooming. I'd seen her only the previous day chasing their pet cat so she could give it what she called "Loves". The quick scarpering cat would no doubt have called them heavy smacks to the head. Michelle was adorable. She was healthy and well.

"What the hell do you mean she's dead?"

"I don't know why, Lauren, but there's a suitcase next to the bed and it's…" Sonya's voice dipped, her breath caught on a sob.

"What? I didn't hear you Sonya. I can't hear you. What did you say?"

Her reply was barely a whisper against the continued wails of the McNeil's. "It's full of cash, Lauren. The suitcase is full of cash."

Chapter 2

Some people think life's shit. No, it isn't. It's a magical gift. To be alive, created from nothing, to be a person, I mean it's amazing.

Forget about God, religion, evolution, apes or little green space men, I don't care how you think we got here, the simple truth is we're here. Not just us, but every living thing is here and it is all down to that vitality, that life spark that infuses everything from the one-celled amoeba to humankind's most majestic achievements. From our elusive thoughts and feelings to the permanence of our words and songs and the majesty of our dance and art. Life is so not shit. Life is amazing. The world can be shit. Politics and politicians are shit. People, even with their gift of life, can take it and make it shit. But life itself. That's precious. Or so I thought.

I'm not sure when I realised that Michelle McNeil's death had been the start of it all. Certainly not straight away. Later, much later I'd realise she had been the test case. The prototype to see how we all would react. How the masses could be controlled and fed a diet of lies and confusion. It turns out we can be controlled easily. Provided false news and kept sweet by more and more banality on our screens and in our lives. Eventually coming to question nothing that we see, other than to comment, outraged. But comments mean nothing, do nothing. Comments aren't real protests. Comments are the crying of voices in a wilderness of angst. No one reads the comments.

On reflection, what they did to us was achieved without much disruption and without much real effort. Those in charge simply changed the world to suit their needs. I was, like all my friends, relabelled. No longer the working class. No longer the proletariat. I was now referred to as a "character". A character in a game that was shaped completely by the new disease that had taken little Michelle McNeil. It was nature's cruelty in her most raw form. Not only for the way it killed its hosts, but in its exclusivity. Not that it cared for race, religion or gender. No. This disease had only one target. It would take children under the age of six.

I said nature's cruelty at her most raw. That's not quite true. Yes, she was a bitch by unleashing the disease, but what the doctors and the scientists discovered and what they managed to unleash on us made Mother Nature look like Mother Theresa. You see, once contracted, there was no cure, unless you had money and a host to take your child's place. A host like Michelle McNeil.

If you had both of those, then you could choose to blow out the candle of life in the most horrific and painful way.

Chapter 3

The night Michelle died was the start of the end for anyone that made less than six-figure salaries or hadn't got obscene amounts of money squirrelled away. She was the prototype. To gather not only information on how the public would cope, but also to see if we would revolt or if we were so diluted from reality we would accept that money was more important than lives. Unfortunately for us, it was the latter that the public accepted being spoon fed to them.

Don't get me wrong, it didn't happen overnight and there were a few that risked not only their reputation but the lives of themselves, their family and their friends to try and stop it, much to their sorrow. We were so desensitised to corruption and violence that we were blinkered by "truths" and gobbled up the "facts" like a good Sunday roast. We had given up fighting the real fight, so much so, that anyone who tried did not receive the backup necessary to suck out this deadly poison.

Our defenders, our heroes, those who could have been our best hope for survival soon gave up fighting a lost cause. Or worse, were removed from the public eye and forgotten about.

Unknown to us "characters", this new disease, this Child- Killer was to become our reality. We felt powerless in its wake as we watched the children of the poor die in droves.

Chapter 4

Paedo Organ Deterioration Disease - PODD

Origin - Japan, 2019
Affected- Children from newborn to six years of age
Cure - None known
Prognosis - Terminal or transferable
Symptoms - Acute leg paralysis followed by incontinence, hallucinations, complete organ failure, death
Progression - Forty-eight hours
Transference window - The final hour before death
Cost - £10,000,000 to initiate the transfer, £1,000,000 to the newly deceased's family

Chapter 5

I didn't hear back from Sonya that night. She left me to pace my kitchen like it was prom night and she had stood me up. I rubbed my face and pulled on my eyelashes so much so that when she finally came to my door the next day, she thought the Grim Reaper was tapping on my shoulder.

"Jeez, Lauren, you look awful," she gasped, when I swung the door open with far more force than was needed.

"Yeah, thanks, you look fucking great too," I snapped. "You were supposed to call me. It's like World War 3 out there and I'm up here at my wits end not knowing what's happening."

I realised by the look on her face, that my isolation was probably the least of anyone's worries. I relaxed my shoulders, softened my expression, took her elbow and guided her into my living room.

"Is she... is she really dead?" I whispered. I already knew the answer but I felt I had to fill the void of despair that was hanging round us like a ghost unwilling to go into the light.

"Uh, huh," Sonya replied, biting her bottom lip to stop the tremble that had set up camp there for the foreseeable future.

"There's something going on. Something dark and evil, all around us. I don't mean evil spirits or ghosts, or something that I've made up in my paranoid mind. I mean real evil, Lauren."

Her tone was sinister. Dark to the point I physically stepped back, like I had been pushed. Before I could fully process what she was saying, she grabbed my hands, squeezing them together and raising them in front of her, almost prayer like and whispered, "We need to pray and pray hard." She dropped my hands as quick as she'd grabbed them and headed to the kitchen.

In her grief and distressed state, she stuck her head under my tap, drank some water and washed her face like she was trying to remove an invisible stain. I think back now and perhaps she was. As she became aware of me watching her, bemused, she marched over to me and cupped my face.

"Michelle is dead. She was alive when Mary and Jonathan put her to bed and she was looking forward to going to the park today. She wasn't ill in the slightest, yet she died of organ failure. Every one of them, Lauren. Every organ in her body stopped working," Sonya stuttered.

"She must have been in so much pain yet she never made a noise or told anyone. The Medical Examiner can't get his head round it at all. He knows of nothing that can work this fast without her showing some kind of symptoms MONTHS before death." Sonya gasped a breath and shook her head in incredulity. "And there was a suitcase lying on her bedside table with money in it, not spare change, hundreds of thousands of pounds and a typed note with a single word." She paused, not for effect but to pant a few breaths, to take control of her voice. I waited. "It said, sorry."

My mind was buzzing. I was devastated such a young girl had died in what looked like suspicious circumstances. I was overwhelmed watching my friend having a mini breakdown and I was unnerved by the fact that someone had left so much cash in a child's room.

"I don't understand, was it an attempted kidnapping? Was she poisoned? Was it, a, a, sexual thing?" I scrunched my nose up at my pathetic attempt to solve exactly what had gone on in that room, with only the barest of information.

"I honestly don't know, Lauren. All that's certain is she's dead. There was money, the note, there were no signs of anyone having broken in and her poor body had completely stopped working. The ME is stumped and I overheard him making a phone call requesting outside help to get to the bottom of it. He wanted full body scans done, blood works, the lot." Sonya stopped talking and seemed to stare off into space. It's like she was suffering from delayed shock.

"But, the thing is," she suddenly glanced my way again. "He was ushered into a black van with Mary and Jonathan, by what looked like the military. Michelle's little body was taken as well. No one is allowed near the house and no one will answer any questions. I've tried ringing them both, but their phones have been disconnected. I'm scared this is some kind of outbreak and we are being left here to rot."

I could see that she had given this a lot of thought during the trauma of the previous night and I could also see that she was getting more and more panicked. She was close friends of the three of them; I personally couldn't connect with many of my neighbors and always referred to everyone as Mr and Mrs such and such to keep them at arm's length. Sonya was exhausted and her mind was going to pot, I mean, come on, she was describing something from one of the conspiracy shows, advocating the end of the world as we know it. That was just ridiculous.

I suddenly felt exhausted. I took Sonya's hand in mine. "Sweetie, come on over to my bed, we can both do with a rest," I soothed to her as I ushered her into my room. She was shaking with fear, or cold, or both. I pulled my blanket over the two of us and lay with her until we both feel asleep. My last thoughts were a heartfelt prayer that we would both wake up.

Chapter 6

I rubbed my eyes so hard that I honestly thought that my eyeballs would never roll back to normal and I would be left seeing red squiggles for life. As I stretched out, I was aware that I was in my bed alone, but I could feel someone in the room with me. My mind became instantly awake and even though I knew it was Sonya, I felt uneasy.

"Morning," I whispered.

Sonya stared at me. With a blanket half wrapped round her and a mug cupped in her hands, she sat motionless on my rocking chair that I kept in the corner of the room.

"They're back," was all she said.

"Who's back? The McNeil's?"

"Yeah. He's been round the block for a run and she is… she is hanging out washing like nothing has happened." Sonya sniffed away some stray tears that had snuck down her face, resting on her top lip.

"I mean really? REALLY? Like their daughter hasn't just fucking died!" She threw her mug at the wall just beside me. The cold tea splattered across my face and hair. I jumped, but Sonya didn't even blink as tiny shards flew over the room.

"Look, you need to calm down, Sonya. I know you're upset, but trashing my house won't do anyone any favours. Except maybe a furniture store."

I bent to pick up some of the broken mug, but when I cut my finger, I conceded to just use my foot to gently sweep it all into a pile at the side of my dressing table.

As I removed my sock and gingerly turned it inside out, I threw a look of confusion at Sonya, who still hadn't apologised and didn't look remotely close to doing so.

"I can't comprehend why they are acting like it is just a normal day, like their daughter didn't just die, like they don't care," she blinked some more enormous drops of salty tears.

"Sonya, I know you are devastated about Michelle's death. I am too, but people grieve in different ways and you can't just break stuff and accuse people of all sorts of crazy shit. I mean, come on here, you're practically insinuating that secret Government operatives came and blanked their memory this morning."

"Well, believe what you want, Lauren. I thought we were friends and you would have my back. I don't need you telling me I am insane when this whole thing is insane!" She gestured out the window towards the McNeil house. Then she scrunched up the blanket and threw it at me like she had discovered it was covered in maggots.

Grabbing her bag and shoes she thumped her heels all the way to my front door, but not without turning and stabbing her finger towards me.

"Just you wait and see… just you wait."

"Wha–" but the door was slammed shut before I could ask what she meant and I was left with the sound of her muttering all the way down the path.

I won't deny that it was all very odd and didn't add up but, what else can you do in times like these? Everyone knows the drill with deaths of those you know but who aren't family or close friends. You hang about your window for a while (or phone if they aren't local), you watch the news for any updates (only on suspicious deaths), you call everyone you have ever met for any significant bit of gossip, even Senga the cleaner, whom you have never said more than two words to. After a day or so you send a card, which leads up to you visiting with some food that they a. probably won't like and b. probably won't eat even if they did. You offer your condolences and say you'll help in any way you can, then leave hoping that they won't take you up on your offer because you are the worst at organising and wouldn't know where to start with a funeral anyway.

I understand that, for Sonya, she is a little more emotionally involved due to her friendship and "neighbour-ship" with the McNeil's, but, she was being extremely paranoid and ridiculous. Wasn't she?

The longer the day went, the more I started to feel guilty. The more I thought about it and the more I stalked the McNeil's from my window, the more I could see Sonya's point. They *were* acting suspiciously.

I started to wonder if we hadn't all been wrong. Maybe Michelle wasn't dead. Maybe we had taken everything out of context. Maybe the rumour mill had gone into premature overdrive and in fact, Michelle was fine. Maybe. I mean, I had just seen Father McNulty scurrying down the path clutching his bible like it contained the directions straight to God's condo. He looked flushed and preoccupied. Like someone who had just tried to console grieving parents of a dead four-year-old child however, the parents of said child were standing at their front door waving him off and smiling like

15

they were on a float at a parade. They caught me watching and gestured me over to their house.

"Oh, fuck," I muttered through gritted teeth. I smiled and gave them the thumbs up

I paced the room with my hands on my arse, patting my cheeks to a random, chaotic tune, arguing with myself that my thumbs up was non-committal and that I didn't need to go over to see them.

"Do I go over and have them shout at me for invading their privacy by watching them? To be told how insensitive I am?" I asked out loud.

"But then, they look so creepily happy, maybe Michelle is ok and they want to explain the misunderstanding?" I mused, whilst biting my nails. I puffed my cheeks out and headed to the door to put my trainers on. I continued shaking my head and whispering, "Fuck it" to myself.

As I crossed the street I could feel a hundred eyes on me, yet I could see not one soul. The air itself seemed to be bristling with eeriness and as I pulled my jacket round as tight as a strait jacket; I felt as if I was walking to my execution. My every step echoed around the street and startled me so much that I started trying to walk practically on my tip toes. I realised it made me look pathetic so I reverted to my normal stride. I was raging with myself that this was bothering me so much. I willed myself to be calm, but by the time I reached the McNeil's front door, I was practically hyperventilating.

"Lauren, do come in," Mrs McNeil waited until I stepped into the hall before putting her hands on my shoulders to remove my jacket.

"Oh, no, I won't stay," I stuttered, carefully twisting myself out from her vice like grip and shuffling into her living room.

"Thanks for coming over," she gestured for me to sit down on the sofa, next to an occasional table that was inexplicably set with a tea pot, cups and a milk jug.

"I take it you have heard the news?" She asked pouring me a cup of tea that I neither asked for nor wanted.

The room was tense. What with me squeezing my arse cheeks so tight and grinding my teeth, to Mrs McNeil pouring out tea in an overly dramatic way, to Mr McNeil, who nearly gave me the fright of my life when I saw him staring at me, silent, unmoving in the corner of the room. To be perfectly honest, I thought he was the grandfather clock, until he coughed.

"Jonathan, will you sit down! You scared the poor girl," Mrs McNeil laughed, a little too much than was warranted.

"Erm, well you know, ahem, I haven't heard any news. I don't actually know anything," I whispered, taking a sip of my unwanted cup of tea. "I just wanted to offer my condolences on Michelle's death, Mrs McNeil, it is such a tragedy," I managed to somehow make it sound more of a question than I intended, but thankfully that went unnoticed.

"Yes, well, we were devastated at first, losing our precious baby girl, but now that we know she died for the greater good, we are at peace," Mrs McNeil smiled a strained smile as Mr McNeil scoffed incredulously. Hardly even waiting for her to finish her sentence, I piped up, "I completely understand and agree with you." This was a big mistake.

You see, this reminds me of an old friend that says no one truly listens to the words another person is saying, they just wait until it is their turn to speak. This was a perfect example of this because; I thought she was going to say Michelle had gone off to a better place. Not that I believe that, but I know it is used worldwide and recognised as an acceptable thing to say when someone has died; to bring comfort to those affected. As soon as I said it, several things happened: 1. Mrs McNeil relaxed her shoulders a bit and her face softened 2. Mr McNeil's eyebrows looked like they were having an affair together 3. I cringed because my response didn't make any sense at all and 4. I blinked many more times than was necessary because I couldn't decipher what Mrs McNeil was talking about. What greater good?

"So, you know about the plan?" she gasped at me, "It feels so good to be able to talk to someone who understands," she was almost breathless.

"Oh, erm, yes of course I do, you can talk to me anytime," I croaked. My heart was beating so hard I thought it was going to burst out my chest and my head was spinning like the waltzers at the fairground. I knew I had to leave, because I had no idea what this plan was and I didn't want to. Yet, something kept me from making my excuses and rising from the sofa. I swallowed hard and decided to wing it.

"So, you're happy with the plan?" I asked, gripping my hands together to stop their shaking from being noticeable.

"HAPPY?" Mr McNeil shouted at me and then stormed into the kitchen.

"Please excuse him, he is still in shock. He doesn't give a flying monkey's about the greater good or the money, he just wants Michelle back. I mean, we all do, but we need to move on. For everyone's sake," she sniffed as though she was going to breakdown, but then recomposed and gave herself an inside talking to, nodding that she understood.

"And what did they tell you were the plans for the greater good?" I asked, hoping it came across as concern and not that I hadn't a clue what was going on.

She looked up at me and held my stare for what felt like hours, when in reality, it was only about half a second. That half a second glance was enough for her to decide that I was in on the secret and she continued.

"Well, they explained that PODD," she gestured to me, looking for agreement to continue.

"PODD, yes," I nodded.

"Well, they explained what it is and even after numerous studies and research into the disease, they still can't pinpoint the trigger. All they know is that it affects children, wealthy children, children that are going to grow up and make a difference to the world. Hopefully find a cure for PODD so the transfers are no longer needed, you know?" she was looking at me like she needed my approval.

"Absolutely," I nodded.

"They told me Michelle died peacefully after the transfer, felt no pain and the £1,000,000 can help us try to move on in comfort. I know you must be thinking how terrible a mother I am, but, it has already been done and to be honest what can I do anyway? I don't want to die; I can't fight it like Jonathan is trying to do. We need to accept it for what it is or her death has been for nothing."

I could see she was saying the words, but her conviction was empty. She didn't believe a word of it. She was heartbroken and wanted her baby, but she was scared for her own and the rest of her family's safety if she pushed any further.

I couldn't risk asking anymore without raising suspicion that I had not one iota what she was talking about.

Would she alert someone that I knew? Would I be next? I had to get out of this house.

Mrs McNeil must have read my mind to some extent, as she jumped up, interrupting my panic ridden thoughts.

"They said they have completed the transfers a few times but, Michelle was the first to be done this way, you know, in public. Not that it will be advertised; it will just become an unspoken way of life. Something that goes on in the background that we can't do anything about, like…" she seemed to grapple for the right words. "Like how we continue to send money abroad to help starving children, yet we let our own people starve and be homeless. It will be added to the other great injustices that is actually a catch twenty-two, no one wins, but unless you are a millionaire, no one cares," she was starting to look really sad, like she regretted not trying to fight this.

"I'm really sorry, Mrs McNeil I have taken up enough of your time. Please do let me know when Michelle's funeral is and I of course will be there." I stood quickly and almost tumbled over the table.

"They want everything tidied up relatively quickly; they have chosen MDs, florists and funeral directors that step in with PODD cases, so, she will be cremated tomorrow. I would have preferred a grave to visit but, I can understand that her body needs to be disposed of safely in case any disease remains," she looked down again, subtly distraught.

I gave her a hug and said my goodbyes, but stepping out into the street, my head was spinning. It took all my strength not to throw up into Mrs McNeil's roses. If it wasn't for Mr McNeil being present and unable to hide his anger, I would have thought she was in some kind of post-death psychotic state. I had to find Sonya.

Chapter 7

I opened a bottle of whisky and popped a straw into it; there was no way I was going to stop drinking long enough to put the lid back on.

Sonya wouldn't return any of my calls, despite me leaving her over twenty voicemails and thirty texts. I prayed nothing had happened to her but the panic began to rise in me. A long sip of the familiar Scottish whisky calmed me down somewhat.

I kept playing the conversation over and over in my head; you could see Mrs McNeil was devastated by Michelle's death and everything that has transpired thereafter, but it seemed she had convinced herself that she was right, what could she do? My mind starts to wander and wonder. Who exactly are "They"? Is it the government? Is it a terrorist group? Is it just a bunch of rich people buying their way in life? The most logical way of thinking is that it was indeed the Government. I mean, if it was a terrorist group, it would have been heard about by now and the Government would be doing all they could to eradicate them. If it was a bunch of rich folk doing as they pleased, the police wouldn't be able to cover it up at all. Hiding the death of children? No way. And who are the only people that we cannot fight against? Who can do as they please to protect themselves? Who already manipulate the people into thinking their way via the news and press? The Government, that's who.

To be honest, I am not as surprised as I thought I would be that they would kill people as a means to an end to suit them and their socialite chums. I am more scared than surprised. Scared because I am not part of the elite. If ever there was going to be mass genocide again, the odds were always going to be high that I was on the shitty side of it. I didn't have millions handed to me. I didn't have a lucrative job. I wasn't part of the political "in" crowd and I didn't have friends in high places.

"The writers" as we later called them, were slowly but surely taking over the world. Most of us could see it, but we were just "characters" in their little script called life. It was almost as if they had prodded us towards a dark tunnel and only a few dared to look around to see their full surroundings. What was the point? The truth would either fill you with anger, making you fight a losing battle or fill you with so much despair and aguish that you could no longer live anyway.

Still, it was a new low they had reached. They were now publicly displaying their feelings towards us; arrogance, believing we would accept money over love. Disdain, not caring whether we lived or died. And now, they even get to choose who dies specifically, not just any old one of us, but the purest and innocent of all, our babies.

I can't even comprehend how their children feel about another child dying to enable them to live; do they feel guilty that they have cheated the natural order of life? Or have they adopted the same egotism and sense of entitlement as their parents and peers? I already know the answer, which makes me shudder causing bile to rise in the back of my throat.

Actually, I am unsure if the bile was caused by the thought that people's lives are being rubbed out like an unwanted smear on a newly cleaned window, or, if it was the fact I had drunk almost half a bottle of straight whisky in the afternoon.

My phone buzzed and startled me, making me spill some of my drink on my legs, much to my annoyance. When I looked over and saw Sonya's smiley face looking at me with a happy tune trilling out, I pounced to answer it before it rang off or went to voicemail.

"Sonya?" I asked, as if I expected someone else to be phoning me from her phone.

"I heard you were at the McNeil's, do you believe me now?" she asked in almost a vindicated tone.

"I'm sorry."

"I bet you are. Did you get the story about PODD?"

"I did. She thought I knew about it. I didn't correct her."

"By this time next week, they will have concluded their investigation into how people and the public will handle this power shift. Some people are so desperate, Lauren. They will accept £1,000,000 for a child. Do you know how many people will deliberately get pregnant for this? Women will be raped and held hostage. For some people, it is like the new age lottery."

"I didn't think I could weep for humanity any more than I did," I sighed.

"Yeah, well, you were wrong. What do we do now?" Sonya asked, intrigued.

"We get sterilised."

Chapter 8

When it circulated online, it was brushed off as a hoax, propaganda created by the poor and uneducated to get a rise from the big wigs. Even when they pulled out witnesses that it had happened to, they were called "out of their depth" actors. For a while, the tables were turned, the families were persecuted by the media moguls; it was probably the only time they were glad to have the money, to run away from it all.

It didn't last long of course, there was no way on this green earth that they could hide it forever. It was just a case of slowly feeding it into main stream media until it had reached an acceptable level. It was most certainly not all plain sailing. We as a race seemed to experience the seven signs of grief in regards to how it affected us:

Shock

I think we were most shocked that in the end, the writers ended up confessing live on TV what they had been denying the whole time. The speculation was rife, the allegations ranged from spot on, to the downright crazy, bonkers, acid taking realms of disturbed. They thought it was better to take the removing a plaster approach. Once the drip feed approach was no longer helping their cause their plan was to unleash the truth onto us in one fell swoop

Everywhere you went people were constantly asking, "So, what do you think?" and you knew exactly what they were referring to.

Denial

It didn't matter that the writers themselves had crawled out from under their rock and confirmed it all to be true, with no show of shame. Or that there was a list of confirmed transfer deaths on their online forum. Some people still refused to believe it was happening. It was so surreal; it was almost as if the nation was divided about who they were supporting in a football match.

Anger

Once it became evident and abundantly clear that this was no hoax, the characters finally woke up, and boy were they fucking angry. Protests before this seemed to look like teenage house parties in comparison. Buildings were vandalised, streets were wrecked and people were kidnapped/tortured or killed. Friends became enemies. You could trust no one, and no one trusted you. All hell had broken loose here on earth and it looked and felt like the end of days for humanity.

Bargaining

This was probably the most disturbing phase to be part of, mainly because no one had anything worth negotiating. It was simple, if you weren't part of the writer's club, the only thing anyone wanted, was unfortunately your child. This conjured up some evil and twisted plans that caused desperate and sad people to conspire in vain hope that their child would be left alone.

It was horrific enough that your child was on the radar of rich untouchables, but to also be a target not only for other desperate parents, but money hungry scumbags that did not understand the process. Well, to be frank, no one understood the process.

Everyone thought that anyone that had a child in their possession was automatically entered into some kind of draw, like a raffle ticket at a summer fete. Kids were being sold by struggling or desperate parents to greedy individuals hoping to have their "number" pulled out of the bag. Others were being kidnapped by money-grabbing gangsters and held captive until they either gave up waiting and let them go, or killed them out of frustration because the plan wasn't working.

It was also known that some families were smuggling their children away to relatives with adequate room to hide them. This also failed, as there were monthly sweeps, not dissimilar to the Germans hunting for Jews. Any children found that were not shown on the Births Register for that address, were removed from the premises and returned to their immediate family.

It became apparent over time, that there was in fact no rhyme or reason to the choice of the transferee. There were two electronic lists. Any person or persons that had money of more than six-figures were inevitably entered into a database marked as transfers, as were their family. It meant that their family's children would never be chosen to be a transferee. The other list was of the transferees, which basically meant all the remaining poor buggers' children. The symptoms of PODD where so precise in the order in which it attacked i.e. acute leg paralysis, incontinence and then hallucinations. This alerted the family to act swiftly in reporting the infection to their designated PODD registrar. The PODD registrar would then activate the transferrer as being contaminated with the disease, thus initiating the database to search out a transferee that was of the same age and locale. Once located, the system would automatically transfer £1,000,000 to a transfer holding account, which then triggers the vault administrator into action. He must remove £1,000,000 cash from the vault and place it into a briefcase, alerting the transfer team there is a job to be completed.

It is all done so seamlessly, so quick and so, dare I say it, professionally that no one even knows that this is going on in the background.

Because there is only a short time from diagnosis to transfer, the writers must have already paid the £10,000,000 fee upon joining the list. This covers a range of things from being on the list itself, to paying agents to locate the transferee, sedating the family to allow the transfer, completing the transfer and finally disposing of the remains once cremated.

Depression

There was so much to be depressed about it is hard to know where to start. I mean, we were the epitome of being under a microscope. Our civil rights and basic human rights had been removed. Our children were essentially being ripped from us against our will to be murdered and we were being compensated for the inconvenience, like they were buying the last bottle of wine for a party and handing us a bottle of pop to apologise.

The questions and conversations between young couples in love were no longer "Can we afford a child? Would we cope? Could I go back to work or stay at home?" No, they were now replaced with one single question. "Can our heart cope with the devastation if our child was taken from us?"

The risks had shifted from wondering if you could still go partying once a month and could you afford part time work; to could I live with myself that my yearning for a baby effectively puts a target on its back?

You were selfish back in the day if you didn't want children. It was what we were here to do; childless couples were seen as irresponsible and pointless to being alive. Now, the tables had turned. Couples that had children were now selfish, bringing a child into the world where there was a risk they would not see beyond the age of six, who the hell did you think you were you to make the decision to create a short-lived life?

Every time a child laughed, everyone around them smiled briefly, until they remembered it could be the last day that they laughed. The sadness tinged everyone's eyes like a cloud of helplessness; the atmosphere was like a dust blanket thick with depression. It was as if literally everyone on the planet had lost the ability to feel anything except anguish. Oh, sorry, everyone except the writers they were untouchable.

There was also so much hatred for the offspring of the writers because, well, you never knew if they were alive because your friend/nephew/brother had died. Even if it was someone you didn't know, the thought that they were possibly walking about because another child had perished made it difficult not to punch them in the throat.

Testing

This stage is when people started to move towards the road to acceptance; they were at last on their way out of the mire. Even in the pit of depressive despair, reality eventually started to bite and people realised they could not stay in the deep, dark hole forever. They started looking for realistic things to do or experiments to see if anything could help the situation in any way. As this activity started to work, in some ways, it was found to be preferred to the depression and so people were crawling and pulling themselves back to life and away from the epidemic of grief.

Acceptance

We were unaware at the time, but we had all finally shifted into the acceptance stage without knowing that we ever could. We were so convinced that the rage and hatred that burned into our very soul would keep flickering like a star deep in the night sky. It was inconceivable that we would ever stop fighting against this injustice and horrifying treatment wasn't it? But, we did.

Our voices became quieter, our resolve became a shadow of its former self and our determination to overturn this new empire became jaded. As disgusting as it sounds, we were exhausted fighting a war that we just could not win. Our soldiers were tired and emotionally destroyed, we were no longer living life and we were wasting it with constant battles, like we were fighting against the grim reaper himself. Transference was our new inevitability, a new tide in our life that we could either surf in or drown.

We pretended that we still had a choice in how we lived. We could accept it or fight it. It was the only way that we could survive, believing it was *our* choice to give in and embrace our new reality.

Thankfully, to the writer's convenience, the majority of the population flowed into the acceptance stage without much commotion. There was a few that sadly succumbed to complicated grief, which is like being in an on-going, heightened state of mourning that keeps you from healing. Those tortured souls that could not move on, sadly, took their own lives and saved the writers the effort of having them disposed of.

Chapter 9

As the days turned into weeks, and the weeks turned into months, it became apparent that the government had every intention of trying to slot this into our lives like a new cancer.

Everywhere you went, there were posters seeking charity donations or begging for fundraisers to help boost the PODD research fund. Our NHS was already on the brink of collapsing before PODD had come traipsing in like a last minute, unwelcomed guest at a house party. They were strained as it was from being constantly looked over by our government for ludicrous, money wasting and elaborate proposals that benefited their lifestyle, and their pockets.

I always felt that if the NHS was to be summed up by a metaphor, it would be the girl in the pub sitting alone reading a book and drinking a gin and tonic. No ice. She was naturally beautiful and had a warm smile that, if you caught a glimpse of it, would leave you feeling safe and content. She would be reliable and fit straight into your life with the full approval of your family and friends. The relationship would be secure and you would live a full and happy life together with no regrets about anything. When you died, she would be there to hold your hand and kiss your lips before softly whispering, "I love you" one last time as you departed on your next journey.

The government, on the other hand, would be a man that walked into said pub, straight past the girl reading her book, with such an air of arrogance, that he would tip her glass over without even noticing. As patrons rallied round the girl to assist her and shout contempt at the man about how rude and disgraceful he was for tramping all over someone so precious, he wouldn't bat an eye.

He would make a beeline for the bleach-blonde, size zero, glossy-lipped dolly-bird sitting at the end of the bar with a hoard of men around her. He would wave copious amounts of money around, that she could sniff out like a blood hound and fondle his car keys wide eyed like a child with a new toy.

His family would beg and plead with him not to waste his time and money on her and concentrate on someone like the gin and tonic girl. He would scoff at the thought of her and continue to put all his efforts and attention into bimbo girl, much to the annoyance of his disgruntled peers.

Everyone around him would try to defend him and back him up in his poor choices however, it would become increasingly difficult not to be embarrassed and disappointed in him. One by one his support would dwindle and all he would be left with were reminders of his repugnant and sometimes criminal behaviour. He would eventually die by the bimbo's hand as she decided to betray him. She would not grieve as she was already looking for her next victim to cast her spell on and dazzle into incompetence.

Let's not get confused here; PODD only appeared to affect wealthy children and not the general public. Was it some new unknown organism that was lurking in one of the many random and luxurious food delicacies of the rich? Was it burrowing into them from deluxe materials from far travelled cities? No one seemed to know. All we did know was no one over the age of six was ever affected by it.

There was a mass burning of Almiya wool by the writers in their desperation to expose the culprit of the disease. The wool from Almiya is the most expensive wool in the world because the animal can only be shorn every ten years. The fabric can be used for apparel and home décor. The Almiya wool ranged from £5,000 - £10,000 per yard, so a scarf would cost around £20,000, and it was the "in" thing at the time PODD raised its ugly head. So, as it seems, were Almiya wool socks for the poor tired feet of the rich children who just couldn''t evolve into adulthood without them.

Alongside the Almiya burning was the make shift decontamination camps that were created for Domicos caviar, and the destruction of Vocium pendants. Domicos caviar originally came from Kuwait which made it rare and extremely expensive. The only known outlet was a company in Chelsea, where a tin cost about £25,000. It was soon run out of business by wealthy vigilantes a few months after PODD arrived on our shores.

Vocium was a stone that was so rare that very few people even knew it existed. It was a mineral of a silver-grey colour that had only been discovered about eighty years prior. At the time, there was only a couple of hundred of the stones in the world, costing about £12,000 a gram.

Obviously, we, the poorer of society, had never heard of such items until the writers went crazy and blamed them as the cause of the outbreak. They were so desperate to find some item in common, something, anything, that they pranced about with or ate and that we didn't. I truly believe that this bothered them more than their loved ones dying. The fact that we who were slumming it were unaffected and their money could not save them, or buy them exclusion.

Before long we had Lord and Lady Zebedee and their offspring turning up in high rise flats as your new neighbours, because they believed there was some secret we were hiding in our water supplies. They projected the sale of bottled water would plummet into the back of beyond (because you know, us poor folk didn't even know what bottled water was). When that barely budged, they started thinking it was living in close proximity of other people and not the seclusion of a manor house on a country estate that was the key.

Eventually, when we learned about transference, they ceased their mass integration and invasion of us poor kinfolk and scarpered back to the overindulgence of their contented lives.

We wouldn't have minded had they decided to mingle with us of our own free will and wanted to be part of our lives, which would never have been an issue. It was the almost instantaneous gag reflex and disdain that they tried to hide from living amongst us day to day.

The atmosphere was so thick that you could wear it as a coat whenever we had to communicate with each other. The fake smiles and garbled small talk was too much to bear at times, that we decided to start avoiding going out unless it was for work, or it was absolutely necessary. This just made the situation worse when they were convinced it was physical communication that was protecting us, so they started dropping in to borrow sugar and for daily catch ups with the neighbours and invading our personal space.

When I say invading our personal space, I truly mean invading, in every sense of the word. They became increasingly creepy and their behaviour was bone-chillingly unnerving. Have you ever entered a lift and there has been a shifty looking person in there that makes the hairs on the back of your neck stand up? Remember how you felt? You clenched your teeth so tight that you could feel a pulse in your gums. You mutter inside your head, "Oh, please, make the lift crash down to the ground and kill us all." The air around you feels like it has suddenly been sucked out the room. You struggle to take a deep breath and you honestly believe that the awkwardness and uncomfortableness is going to make you combust right there and then. Well that. That is how they made us feel each and every time they forced themselves into our company.

It was quite traumatic at the best of times for rational people however, if you had even a modest issue with slightly elevated anxiety, then you my friend, were living in actual hell itself.

If they were alone when they approached you, they would over enthusiastically shake your hand, lean on your shoulder whilst talking to you or in the worst-cases, try and embrace you for a length of time that was unnecessary.

If they came at you in a pack, it was a much more terrifying and traumatic experience as they all wanted a piece of you. Talking at you in unison like clucking hens round the only available cock in the farm. They would circle you until your head was spinning and you prayed they would just kill you. These incidences and the aftermath of them became so severe that, the GPs and hospitals were authorised to sign people off sick from work after one had occurred. They called it transference prevention attacks, or TPA.

The police couldn't act on any of these attacks because in effect, no one had actually been physically assaulted, no matter how intimidated or scared you felt. Plus, hello! These people were the cream of the crop, the richest of the rich, who would actually dare try to have one arrested for asking how you were and being interested in you as a person? We should be grateful that these socialites wanted to mingle with us and breathe the same air. Oh, man, lucky us!

Much to our disbelief, this was the only sick note that no one wanted to scam or pretend had happened. Not because of some moral backbone people had grown, but, to put it nicely, there was no acting school out there good enough to teach you how to act out the trauma of a TPA. Especially, repeated ones.

This leads me back to the NHS and their struggle with this pandemic; it wasn't just the writers that became award winning armature dramatics overnight, it was the characters as well.

You see, before it became known who the intended targets were, and what the symptoms were, it was all kind of he said… she said. You know, "My aunts, neighbours, estranged son's hamster's adopted gran had PODD, and it was like watching an exorcism!" Information was scarce, but the whole world started contracting their own imaginary, over-exaggerated version of PODD.

Hospitals and doctors waiting rooms were crammed to the hilt with people of all races, genders and creeds, acting out a full range of symptoms. From colic to heart attacks, common colds to nosebleeds, and the odd ingrown toenail was thrown in for good measure.

When there is a crisis unfolding and the general public is trundling down the road to mass hysteria, every single minor or insignificant ailment is magnified as certain death. Pharmacies were being broken into and raided for antibiotics and tranquillisers, the reckoning being, if they couldn't kill it or at the very least keep it at bay with the antibiotics; the tranquillisers would make you not give a flying fuck what was going on. This was creating a vicious circle that was killing people, when there was no reason that it should.

This is how it carried on for a little while: People were storming hospitals with non PODD, in fact, non-emergency symptoms, this put the hospitals and staff under tremendous stress, which caused mistakes to be made and people to die. That also took the specialists away from real emergencies, which made people panic because the death rates were rising, which made people take their fate into their own hands by robbing pharmacies, which meant they took drugs unsupervised, which resulted in them either overdosing or having allergic reactions, which had them rushed to hospital, where the cycle started again. It was horrendous and horrific. So many people died needlessly. If everyone had remained calm and listened to the daily updates, it could have been avoided. But then, this is how our downfall all started… listening to the corrupt government and media to begin with, dancing to the tune they played on their financially driven fiddle.

Chapter 10

You never really know what to expect at a child's funeral. I mean, it's just not the natural cycle of life, is it? Children aren't supposed to die. Why allow a man and woman the ability to create a new life together, only to snatch it away so cruelly from their very grasp? To allow a mother to feel it's every movement as it grows into perfection. Even if it is born not perfect in the eyes of society, every child is perfect to its parents. How could it be anything but perfect? The child is a beautiful mixture of both of you, like a little cake you have blended up in the kitchen without a recipe to hand.

It doesn't matter if your baby is one week gestation in your tummy, born sleeping, or stolen from you when they are forty years of age, your child is part of you. The bond will always be there regardless, even if they are not. The pain remains with you, you could almost pass it off as hunger, until you concentrate really hard and realise and it is in fact emptiness. Not too dissimilar to someone that loses a limb, and when they close their eyes they swear it is still attached to their body. That connection may be physically severed but, they are very much still linked to you emotionally, mentally and spiritually. The devastation of your little miracle no longer being on the same mortal coil as you, is unlike any other anguish you will ever feel in your entire life.

The look of desperation was etched across the faces of Mr and Mrs McNeil like a coat of plaster that had been roughly applied. I wasn't aware that a person's face could physically change so much, in such little time, but here we were, staring at the raw pain they were feeling right in front of us.

You could almost see the last of their very soul, vacating through each tear that bounced off their jackets.

Mrs McNeil had changed her composure from when I had spoken with her last, from calm and collected, to inconsolable and struggling to stand up. She was draped over her husband, almost like a pashmina, clutching her heart as if it had forcibly been removed from her when she wasn't looking.

He was trying his best to keep her just this side of sanity but, you could see he was lost in his own thoughts, thoughts of betrayal and revenge. His eyes had morphed from having a blue tinge of warmth and cheekiness, to black pinholes of hatred. With every fake smile he offered to friends, family and nosey buggers that were offering their deepest sympathy, you could see he would rather have been cremating himself, alive.

Mrs McNeil was completely unaware of anyone or anything that was going on round about her, I truly believed that in any given minute, she was going to fold away into herself and disappear into thin air.

What do you do? Do you go over and utter some useless, cliché bullshit about how time is a great healer and she was a beautiful girl? Which, by the way, always bothered me.

What has looks got to do with anyone dying? Every, single time, a young person died, news reports and anyone that knew them always felt the need to say, "Oh, it is such a shame, such and such was such a beautiful, talented, kind person." So, what was happening here? Was it a case of not speaking ill of the dead? Was it just all beautiful, talented, kind people that died? Would it not have been so terrible for them to die if they were unattractive and unemployed?

I could never understand how the tragedy of a death was rated on how someone looked or conducted themselves. Every death is tragic and reminds us all of our own mortality, the only deaths that are harder to swallow, is those of children. Just once, I would love to switch on the news and see a report of a teenager that had been killed, and all the friends were gathered round the news reporter and one piped up, "She was a bit of a cow, and ugly as a dog's arsehole but, I will miss her terribly." Just once would appease me.

As I tentatively approach the McNeil's, I can't help but think, if I left now, they probably wouldn't even notice. It's not like a funeral has a guest book and a photographer. Well, that's not strictly true. The writer's funerals do. Centrefold story, with a detailed breakdown of the food that was served at the wake and tasteless selfies of the designer-clad mourners with the deceased. It was what he would have wanted. Of course, it was.

I curse at myself, because yet again I digress into a discussion in my own head and before I know it, my legs have betrayed me and shuffled me right in front of the McNeil's.

There was a flicker of acknowledgement in Mrs McNeil's marble-esque eyes, as she stared at me. I was unsure if this was a good thing, was it because she recognised me as a friend and felt that she wanted to embrace me or, did she think I was part of all of this and want to lash out at me?

Whatever it was, it seemed to pass through her like a ghost as she gazed off behind me as if she was admiring a painting in an art gallery.

"I'm terrib—"

"Sorry? Yes, I know, you and everyone else that has turned up today," Mr McNeil interrupted my pathetic attempt at sympathy.

He paused and looked annoyed with himself. He took a breath and tried again, "Look, I'm sorry, I'm heartbroken, I'm lost and I'm really pissed off right now. I haven't had enough time to absorb all of this, whatever "this" is," he waved with his spare hand. "Then I have hundreds of unanswered questions to chase up, from people that do not want to answer me. And finally, I have her, she is winding down like an old clock that cannot function anymore," he gestured to his wife. I winced at his words and glanced at Mrs McNeil waiting for some kind of explosion of emotion or reaction about how harsh and unsupportive he was being.

"This transference malarkey," he inhaled deep through his nose and shook his head. "I WILL avenge my daughter's death, and you, Lauren, you WILL help me."

"I will?" I said, in more of an asking permission tone. He had completely thrown me off my guard. How the hell can I help? I didn't know anything.

"I know, you know? When you were sitting in my house shooting the breeze with my wife. You had no idea what was going on or what she was twittering on about, you still don't, which means I can trust you. They haven't killed you off, so they either don't know that you know, or you are no immediate threat to them. Either way, you are an ally, and right now my only one," he pointed to the ground with one shaky finger.

41

"Please, don't drag me into this," I mouthed whilst holding my breath at the same time.

"I'm sorry, you are already involved."

"I didn't choose to be," I sniffed.

"And I didn't choose for my daughter to be murdered, so suck it up, sweetheart."

Fuck.

I backed away as slowly as was deemed acceptable from grieving parents at a funeral. I mean, running away would have looked odd. But man, did I want to run away. I wanted to kick off my ridiculous heels, rip off my tights that had somehow become a sauna for my lady's bits and head for the hills.

I had sweat forming from every single pore on my body, but it was the worst kind, it was cold sweat. From my top lip, to under my boobs and even between my toes. I was beginning to think they had poisoned my drink and as I thought that, my hand automatically rose to my throat.

"Oh, God," I swallowed hard. My head was spinning like that week I spent in Ibiza and my heart was fluttering fast, like a trapped pigeon.

"Help," I squeaked as I stumbled backwards. I could feel my throat narrowing and my pulse quickening at the same time. Panic had set in and I didn't care who was watching or how much I embarrassed myself as I fell in slow motion. There was literally nothing gracious about how I fell, neither was an ounce of grace shown as I flapped about on the grass like a fish out of water.

Sonya had been summoned over to me by panicked mourners along with a priest, presumably to give me my last rites.

"Lauren, talk to me, who did this?" she questioned as she cupped my sweaty face.

As I lay on the grass, gasping for air, my life flashed in front of me like you see in the movies. But not all the amazing parts, the shitty, non-important bits that you struggle to remember. Like the time when I was twenty two and bought the last ice cream in the shop, stepped outside, and dropped it on the pavement. Or when my work colleague didn't hold the lift for me and I wanted to beat her with a stapler.

"Sonya," I pulled her closer to my face by grabbing the collar of her shirt and her necklace.

"I am getting weaker, and cold," I shuddered.

"The ambulance is on its way," she tried to soothe me, "Try not to talk."

"Promise me, promise me you will let it drop," I pleaded, more with my eyes than my words.

"Transference?" she whispered.

"Mmmm hmmmm," I nodded.

And with that, I felt the life draining out of me as the paramedics approached and my eyes closed for the final time.

"Clear!"

Chapter 11

"I'm afraid; there is nothing else I can do, Sonya,"

"Are you sure?"

"Yes, I must call it."

I could barely make out the voices, of what I can only assume was a paramedic or doctor and Sonya. Everything sounded garbled, like I was submerged in water with only tiny fragments of the conversation able to be picked out.

It reminded me of the time when I was seven years old, at Berwick upon Tweed for a week with my family. It was our final day, and my mum had decided we were all going to spend it at the beach, picnic in one hand and raincoats in the other. We were warned on more than one occasion not to go anywhere near the rocks at the far end of the beach, but of course, seven and ten year olds know better, right?

My older sister, Sarah, had taken it upon herself to be the leader of our little beach trip, well, just of me really and plotted to sneak us away to the rocks. Thankfully, every attempt she made was thwarted by our eagle-eyed dad, who knew her every move before she even knew herself. That was, until our baby brother, Nathan, had grabbed a handful of sand and proceeded to shovel it all into his mouth like he was eating a chocolate cake.

"Oh, for goodness sake, Nathan," my mum grabbed him and tried to unclamp his toothless jaw.

"He's choking, Barbara, HE"S CHOKING!" my dad shouted, practically hysterical, grabbing him and bending him over his knee. At this point, watching your dad batter seven shades of shit out of your baby brothers back, you would expect us to be terrified. Wouldn't you? Terrified that our baby brother was dying, seeing how petrified our parents looked and not knowing how this was all going to pan out. We should have been clutching onto our mum, whilst pleading with our dad to save Nathan, and make our family happy again.

But no, it didn't happen like that. Not one bit.

Us sneaky little toerags giggled at all the commotion that was unfolding and saw this as our opportunity to flee unnoticed, and head for, as we called it, Rock Mountain. Nathan was brand new. So, in our childish minds, if he broke, mum and dad would just go out and buy a new one.

Sarah whipped me away so fast that she almost dislocated my arm out of its socket. Even when I tumbled slightly, she still dragged me behind her like a bag of washing.

"Ouch," I shrieked, "let me go, Sarah!" I held on to my arm in a sling like position.

"Shut it you!" she seethed to me and continued to drag me along to the base of Rock Mountain, where she threw me down on top of a pile of muscles. With a throbbing arm and stingy bum cheeks, I climbed behind her in fear that if I moaned, the highly strung little witch would chuck me head first into the water.

Sarah had always been high maintenance as a child. She was the oldest and I was just an inconvenience to her getting everything she wanted. She wanted mum and dad back to herself and jealousy poured out of her in spades whenever I was in the spotlight. She always made it perfectly clear that even though sometimes she did enjoy my company, she would slit my throat as I slept if she could get away with it and make it just mum, dad and her again.

Despite her murderous tendencies towards me, I adored Sarah. I would follow her around whenever she allowed me to, because the small glimpses of love from her or a rare hug made it all worth it.

Anyway, what else could I really do? Mum and dad thought her little acts of jealousy were cute, which only egged her on to act like a brat even more.

We clambered up the mountain as quick as our little legs would allow us, giggling and tripping over as we went. We didn't stop until we reached the very top, where we could see that Nathan was alive and well and mum and dad were cradling and fussing over him.

"I knew it would be ok," Sarah snorted, looking completely unimpressed that he was still breathing.

"Yeah, I know you did," I sighed. I was relived and excited to be spending some time with her alone on our secret mission.

Now, Sarah had chosen wisely that morning when she had got dressed, donning her super sturdy construction worker type boots to the beach. At the time, I recalled shaking my head at the sight of her in them as I pranced about in my much more appropriate beach wear attire. Bloody jelly sandals. I stood there feeling every shell, cockle and grain of sand through the soles of them as the cold air teased my exposed, red toes. Without saying a word, Sarah looked at me with her big, brown, smug eyes and for the first time in my life… I hated her.

As she turned and skipped away humming the most patronising hum I have ever heard, I felt a pang of jealousy that I could not skip alongside her. Instead, I had to take each step carefully, because not only had the jelly rubbed all the skin off my feet, but the jelly soles on seaweed was like walking on ice.

I remember seeing my sister dancing on the rocks looking so happy, free and smiling! What a beautiful smile she had when she wasn't scowling and burrowing her eyebrows into her nose.

"Come here, Lauren, come dance with me," she laughed and stretched out her arms to me whilst wiggling her bum.

"I'm coming, Sarah," I gushed. I was so ridiculously elated that she wanted me to share this moment of happiness with her. Together, our adventure, she wanted me by her side. She loved me!

"Wait for me," I squealed in excitement, completely losing all awareness of my surroundings and ultimately, my footing.

It was the pain that kept me from passing out, every piece of my body was in agony and I couldn't move an inch. I lay there floating in the water, like a piece of driftwood. Teasing that it was coming into shore, when in all probability, it was stealing into the depths of the unknown. I could only hear two things as I lay there. My own pulse swooshing in my ears like the ultrasound of an unborn child and Sarah screaming my name like a continuous echo.

As the water lapped over me, I felt calm and almost at one with the ocean, even though I knew this is where I would likely take my last breath. My tiny body had bounced and scraped off every surface of Rock Mountain on my way down to the sea, where I then flapped about trying to remove myself from its grip. I realised

47

that, not only was this making the situation worse, but also that I didn't want to fight it anymore.

I thought I could hear some more voices join in the panic, but I couldn't make out who it was, or even if it was just seagulls playing tricks on my mind. The sea was embracing me into its soft, silky arms and I just wanted to roll over and snuggle into it until I fell asleep.

I snapped my eyes open and was overcome by so many different emotions that were surging through me at the same time. I was gasping for air as I tried to focus on what the hell was going on. Pain surged through me like a lightning bolt, it was simultaneous and indescribable. I genuinely didn't know what body part to weep for first. My skin was red raw and shivering from the freezing cold, my lungs felt as if they were on fire and each breath was burning my throat. Confusion, panic and pain rattled through me like an old steam train but, I was also overcome with anger. Why had the sea, which had made me feel so welcome, so at home, abandon me? Did I do something wrong? To go from such love and comfort, to feeling spurned and desolate was a rejection that was hard to bear.

"How many fingers am I holding up?" a gruff voice shattered my daydream.

"I, erm, three?" I blinked to try and focus on the task at hand.

"What the bloody hell were you two thinking?" My dad raged, more to Sarah than to me.

"Did you not think we had enough to deal with, with Nathan choking to death, without you two idiots plotting a great escape from us?" You could see he was more panicked than angry.

"I'm sorry, Dad," Sarah gulped. "We just wanted to explore together, and you are always asking me to spend

·more time with Lauren…" She was almost making out as if it was their fault and not ours.

"You know fine well that is not what we meant young lady, passing the buck is not going to be accepted as a get out of jail free card."

"Maybe we should concentrate on getting Lauren to hospital," my mum interrupted, seeing the pain engraved on my now depressed face.

That trip and incident, brought our family a little closer from that day on. Sarah's guilt for bullying me almost to my death meant she became over protective of me. Sometimes too much that I longed for the days she threatened to murder me again. Couple this with my mum and dad's close encounter with nearly loosing not one, but two children on the same day; to two separate incidences I might add, made our family truly appreciated each other.

I learned over time that my succumbing to the sea was not me giving up my will to live nor was it the sea offering me the relationship it portrayed but, more of a defence mechanism.

You see our wonderful, complex and completely underestimated bodies have a natural defence that kicks in when imminent danger presents itself to us. You don't choose to cough when a piece of chicken decides to go on an adventure to our lungs instead of our stomach; the body initiates the cough to rid the little trespasser. You don't decide to make yourself shiver when you are freezing cold; the shivering reflex is triggered to maintain homeostasis. Basically, your muscles begin to shake in small movements, creating warmth by expending energy. What I am trying to get at, is my body reacted to the distress of impending drowning by generating a sense of calm. My mind tricked me into believing I was not in any danger, this allowed me to form a false bond

49

with my surroundings, keeping me calm and allowing me to remain in a buoyant state until rescued.

This is exactly how I was feeling in the back of the ambulance at Michelle's funeral, yet somehow different.

I was numb, I couldn't feel myself breathing and no one was showing any indication that they were concerned for me. Was it too late to show concern and my body was left in the ambulance until the Medical Examiner arrived? Plus, saying there was nothing more they could do and calling it, are they calling my time of death? It took me longer than I should confess to admitting, to realise there was a sheet over my face. Fucking great, I was dead.

"Look, I'm not being rude here; Sonya, but I really need her out of this ambulance."

"Yeah, I know, leave it with me."

"Like, now."

Yeah thanks for that, best friend and professional person, I'll lie here dead and you two plot to dump me out of the...

"You need to get up," Sonya said solemnly as she pulled the sheet from my dead body, startling me.

"What?" I huffed.

"You. Need. To. Get. Out. Of. The. Ambulance," Sonya replied, very slowly as if she was dealing with a mentally underdeveloped person.

"You can see me?" I quizzed.

"Of course, I can bloody see you, what is wrong with you?" she laughed, guiding me out of the ambulance whilst thanking an impatient paramedic.

"Take care of yourself, Lauren, go and have a rest." He smiled, a warm, sympathetic smile before slamming the doors shut, making me jump a little more than anticipated.

"So, I'm not dead?"

"Dead? Ha! Nope, not this time," Sonya smirked, "but you did give us all a fright."

"But I heard you talking; he said there was nothing he could do, that he was calling it..." I trailed off as I stumbled into a chair that Sonya was placing me into.

"Talk about hearing what you want to hear, sweetheart. James, the paramedic, was explaining to me that there was nothing else he could do, as in; he couldn't take you to hospital. He was calling it a panic attack. A great, big ass panic attack. You said the light in the ambulance was making you feel sick, so you pulled the cover over you like a creep. He was giving you some time to calm down and come around a little, but dying you are not." She brushed some stray hairs from my face with the back of her fingers.

"I won't lie, Lauren. I did think for a split second they were out to get you. What did Jonathon say to you to cause all of this?" she softened her face as she asked me.

"I can't remember," I lied. But, you can't lie to a best friend, can you?

"Yeah, ok," she rolled her eyes at me and pulled me close for the tightest hug of my life.

"You *will* tell me later," she wiggled her finger and pursed her lips. "With all this nonsense that's going on, I need you by my side more than ever. Don't ever scare me like that again."

"The McNeil's must really hate me, I ruined their already difficult enough funeral for Michelle," I rubbed my eyes embarrassed.

"Oh, seriously, I wouldn't worry about that, honey. Mary didn't even bat an eyelid and Jonathan acted uninterested in the whole episode. Everyone else thought you were drunk to be honest and left me to deal with you."

"Great, so I am the pisshead that ruins a four-year-olds funeral. Who phoned the ambulance then?"

"No-one called one. James is an old neighbour of Mary and Jonathan and snuck here on his break to pay his respects to Michelle."

"Well, at least I didn't waste any taxpayer's money," I quipped.

Our conversation was cut short by Mr McNeil announcing to the remaining grievers, that he would be grateful if everyone would vacate the crematorium.

"Unfortunately, as you can understand and see," he gestured to Mrs McNeil, "we are in no mood to continue this funeral, if you can call it one," he glared, at two men hiding at the back, wearing sunglasses. "There is no meal, no gathering of people to talk about how beautiful our daughter was. We just want to stay here alone for the time being and then go home to try and get our head round all of this," he kept his steely gaze.

"Let's boost, we have a lot to discuss, like," Sonya said and looked around before whispering in the same way as you do when you are talking in public about periods, "Transference."

As we waited patiently in the orderly line that had been formed to escape, Mr McNeil wasn't shaking anyone's hand or thanking anyone for coming. He wasn't acknowledging anyone at all and truthfully, no one wanted him to. Everyone was skulking out the door in liberation that they were excused from this tragic funeral. I could even see a few friends just outside breath large sighs of relief and we were just inches from joining them in the fresh air.

As we were about to pass the threshold to freedom, Mr McNeil peeled Mrs McNeil from his arm and almost launched her into a coat rack. He grabbed the back of my jacket and twisted it like a stopcock.

52

"Except you," he whispered into my ear, "You aren't going anywhere."

Chapter 12

Hostages. That pretty much sums up what we were right now. Captives, prisoners, detainees, yup, that was us alright. Well, hostages that could drink alcohol and have bathroom privileges. Ok, well we were never actually told that we weren't allowed to leave however; Mr McNeil had adopted the old crazy eyes when he man-handled me after the cremation.

He had propped Mrs McNeil up in a chair that was leaning against the wall, and she hadn't moved from that very spot. In fact, I'm positive she hadn't even blinked. The two secret spy wannabes that were previously hanging about like an unwanted fart were clearly confident that if anyone could have attempted to foil their plan, it was not going to be a drunken lush (me) or her stroppy sidekick. They skulked off giving us the chance to talk.

Mr McNeil produced a flask of vodka from a concealed pocket in his jacket. I don't usually drink vodka, especially warm vodka that has been so close to an older man's genital area that I swear I could smell his urine splashes. I could feel myself staring at his crotch area with every swig that I took and had to remind myself that there were much, much bigger issues going on here. I craved the warm, burning taste of the vodka to try and block out everything that had happened over the last day or two and prepare me for the shit storm that was still to come.

As we sat in a circle, if you could call four people a circle, passing the vodka flask round like an alcoholic's version of pass the parcel. Mr McNeil, after an age, finally cleared his throat.

"Ahem, so, if you're not against me, am I safe to assume you are with me?" he asked, squinting his eyes and pointing the flask at me like he was conducting an orchestra.

"Well, I am certainly with you just now," I attempted humour as my armour, which was not well received. Not in the slightest.

"What the hell, Jonathan?" Sonya piped up; impatience was not her strong point. "Who were the hired guns that were here earlier, are they part of Transference?"

"Will you keep your voice down?" Mr McNeil stammered, jumping out of his seat as if it had suddenly combusted underneath him. This also startled Mrs McNeil out of her grief coma. This made her blink uncontrollably whilst trying to absorb her surroundings.

"Jona… Jonathan?" she reached out to him almost tumbling out of her seat.

He rushed over to her and held her shoulders delicately but firmly at the same time.

"Sweetheart, I'm here. Lauren and Sonya are here as well," he gestured to us to make our presence known. All we did was shuffle a tiny bit in our seats and nod in her direction.

"Where is Michelle?" She suddenly darted her eyes around the whole room. Oh Christ, I cannot watch him break this to her.

"We have been over this, Mary, darling. Think," he urged her.

"She's dead, isn't she?" she dropped her head, weeping silently. She soon slowly reverted into her previous state of oblivion.

"It's ok, she does this every couple of hours and she keeps reliving the torture over and over again. I'm not sure how long she can keep this up before it completely consumes her and traps her into wherever it is she keeps disappearing off to."

"Jonathan, I'm so sorry this has happened to you both. I loved Michelle like a sister, I can't believe they have stooped to these kinds of tactics," Sonya raged.

"All for the greater good, or whatever crap they want to sell it as. The bottom line is they have murdered my daughter to save one of their own. They are planning to murder hundreds if not thousands of more innocent children in the name of supremacy. They are planning to roll this out to the public over the next few months and I will risk my life to stop this being the new future for generations to come."

"But, if they are rolling it out, what can we do? We can't expose something that they are admitting to and we sure as hell can't make them stop doing it. Can we?" I chimed in.

"There are two issues to tackle here, Lauren. If we expose them before the brainwashing starts, it can be nipped in the bud, right? And I'm telling you, there is something about this that doesn't add up."

"Do you have any specifics?"

"Well, for starters, have you ever heard of a disease that targets certain age groups?"

"Yes, there are many childhood illnesses that—"

"Right, right, ok. Have you ever heard of an illness or disease that affects only certain minorities?"

56

"Again, yes," I stated to him, quite bluntly.

The frustration was growing on Mr McNeil's face and tone at an alarming rate. I did understand what he was getting at but if he was to highlight this with no proof to the public, he would be laughed out the door.

"Jonathan, we need to compile proof, we need witnesses, or something to back this all up," Sonya soothed.

"And when exactly did you become cool, calm and collected?" I raised an eyebrow and glanced in Sonya's direction.

"Well, ok, I know I was a bit off the chart in yours."

"Way off the chart, like another planet," I interrupted.

"Ok, yes on another planet, but to be fair, I was distraught! I also hadn't slept for like thirty two hours, my mind was creating all kinds of crazy scenarios."

"More crazy than this?"

"Don't even ask, for your own sake, but to be mild about it, this is the sanest out of them all. I've had a sleep and I have you guys by my side as well, not making me feel like an idiot." She didn't look at me but I knew that was a dig at me.

"So, why is Mrs McNeil breaking down now, I mean, she was fine when I was at your house. Well as fine as you could be, I suppose," I mused out loud.

"I honestly have no idea." Mr McNeil said. "I think she was going along with it all in some kind of shock like state, or trying to convince herself this was all normal. To be honest, she was truly infuriating me the way she was prancing about as if it was her goldfish that had died. I prayed and begged her to feel her emotions like a grieving parent should. Be angry! Those murderers had taken our baby and she was making cups of tea. She decided to do yet another load of washing and had gone into Michelle's room to change her bedding and came out like this," he sighed and rubbed his temples.

"It was the lid," Mrs McNeil whispered. A dry whisper that startled the three of us out of our skin.

"Mary!" Mr McNeil exclaimed.

"It was the lid of a syringe," she proceeded without prompting.

"I was stripping her bed thinking about how she loved that silly octopus bed cover, she begged me to buy her it for a week. Kids usually want computer games or expensive clothes but not my Michelle. She clocked that cover in the supermarket when I had popped in for some new hand towels. She had tried to flush one down the toilet the night before," she explained. We didn't dare interrupt her memory.

"You know that washing it in a ninety-degree wash and adding antibacterial powder will rid it of any germs but in the back of your mind, it's been down a toilet pan and I just couldn't use it again," she shuddered.

"I looked down and saw the lid, the lid they pulled from the syringe that they used to kill her. They plunged it into my baby's body and put something in her that made her take her last breath. All alone. With no one to hold her and tell her who would be waiting for her on the other side. No one to kiss her and tell her how loved she was. No one!" she shrieked, clenching her fists so tight, her nails drew blood in her palms.

The air was as thick as homemade soup, filled with sadness, anger and dare I say it, awkwardness. It felt as if Sonya and I were ghosts intruding on The McNeil's sorrow. I held my breath because I didn't want to remind Mrs McNeil that we were there, in case it startled her back into her own world.

"I know you are hurting, sweetheart, trust me I feel it with every fibre of my being, but hurting yourself is not going to bring her back," Mr McNeil gently unfolded her hands to reveal the half-moon shaped wounds in her palms.

"Maybe we could take you home, Mary, we are very concerned about you," Sonya sounded a little heartbroken about saying what we were all thinking.

"I'm sorry if I am making you uncomfortable, Sonya, but you can't just ship me off out of sight, out of mind to make YOU feel better," Mrs McNeil replied abruptly.

"Now, come on," Mr McNeil rolled his eyes up to heaven. "This is the last thing we need right now, turning on each other. It's what they want, us to be isolated and to trust no one, Mary. These two girls know the truth, they want to help us stop this happening to anyone else and bring them down. Right?" he urged us to confirm his declaration.

"Whoa," Sonya gulped and bounced her look of astonishment around the room, like a stray squash ball that had escaped from the middle of a game. I was glad she was the one that would be breaking it to them, that no, we hadn't signed up for some bringing down an empire plot.

It reminded me of the time when I was eleven and my friend Maria had convinced me to distract our local shop keeper, whilst she stole some magazines. I say convinced, I really meant she goaded me into it by persistently asking me, moaning at me and eventually blackmailing me into doing it. In my head, all I had to do was strike up a conversation with Samil, the shopkeeper, until Maria had pilfered said magazines. In Maria's head, however, I was supposed to distract him and if he caught on to what we were doing, throw a tin of tomato soup at his head. Obviously, because I was somewhat the rational one of the two of us, when he did cotton on to our pathetic attempt at theft, I said sorry and hung my head in shame. It was my automated response that I had built up over the years from agitating my mum to the point that she considered adoption.

Maria panicked, and decided to turn it into an armed robbery. She picked up the tin of soup and launched it straight at Samil's head whilst shouting "no one goes anywhere!" Luckily, Samil was also brought up with a highly-strung mother and was able to duck and dive like an ice hockey star could only pray to achieve.

When our parents, neighbours and irritated friends of the family finally located us hiding on top of a bin midden two streets down, we were frog marched back to the scene of our crime. Police were rarely needed back then for unruly kids, one look of disappointment and a public dressing down was usually enough to prevent whatever incident from happening again. A tut from the local elders was enough to fill you with enough fear to, at the very least, make you cross the road for weeks if you saw them.

Once back at the shop, Maria decided to spew out a tale of how we were planning on stealing money from the till, along with the magazines, so we could travel into Glasgow City centre for the day and go clubbing. Never once had we discussed this version of events! I mean, we had previously fantasised about going clubbing, at night, like normal folk and travelling the world (to the city) on a bus.

My mouth was agape by Mr McNeil's assumption, just as it was at Maria's "confession" all of those years ago. How the hell did I allow myself to be enveloped into another half-arsed scheme without my prior agreement yet again?

Mr McNeil must have seen my look of bafflement because he turned to me and said, "Don't you?"

"Ok, we'll do It," Sonya stated, with a determination that I had never heard from her before. I swear I am going to nickname her the yoyo because she is always up or down, never in between.

I took the deepest breath of my life, so much so, that I honestly believe that I heard my lungs creak like an old barn door. It was so deep, that I had to stagger my breaths out in small bursts until I could speak.

"We will help you," I agreed whilst sucking my top row teeth with my tongue.

"And what exactly will you be helping with?" a voice boomed into the room so loud, that we all gasped in unison.

"The four of you are coming with us," the voice continued whilst rounding us up like a heard of unruly sheep in a field. It took me a few seconds to register that we had been caught, midst plan, by the Government gangsters.

Chapter 13

I was thirteen when I was first caught smoking with my partner in crime, Maria. I have no idea why I remained friends with her after her earlier bizarre attempt at having us publicly stoned by the street elders.

I still remember it like it was yesterday, her face as she approached me on the lane behind her house. I could tell a mile away that she had either a. already committed some random act of shitfuckery that I was going to get dragged into or b. she had saw or heard some random shitfuckery that she wanted us both to conspire in. Judging by the size of her gormless grin and the fact she was walking with her hands behind her back, I was confident it was the latter.

"Guess what I have?" she sang to me whilst bobbing her head side to side like she was entertaining a small child.

"A gun?" I asked, half joking.

"A gun? Yeah, right, ok, Lauren. Where the hell would I get a gun from?"

"Well, I never know with you, Maria. I honestly wouldn't be surprised in the slightest if you whipped out a brazooda!"

"A brazooda? You mean a bazooka, right?" she had doubled over with laughter as my face went bright red.

"See, Maria, you are the only person who would even know that I was wrong! Since when did you become a gun expert?"

"Oh, come on, Lauren, that was hilarious. A brazooda!" she continued to go into hysterics despite my face looking unimpressed.

"When you have quite finished splitting your sides at my expense, are you going to show me what's behind your back?"

"Oh, yeah! You are going to love this," her eyes were wide with confidence.

"See the bushes on the hill that no one hangs in anymore, because of the clowns?"

"Yes," I hesitated.

"Well, I decided to go there earlier, just to see if there was anything left behind or dead bodies or something," her eyes were now glistening with excitement. Oh Christ, please don't let her have a dismembered limb behind her back, I thought to myself.

You see, every week there was a new horror story circulating in my neighbourhood. There was never any proof to any of them, but they spread like wildfire and put the fear of God into us. This week, it was vans of child killers driving around, dressed as clowns and kidnapping local children. The bushes on the hill were the last place one of them had been spotted lurking around. The week before, it was the community football pitch had quicksand in one corner which devoured any poor children that stood near it. The week prior, our school gym hall had a ghost in it that could only be seen out of hours, from the hills. We spent bloody hours sitting on that hill, desperate to catch a glimpse of the ghost that stole pants from the locker room and waved them like a flag at the windows that were over twenty feet high.

I think you are beginning to understand how active our imaginations were and why I was uncertain about what Maria had hidden behind her back.

"Ta-da!" She presented to me, one half full pack of cigarettes and three boxes of matches.

"Have you ever smoked one?" I asked her, knowing full well that she hadn't because she would have bragged to me about it.

"Nope. I have seen loads of people do it though, let's try it together," she held up a cigarette by the tip and examined it, like it was a new species.

We spent the next hour trying to light and smoke one cigarette between us as it kept burning itself out, due to lack of it ever being smoked. There were five in the packet and a voucher to get free household items if we collected four hundred of them and took them to a shop in town. I remember always seeing my aunt pick these vouchers up from the pavement, bins; anywhere she could to save up for a lamp or an ashtray. Her living room was littered with the tattered vouchers. It was like her odd hobby was simply collecting them because, the collection never seemed to get any smaller nor did any new items ever appear in her house from trading them in.

"Are we supposed to breathe the smoke in?" I quizzed my resident expert on everything.

"No, don't be silly. We will choke on the smoke if we breathe it in, I never see anyone choking. Look, suck it in a little until it is in your mouth, then blow it back out again, like this," she continued to show me what to do.

The whole thing to me felt pointless, I stunk of smoke, I wasn't buzzing or anything and we looked like circus goldfish.

I was in the middle of sucking in the smoke when Maria farted, which caused me to laugh and inhale some of the smoke at the same time. I coughed so hard; I vomited all over my fake, ironed on designer jumper. Once I stopped shaking and used the voucher to scrape some of the sick off myself, I realised that I felt great!

"See, I told you we were to breathe it in," I done it a few more times to show Maria I was, in fact, correct.

"Gimme, gimme," she grabbed the cigarette from my hand and mirrored exactly what I had just done.

"Wowzers, look it's burning down and we even get to flick it now," she tried to flick the cigarette ash from the tip but ended up dropping the full thing into my scraped off puddle of vomit.

Now, as far as we were concerned, our mums didn't ever leave the house, just like teachers do not need to pee. Well, of course they did but in our tiny self-centred minds, we only ever saw our mums at dinner time and bed time so we assumed they remained always indoors. How else could our clothes magically appear washed, starched and ironed? How else could all of our meals be made and then the dishes be cleaned and put away? How else could every surface of the house be polished and swept from all fragments of dust if they left the house? None of this could be completed if they worked full time and had a semblance of a social life, could it?

Oh, to be young and naïve and not fully understand that mums are truly remarkable. In fact, Mary Poppins was basically a normal, everyday mum.

As we laughed and enjoyed our cigarettes, we became oblivious to the two women that were walking up the lane, getting closer with each step. I mean, we were aware of them, just not who they were.

"And just what the hell do you two think you are up to?" a voice screeched at us, on par with a pterodactyl.

The sun was shining bright behind them, allowing us only to see their silhouettes. Terror soon invaded our very souls once we recognised it was our mums, on their way back from jazzercize. Who knew?!

We didn't have time to conceal what we had been doing; we didn't even have enough time to come up with a convincing lie. We had been caught red handed and I could feel my heart fluttering like an excited butterfly. I could also feel my mum's hand grabbing my throat and shouting at me through gritted teeth that she was going to skelp my arse red raw so I wouldn't be able to sit for a week.

I yelped, gulped and shook like a jar of wasps all at the same time as I waited on Maria's mum to save me from this child brutality. Alas, Maria's mum had somehow removed her shoe and was thumping Maria all over with it whilst shouting, "Just wait until I tell your dad!"

Back in my younger days it wasn't seen as abuse to publicly roar at your children or skelp them on the arse. Teachers didn't get the blame if children were failing at school and everyone went out to play, relying on the street lamp coming on as time to return home. It wasn't uncommon to see an exasperated parent dragging their child home by one of their limbs and throw them into the room for the night without dinner.

To be fair, those were the best days for children. You only had to have a look from your mum/dad/teacher/neighbour/relative to know that you were on your last warning to a fate unknown, depending on how much you had wound them up previously. Kids nowadays, just don't seem to have any respect or fear for anyone. They know that if any of the above was ever applied to them, they can have social services at their door within an hour. They would happily sell their parents down the river for a computer game and a packet of crisps. It would provide them with a sad tale of how they were beaten and put into care, to further their chances in a reality television show. Yes, as I have previously stated, our modern world sucked.

That fear of being caught and having no way to dig yourself out? That's exactly how I felt, when the Government gangsters walked in and caught us plotting the destruction of Transference. I almost expected my mum to run in, apologise on my behalf and clip me round the ear.

As they walked the four of us out to their obscenely huge, black tinted vehicle, we all glanced at each other like we were being hauled to the head master's office. They weren't exactly forcing us to go along with them, however, the air was clouded with the collective feeling that this was not of our own free will.

We were bundled into the car and it headed out of the crematorium grounds.

"Why are you all so quiet? You were all super chummy only ten minutes ago," the biggest goon interrupted the awkward air like a knife through butter. The stony silence seemed to drag on for what felt like an hour. My mind was racing, my tummy had collapsed right into my lower bowel and I was already picking my funeral song to be played once they killed me.

"Not that it's any of your business but they were holding an intervention for me," Mrs McNeil spoke in a very matter of fact tone.

"An intervention?" The smallest goon raised his eyebrow, not quite sure whether to believe her or not.

"Yes, dear. An intervention. You do know what that means don't you? I miss my daughter terribly and I wanted to end my life to be with her. My husband sought the help of these two girls, who are our neighbours and friends. You need to understand, I haven't been allowed adequate time to process her death, never mind cremate her. My mind was spinning into a black hole and I was sucking everything around me into it. I am struggling to come to terms with this whole situation, I actually feel quite violated that you imposed yourself into such a private moment."

"Who are you guys again?" Sonya interjected. "I don't recall ever being introduced," she quizzed. We all adopted our unspoken roles of innocent mourners that were in effect, being kidnapped by strangers.

"Sonya, Lauren. These gentlemen work for the Homicide and Major Crime Team. Any unexpected child's death is investigated by the HCT," Mrs McNeil explained.

You could see the goons were glancing at each other behind their shiny sunglasses, unsure if they believed her magnificent tale. I must say, even I had started to believe her and relaxed a little.

"They monitor you like a convict; even though the post mortem has proven to them she did not die by OUR hands."

Suddenly, the vehicle was pulled over to the side of a deserted narrow road; the goons got out and began speaking to each other in hushed tones.

Sonya opened her mouth to say something but Mrs McNeil jumped in before her.

"BUGS," she fretted. "Bugs have got in when they opened the door, be careful, they are nipping," she fake slapped her wrist whilst pleading with her eyes for us to pick up on her warning.

"Gosh, so there is," Sonya eyed the internal uphol- stery suspiciously.

The goons were shifting from side to side whilst ad- justing their ties and jacket buttons respectively. It was obvious that the conversation they were having was not just with each other, it was with separate individuals in their ear pieces.

We waited patiently in the car, with only our synchronised breathing and the sound of our hearts beating reminding us we were alive. Would they believe our version of events? How much had they heard at the crematorium? Who were they talking to? These were the questions that were galloping through my mind like a demented horse.

Sensing that we were unlikely to win any awards for our second rate acting, coupled with the fact that she was never going to be able to live without Michelle, Mrs McNeil took drastic action to save us. Or kill us, depending on your outlook on life.

"I love you, may God forgive us," she whispered so quietly, before removing her seatbelt.

Before we could register what was going on, I got slapped full pelt across the face.

"HOW DARE YOU BLAME HER DEATH ON ME! YOU KNOW NOTHING. NOTHING!" Mrs McNeil screamed at me, whilst pretending Mr McNeil was holding her back. Mr McNeil was as shocked as we were with her outburst as he tried to restrain her and calm her down.

"You know. You know who killed her! You let them take my baby without a fight!" she sobbed, punching Mr McNeil with pathetic little fists.

Mr McNeil looked into her eyes and then understood that she was creating a diversion to try and save us. For that split second, their glance into each other's souls was their final, silent goodbye.

The commotion was enough to make the goons swing the door open and drag her from the car without a second thought.

"Stay here," the bigger one ordered.

"Avenge our daughter, Jonathan. Don't let them win! Take them down. TAKE THEM ALL DOWN!" Mrs McNeil was rambling like a lunatic as she was dragged further up the road.

"You won't get away with this you know, Trans–"

Before we could catch our breath, the bigger goon punched Mrs McNeil in the face four times; bringing her to her knees and eventually face down in the dirt.

The silence was deafening.

She had quite literally taken the hit to allow us a chance to survive this, we couldn't ruin it now.

Mr McNeil sat with his face in his hands, weeping ever so slightly. I swallowed hard and put my hand on his shoulder, which was tense to the touch.

"She was out of control, Mr McNeil, she was a risk to hurting us and the HCT workers, they had to restrain her," I tried to sound as convincing as I could.

"I know," he sighed.

"Our intervention didn't work. She was still convinced we should sue the doctor that said Michelle was fine last week, she only had a cold but she is convinced it killed her. She was never going to stop finding someone to blame, she needs professional help so we can all move on."

It was becoming evident that, not only were we correct in our assumption that the car was bugged; the buggers (see what I did there?) were also in communication with the goons.

They had almost made a bee line for us, to likely cave our faces in as well, when they stopped in their tracks. The buggers (sorry I need to call them that now) had obviously told them to hang fire, so they could hear how we reacted and find out what we knew.

Suddenly, another car pulled up alongside ours and bundled an unconscious Mrs McNeil into the back.

"Where are you taking my wife?" Mr McNeil quizzed, whilst attempting to open the door and get out.

"Mr McNeil, you saw how violent and incoherent your wife had become, we had to use adequate force to restrain her, for our safety as well as her own," the goon stated. We all nodded in agreement with him.

"She has been taken to a private facility to receive treatment, she will be well looked after. Let's get you all home for now."

"Ok, thank you," Mr McNeil sighed.

We truly had no idea if we were in fact being taken home, or to a field, or to the bloody moon for all we knew. Mrs McNeil had taken some beating, and it took Mr McNeil all his might not to get out and do the same to the goons that had assaulted his poor, bereaved wife.

The remainder of the journey was completed in silence. The three of us hung our heads, almost prayer like, and secretly held hands.

As far as the goons were aware, Mr McNeil was the only other person that knew about Transference and they wanted it to stay that way. For the time being. They couldn't risk the experiment being leaked and the whole façade to come tumbling out. Not before they had manipulated everyone to adopt their way of thinking.

Hitler, he was an extraordinary speaker and had the ability to convince people that he could bring them out of their misery. The 1920s was a period of extreme economic hardship for Germany; of course they would believe anyone who could be that convincing. The German people were disorientated by World War 1. They desperately sought answers for the defeat and one young man convinced them that he had the answers. What is scary about Hitler is, that his rise was neither extraordinary nor that sudden. There was almost a natural progress to his rise and this is where the world dropped the ball in the prevention of another Hitler.

Our modern version of Hitler was of course, our Government. The victims that were persecuted were different this time round and the manipulators formed part of a much bigger, scarier structure however, the premise and ultimate goal was the same. Manipulate, control and execute anyone that stood in the way of a superior empire being built. An empire of rich people.

The similarities are explained below:

1. Hitler was convinced that Germans were entitled to more living space than any other peoples, for they were a "tightly packed racial core" who exceeded any other people in number, so they deserved more space.

The writers and their rich associates were also convinced that they were entitled to more land to keep out us lower classes. This spread out to them believing they were also entitled to their own laws and rules, their own unfiltered opinions and ultimately the upper hand on life and death.

2. Hitler's war was never against his European neighbours to begin with, it was against bankers. He became an out and out anti-Semite during his early years in Vienna, saw that Jews were not to be confused with pure Germans, and sought to remove them from Germany's heartland. 70% of Jews lived in big cities like Berlin, so even if they formed only 1% of the German population, he wanted them removed.

The writer's war was never personally against us characters to begin with, it was against equality amongst humans. They wanted to retain the sense of hierarchy that made them feel superior and full of purpose. When the everyday working man decided that they no longer felt threatened by the presence of power or money and that the ultimate goal shifted towards peace and harmony, the writers really got the fright of their lives. We were pulling together for the first time in history to eradicate food banks, homelessness, anything that separated us and made us all in it together.

The writers were not having any of this, they had to work at keeping the common man down, and thus the silent war changed, to between the rich and the poor. In the background their cogs and moguls were working hard to keeping us fighting amongst ourselves, like we were their entertainment. Suffering and hardship was the world's new way of life, whilst the writers sat in their ivory towers and watched. It made them feel like the ultimate race, almost God like, for they had created this stage and we were their puppets.

Sympathy, empathy, basically any human emotions were all removed like some sort of genetic deformity and replaced with egocentricity. God like complexes were obtained and adorned like a vulgar new fashion statement.

So, you see, you may have been thinking that comparing them to Hitler was a farfetched exaggeration but ultimately, they were both executing social cleanses with their own arrogance and hatred in the driving seat.

We were only five minutes away from our homes, were we going to get away with convincing them we knew nothing? The three of us held back our strained smiles and our relief that no one was killed.

"Once Mary gets released from hospital, please do come round for din–"

BANG!

Mr McNeil was cut short from his sentence by the bang of what sounded like a gun going off in the vehicle in front of us, where Mrs McNeil was contained. Before we could ask what the hell had happened, our car sped up and crashed straight into the back of the vehicle.

My ears were ringing, and it was dark. So dark. I had to close my heavy eyes for just a minute.

Chapter 14

"Diamonds are just awesome!" we both sang as we twirled around in our fancy new clothes, adorned with diamonds and rubies.

"Can you believe they gave us these fancy clothes?" I laughed to my trusted friend.

"Nope! And to be honest, we look fabulous in them," she replied.

It was true, we did look fabulous, and we had so much money that we didn't know where to shop first.

"Ok, let's sit down rationally with a pen and paper and break down exactly what we will do with our millions of pounds," I squeaked.

"I can't believe what we had to do for this money, Lauren," she looked remorseful in her statement.

"I know, but we need to try and forget about it and move on with our lives, I mean, how many people are given this chance!" I gushed, stroking the jewellery display box that contained every precious gem you could think of.

"Look, no one will ever know what we did," I paused, to soak in the crushed look on her face.

"But, we will always know, and how do we explain this to our family and friends?"

"It's simple, we tell them we halved in for a lottery ticket and we split the winnings. No one will care anyway once we start helping them out, paying off their mortgages and debts," I mused.

"I can't believe we sold our souls to the devil and for what? Just to look good? To live in a nice area?" her blunt accusations pulled me from my deep thought.

"You're kind of bumming me out here," I looked at her intensely.

"I know, sorry. Ok, first things first, shall we move to Miami?" she asked in a more optimistic tone.

For the next hour, we compiled a list of people who were going to help and people we hated that would get nothing. Thankfully we had more people that we were going to save than people we were going to leave behind.

We pranced about some more, curtsying, practised saying "Milady" and basically acting like stuffed up pompous twats, before falling to the floor with laughter.

"Lauren! Have you been in my wardrobe?" my mum shouted from her bedroom.

"Crap, here, unzip me!" I shoved my back into Maria's hands causing her to topple over and rip the dress.

My mum came bursting into the room to find us giggling and trying to hide her now ripped dress.

"You two!" She tutted.

"I take it you two have been watching that film again and have become the world's most expensive hookers?" she rolled her eyes up to heaven with a smirk on her face.

"Oh, you take that back!" Maria fake gasped. "It was a one-time offer because the millionaire and his friend fell in love with us this time."

"Oh, behave the two of you; honestly you shouldn't even be watching films about prostitution! I don't mind you touching my stuff, but you have ripped my good dress I was keeping for a nice occasion." She helped me to my feet, assessing the damage.

"Sorry, mum, I'll help you fix it and here is your box of gems, I mean collection of seashells," I sniggered.

Beep. Beep. Beep. The three of us stopped what we were doing to try and figure out where the beeping noise was coming from. Maria was saying my name, over and over again in an echoing voice.

"Lauren. Lauren. Lauren."

"What?" I gasped and opened my eyes to see two white coated figures glaring down at me.

My eyes were struggling to focus on who was in the room with me, in fact, what room I was in and where I was.

I rubbed my right eye almost into the other side of my head, and tried to sit up, realising that I couldn't for an array of wires that appeared to come from me.

"Just relax," soothed a voice, clearly sensing I was confused about my surroundings.

"That was some dream you were having, Lauren, you seemed to enjoy it," white coat number one chimed in.

"Yeah, it was actually an old childhood memory. Where am I? Who are you?" I shifted my look between white coat one and two.

"Well," white coat number two decided to speak, "you were in a car crash and for your own safety we had to put you in a medically induced coma," he glanced at white coat number one.

"How long was I in a coma for?" I pushed.

"It was just over a week. Your friend, Sonya, is it?" he urged for clarification.

"Hmm," I nodded.

77

"She was also hurt in the accident and placed into a coma for her own protection. Mr McNeil, I'm afraid perished in the crash. Mrs McNeil also perished however; she caused the crash by stealing a gun from an officer and taking her own life."

"Guns? In the UK?" I asked puzzled. "Plus, we sped up into the car, I'm sure of it," I said out loud, which I instantly regretted.

"Well, yes, some officers in certain government organisations have guns and I'm sure you are confused about the incident due to the head injury you sustained," he stated, pleading with his eyes for me to accept their version of the truth.

"Oh, right, yeah, totally," I laughed. "My poor mind is just a little hazy just now," I gestured with my hand. I was also twirling my hair with my finger.

"It's to be expected," he nodded. "Rest up just now, and we will take you to see Sonya in a little while."

"Ok, thanks," I pretended to snuggle down into my bed, aware that Mr & Mr White Coat weren't the only ones watching me.

It's hard to lie in a hospital bed looking relaxed and nonchalant, when in all reality; you want to scream at the top of your lungs and fight like hell to escape. I thought I was looking too relaxed, so I wept a few times whilst shaking my head and saying "poor Mary and Jonathan."

Had my kidnappers known me at all, they would have known that I never called them Mary and Jonathan, it was always Mr and Mrs McNeil. I felt an almost feeling of betrayal calling them Mr and Mrs McNeil now, like we had shared too much together in our short time we had as conspiracy theorists.

When every aspect of your life is being violated by strangers, you start to wonder if they have access to your thoughts as well. It was in this time, that I felt an inkling to what it must feel like to be a paranoid schizophrenic. It also reminded me of that old saying "you're not paranoid if they really are out to get you."

Time was dragging by so slowly, I tried to count in my head how many seconds were passing me by, but I lost track after 2367.

I tried to remember how I felt when my nana had died to enable me to re-enact my sadness, but then I thought better of it as I didn't know them well enough to warrant that kind of distress. I then tried to remember how I felt after my near drowning, to act out the feeling of shock and panic I had of almost dying, but then I gave up. I had no clue as to how I should be acting, what I should be saying or how I should look. Maybe I was putting far too much thought into this and they could sense I was fully aware of the whole situation.

I curled up into the foetal position and pulled the cover right over my head to hide my whole body. My back was agony, but I wasn't convinced this was from the crash, it felt more like from lying on my back for a week doing nothing. Have you ever had that? When you feel like a really lazy day in your pants watching trash television and lying in bed for hours? Then you feel so much worse for it because you ache all over and your head is fuzzy and tired. It's almost as if your body is rejecting you being so lazy and forces you to get up and move about.

I decided that I would play along with this story and also to check to see if I really was being watched. I turned over under my makeshift cocoon, pulling back the covers just enough to allow them to see me wincing in pain with a very dramatic "ouch." Sure enough, within five minutes a nurse came waddling into the room clutching a clip board and a pen for good measure.

"Lauren, I am Nurse Brown. I am just in to do a routine check-up on you, how are you feeling?" she asked already knowing my answer and looked uninterested in my reply.

"My back is painfully sore when I move and my neck feels stiff as well," I blinked up at her.

"Well, that is perfectly understandable after the accident you were involved in."

"So, what were my injuries?" I asked as innocently as I could. You could see she was a bit thrown by my question, so I tried to help her out.

"Well, I was put into a coma for a week, what the hell happened to me? Will I need further specialist help when I get released?"

"Let me assure you that you are not in any further danger, Lauren," she scraped a chair from the window to beside my bed and sat down.

"You and Sonya both sustained whiplash and deep muscle bruising, which is what you are feeling right now and will continue to feel for a few weeks. A fire broke out in the car whilst you were being rescued and you both showed signs of smoke inhalation, which as you probably know, can kill you. For your own safety and until we were reassured that the fire didn't damage your airways or lungs, we felt it safer to make you both comfortable."

Bugger. That sounded plausible.

"Right, that explains a lot," I fake coughed to prove I believed her lies.

She settled back into her chair with a look of smugness that made it very difficult to not pole-volt out of my bed and jab her in the eye with my finger.

"I'll just pop out and get the doctor to write you up some strong painkillers, so you can get a sleep."

"I've been sleeping for a week!" I laughed.

"Yes, but that isn't a proper sleep, you need to try and rest," she breezed to me.

I sensed from her tone that this wasn't going to be negotiable, so I went along with her.

"Thank you, I think you're right," I fake winced again.

Almost instantaneously, another white jacket clad man entered the room, sucking all the air out of it as he did.

"Now, just you lie back and get comfortable, Lauren. You will feel a little prick, at which point you should start counting back from ten," he grinned.

"I can see a little prick," I thought to myself.

He pulled out a syringe and gave it a flick like they do in the movies, all very dramatic like and entered it into my nervous vein.

"Ten, nine, eight, am I going to wake up again? Six, five…"

Chapter 15

Mum and Dad would never discuss anything in front of us when we were little, not diddly squat. They would pull each other to the side of the room/shop/restaurant/swimming pool to have heated, lowered voiced rantings with straight faces.

To the outside world, or rather other parents, it was obvious they were one crossed word away from some epic public battle, but to us, they were having odd discussions in code with weird bulging eyes and pursed lips.

It was the oddest thing to witness and listen to, especially if it was because of you. The words were always inaudible and the gestures ambiguous, until one of them always lost their cool a little and would belt out a random word from the conversation. "Whisper, whisper, rant, rant, mumble, mumble, CAR!" shifty look whilst composing themselves and then it would continue, like a game of Tourette's charades.

The night time ones were the most terrifying; their voices would flow round the house like a warm unwanted burst of lava. It would vibrate off any surface or material and seek its way to our young ears like a slimy snake, hand delivering incoherent messages in a secret code. It would always end its journey being magnified through my pillow and into my uneducated innocent little ears. It took me much longer than I should admit to realise, that our house was not, in fact, haunted. It was not whispering ghosts that lived in my pillow I could hear.

Sarah, who hated me with a passion, knew very well it was mum and dad's voices I could hear however, that wasn't much fun for her. It was incredibly more entertaining for me to be convinced that we had to perform an exorcism on said pillow. Unbeknownst to me, she had covered a jotter in brown paper and drew a huge cross on the front of it with mum's black bingo pen. She had also peeled the label from an empty, quarter bottle of vodka, and filled it with tap water. Clutching her "Bible" and "Holy Water" she ushered me into my room one night to exorcise the demon in my pillow.

To anyone looking in, this would have probably been the funniest thing you had ever witnessed in your entire life. Sarah had cornered my pillow. She was chucking "Holy Water" at it whilst holding up her "Bible" and shouting, "May the power of Christ compel you!"

Mum must have heard Sarah's rendition of an exorcism, because she flew up the stairs with a baseball bat in her hand and her eyes wild like a feral cat. As she looked around the room and soaked in the scene before her, she dropped the bat and stood with her mouth gapping open.

"What on earth is going on in here?" she demanded.

"Lauren's pillow was possessed by a demon, so I was performing an exorcism," Sarah replied, quite matter of fact.

Mum's eyes swooped around the room and could see my scrunched up, soaking wet pillow in the corner. Sarah was still waving the "Bible" around like a lunatic and there was a little puddle underneath my legs. I was so scared that I had peed in my pants. I didn't even know I had done it until mum scooped me up and breathed, "It's ok sweetheart, and you're not in any trouble for your accident."

Sarah stopped her gobbledygook when she heard this, turned to see my puddle and burst out laughing.

"You're such a baby, I can't believe you peed in your pants!" she doubled over in laughter.

"You! You are just awful!" mum shouted to Sarah. "Scaring a child, nay, your little sister half to death! Get out of my sight, you horrible little witch!"

"It was just a joke," Sarah whined, whilst popping out her bottom lip for good effect.

"Let's clean you up, baby, and then you can sleep in with Dad and I tonight," mum wiped my tear soaked face with her warm fingers and guided me to the bathroom.

"Whisper, whisper, pause, whisper" the voices continued. I lay with my eyes shut tight and struggled to hear an actual vowel that I could associate to a word. I wasn't sure if they were even in the same room as me or if it was the pillow amplifying the chat. It was a good sign that I wasn't dead mind you, but I still wanted to know what they were talking about before I made my conscious presence known.

"Hello?" I asked before I opened my eyes. I got a fright when I heard quiet shuffling in my hospital room.

"I'm terribly sorry we disturbed you," the nurse cleared her throat.

"Oh, no, it's fine. I just wasn't sure if I was dreaming or not," I laughed, shakily.

"We were just discussing whether you would be up for going into the gardens to get some fresh air and visit Sonya today?"

"Really?" My eyes widened as my voice squeaked.

"You don't have to sound so surprised, Lauren. We aren't keeping you here against your will."

"No, no, it's not that at all," I reasoned. "I didn't think Sonya would be up for visitors yet. She can be very dramatic at the best of times, never mind after a car crash and coma," I chuckled to lighten the stilted mood. I bloody well knew that is NOT what they were discussing, but I couldn't twig to them that I knew more than they thought.

"Well, that's sorted then. I know you must be eager to see her, so we shall go to her room first and then you can both get some fresh air together."

"Perfect," I smiled such a creepy smile, that I could feel every muscle in my face and it ached.

As I was wheeled along the clean and roomy corridors, it became apparent that I wasn't in any local NHS hospital that I was aware of. The nurses all wore white tabards with matching white tights, shoes and a hat thing that looked like a doily. The porter never spoke to me, with exception of asking if I was afraid of lifts.

I never saw any other patients and the place was as quiet as a morgue however, nurses and doctors seemed to appear at every twist and turn and were always deep in conversation about something, barely noticing me.

I picked at my nails to try to calm my nerves and almost bit the inside of my lip into a new shape. I was mindful that we couldn't talk about anything whilst still in the hospital. My mind flicked through different scenarios. Most of them ended in me never leaving the place. I sighed heavily at the thought of being kept captive, which caught the attention of my porter.

"Look, don't worry, we are almost at your friend's room. You will see she is perfectly fine," he smiled without showing any teeth.

"Thanks," I nodded.

It felt as if he was wheeling me for miles and at the end of it he was going to guide me out a door and close it behind me, leaving me stranded.

"Here you go;" the porter's voice pulled me from my manic thoughts.

"Lauren!" Sonya gasped. I'm pretty sure it was out of relief that I was, in fact, still alive.

"Man, now who looks like crap?" I giggled, pulling her into the tightest hug that I wasn't aware I could perform.

I could feel her tears dampen my shoulder as we silently clung on to each other in disbelief and fear.

The room door clicking shut interrupted our reunion and we became aware that we were alone, well, alone as in no one physically in the room with us.

I jumped in first with some damage limitation as I gripped both of Sonya's hands, ignoring that her fingers were turning blue.

"How lucky were we? I knew Mary wasn't handling Michelle's death, but I didn't think she would ever do something like this. Poor Jonathan, but then without Michelle or Mary, it's probably for the best that he isn't here anymore," I sniffed.

"Yes, yes, Mary," Sonya hesitated because *she* knew I never called them by their first names.

"God, a whole family wiped out, it's so tragic. It makes you realise how precious life is doesn't it?" She urged.

"Um, totally, I will never moan about being stuck on the train again or having to go to work".

"Work!" Sonya exclaimed. "Do you think the hospital called our families and work so they know where we are?"

"I imagine they did, but they didn't say anything about my family when I woke up."

"They probably didn't want to over stimulate us with too much information, we were in a coma for Christ sake," she laughed, whilst rubbing her throat.

This fake small chat was making me feel ill, my jaws were clenching with every word and my head was spinning so fast I felt sick. Sonya's eyes weren't the usual sparkly blue ovals and her face looked sad.

"Are you up for some fresh air?" I asked her.

"Yes, 100%, I feel really stiff and stuffy," she rolled her shoulders back a couple of times.

Suddenly the room door swung open and two porters confidently rolled in sturdier wheelchairs for each of us.

"All aboard," my porter laughed whilst holding his right hand up into a salute. "We have been assigned to take you lucky girls to a better place. To a place we call Paradise."

"Talk about messing with our heads," I thought angrily to myself.

My chest tightened like a corset and I shifted uncomfortably in my wheelchair. Where exactly was Paradise? Sonya seemed to share my feeling of unease as she stared at me and gulped.

We weren't as gullible as children being told their old dog was going to live on a farm or as it was also called, Paradise.

Have we really come this far to be disposed of? Did they know that we knew?

Chapter 16

"No, please, no!" she kicked and screamed right in front of me, but I couldn't do a thing to help. I froze and felt helpless as I watched a team of five nurses restrain her and pin her to the ground.

"Get off me! Let me go!" she pleaded, but it fell on deaf ears.

"You will never leave here alive," the man barked at her as he held some tissue to a wound on his cheek.

"Jesus," I gulped, trying not to stare.

She bit another nurse on the finger and he responded by punching her square in the face, causing her to pass out.

"I know what you're both thinking," my porter interrupted my thoughts.

"That woman was Slasher Susan," he pursed his lips and widened his eyes to me as if I should know who he meant.

"Christ," Sonya piped up, "the woman that slashed and stabbed thirty men?"

"That is the very one. She is serving thirty life sentences, but she is kept here instead of jail because she is, well, mentally unstable."

They must have sensed our panic at the mere thought of this being a mental institution.

"This is a private hospital, but there is a section at the end of the building that has been adapted to house mentally unstable prisoners of the rich and wealthy. She is wired to cloud cuckoo land that one, but she hurts herself to get taken for medical treatment. She knows we can't deny her treatment and then she tries to escape. At least once a bloody month, she is a nightmare, people don't pay top notch to listen to her ramblings."

"Brutal," Sonya agreed.

"Anyway, don't give her a second thought. Welcome to Paradise."

He pushed open the double doors and I must admit, I gasped at the beauty that was before us. The most majestic and stunning garden that I had ever clapped eyes on, in real life, or in films.

"Wowzarooni," I gushed, trying to absorb the exquisiteness.

"It's something alright, isn't it? They believe that nature's surroundings calms and heals just about anything," my porter sighed. "Except Slasher Susan, the only thing she sees is her four padded walls. Then she must account for all her slayings to the man downstairs when he finally beckons her to join him," he sucked in air between his teeth.

"Anyway, you two enjoy your fresh air; it will do you the world of good. We will come back in a little while for you. Do you want us to have some tea brought out?" he asked.

"Yes, please and a biscuit," I asked, cheekily.

"Ma'am," he bowed down and tipped an invisible hat towards me and then left.

We sat in silence right up to our tea being brought out to us and for at least ten minutes after that. What could we say? What could we do? There was every possibility that this was a setup, leading us to a false sense of security to find out what we knew. We both knew this, and it was killing us both in equal measures.

A single solitary tear rolled down Sonya's face, as her bottom lip tremored like a jacketless teenager on a night out in Glasgow. She was swallowing hard and almost choking trying to hide how upset she was.

"I can't wait to see my mum," I burst through the thick atmosphere.

"Me too, I mean, my mum," Sonya failed at her attempt of humour.

"What do you remember?" I asked, praying she knew we were still in acting mode.

She shot me a blank glance and then cleared her throat. "Well, I remember we held a make shift intervention for Mary. We were being taken to get Mary help; she went berserk and had to be calmed down. There was a loud bang and then finally waking up in here."

"Yip, same here, I thought a tyre had blown or something, but it was Mary shooting herself. Man, I knew she was unhinged, but you never really can tell someone's state of mind, can you? Especially after their daughter died from a cold or whatever virus she had," I tapered off at the end, scared that I had said too much.

"Remember that time Leanne's boyfriend burst a spot on his nose and ended up on life support? What was it? Was it septicaemia? Our bodies are incredibly complex at times," she nodded to herself.

"That's right, I forgot all about that. And don't forget Sarah had the flu that mutated into her eye and made it that gross greyish colour. Like a giant lizard," I snorted at the memory of Sarah's eyes bulging and poking her tongue in and out.

As we sat sipping our tea from bone china teacups, I prayed inwardly that our innocuous chat was being believed. I mean, I almost believed it myself and I had

90

started to feel a smidgen less anxious about being here. It was far more unnerving attempting to drink from these delicate and flimsy teacups without destroying them with my heavy handedness. I was more used to my cups of tea being chucked into whatever cup was to hand, being that I lived alone and was not gracious in any way shape or form. I have been known to drink tea from a glass and my toothbrush holder. Gross, I know.

"I actually can't deal with these cups," I slammed it down and broke the handle. "I mean honestly, I want a big ass mug of tea and a slice of cold pizza."

"Ha! Yeah ok, like they would have any of our lower class, processed, 'one ingredient away' from being plastic, bottom feeder crap that we eat," she laughed out a hearty laugh.

"Harsh, much?" I raised my eyebrow, mainly because she was talking about my diet not necessarily the whole of the lower class's diet.

"I'm just saying, Lauren, I have seen plates of food in your house left out for weeks, that even mould doesn't grow on them!"

I stared at her in disbelief, disbelief that she remembered that, ONE time may I add, when a plate had slipped under my couch and lay there like a forgotten, fallen soldier. She was correct, there was no mould on whatever it was I had been munching on weeks earlier.

It felt good to distract ourselves with funny anecdotes of our past, because if we didn't try and regain some brief sanity, we would never leave this place.

I stood up, slowly and noisily, grunting with every muscle and stretched like a pensioner that had been folded up and kept in a drawer for a month.

"Cat stretch, cat stretch," I breathed out, whilst standing on my tip toes and reaching my arms up and up, away up towards the moon. I enjoyed the thirty seconds of pleasure the stretch brought me, and then regretted the immense, unforetold top to toe pain it unleashed on me. It caught me off guard and caused me to stumble over my seat onto the freshly watered lawn.

"Lauren!" Sonya pretended to catch my fall, you know the one? Where there is literally bugger all, you can do for someone and you feel so helpless, that you act out what you would have done had you been closer? Like a robot that was sad and winding down.

I could hear the thudding of feet running along the grass as I lay spread out like a starfish.

"Lauren, are you ok? Please, don't try to get up," a voice urged to me.

"I'm, I'm ok. I think. I feel quite weak and woozy;" I used the porter's forearms to gently pull myself to the sitting position and tried to get my bearings.

"I think we ought to get you both back to your rooms, this has evidently been far too much for you after all you have been through," my porter guided me gingerly to my wheelchair.

"I agree," I wiped the cold sweat that had formed on my forehead with the back of my hand.

I felt so ill that I welcomed the coolness of my hospital room and didn't argue about being confined in my bed until further notice. They may have secretly harboured plans to kill us off, but for now, they were taking such good care of me in my time of need. I subconsciously forgave them for all their shenanigans. Don't get me wrong, what they were doing and had done was completely immoral and despicable however, right here and now, as I snuggled my damp face into the Egyptian cotton bedcover…. all had been forgiven.

A couple of hours must have passed me by because when I opened my eyes the room felt freezing cold and eerily dull. There had been a drip placed into my arm, which I imagine was fluids or painkillers, or both and I was feeling the polar opposite of how I had previously felt in the garden.

I lay on my back wiggling my toes and smiled to myself how cosy I was. Was I letting my mind get carried away with this whole thing? The hospital had shown nothing but kindness and attentiveness towards my wellbeing, not once had they revealed themselves as big bad conspiracy concealing murderers. I think we may have gotten a little paranoid.

I rolled over to my side and I felt my heart momentarily stop and I held my breath for longer than was deemed acceptable to stay alive. There on my dresser, was a perfectly timed, huge, steaming mug of tea and a slice of congealed, cold pizza.

Chapter 17

You just can't beat a mother's hug. No matter what age you are, what stage of life you are at, or how often you see her, a squishy hug from your mum will always calm you down. My mum always told me that she had magic powers in her hugs, that for saving the life of a young fairy in the woods, they had given her the power to melt problems away in her arms.

Bit of two by two wood stuck in the sole of my foot with a nail? Tick. Sarah stretching my favourite leg warmers? Tick. Being dumped by Charles Smith, the local stud? Tick. Being sacked by a prima donna old cow of a boss? Tick. Any problem, heartache or injury in my life was always hugged away by the warm embrace of my mummy bear. I had no doubts whatsoever, that when she came to visit me in hospital, she would make all of this seem like my birthday.

Sarah and Nathan were the resident creeps of the family, no touching of any kind. No showing of any emotion, except anger and nothing was ever an emergency or urgent (unless directly involving them).

I could imagine trying to reach out to Sarah about Transference; she wouldn't see an issue with it. Kill or be killed, and being in hospital would have been my own making because I was too nosey. I could see her in my mind's eye, sitting in the chair, eating the grapes that she would bring me, sniffing matter-of-fact like and rolling her eyes at every opportunity. She would liken my injuries and coma to her worst hangover and tell me how lucky I was to be waited on hand and foot; like being in a spa for two weeks. She would then make me order "room service" so she could have a cup of tea and whatever freebie she could blag along with it. Then she would wave me goodbye (literally stand beside me and wave) and bounce out the door, leaving it slightly ajar.

A shiver ran right down my spine at how accurate my mind can generate Sarah at such short notice, like she was here in spirit, bothering me. Don't get me wrong, I still adored her and somewhere in her ice cold black heart, she loved me too. She just wouldn't ever show it, or say it.

Once when we were at my Aunt Loretta's funeral and I was understandably absolutely devastated that she was dead. Sarah tried to tell me she loved me, but instead mumbled and uttered "I muff you" in front of our giggling cousins. This only reinforced her mantra of "no talking, no touching" and she vowed never to give in to the commercialised way of living with your emotions on your sleeve.

As time crawled past me at a snail's pace, I actually longed for creepy Sarah to come in and talk down to me from her clinical, secluded shelf that she lived on. In fact, in that instance, I was positive I would probably see a flicker of concern in her closed off eyes and possibly even be allowed a stroke on the shoulder with her finger. As cold hearted as she was, if she even sniffed that I was in any kind of danger in here, she would assemble a make shift petrol bomb using a can of deodorant and whatever she could grasp to ignite it. For as much as she didn't care for me, she would never let anyone else bully me or be responsible for my death, before her.

Nathan was just as weird as Sarah, but it was socially more acceptable for a man to be emotionally detached (or unhinged) than a woman was allowed to be. Women looked upon them as strong, dark men that they could save. Women were deemed troublemakers and high maintenance.

That's why, as much as my mum tried to protest it with every fibre of her being, I was her favourite. Her little dolly bird that needed protection and shielding from the big bad world, which ironically was filled with Sarahs and Nathans.

My dad would always try and come across as the Devil's advocate, but would light the fireworks fuse and walk away, so we discussed at length who was normal and who was abnormal. He liked both ways of thinking, but would have preferred if his three kids had been rolled up into one master human being, that could kick ass, but cry about it later in the shower.

I could feel my eyes watering. I missed my family and desperately hoped they would all come to the hospital and save me. Then my mind jumped to seeing them all lined up and shot in a secret garden out the back of the hospital, whilst Sarah was shouting that it was all my fault. I wanted them, but I didn't want them, this was a real-life version of Sophie's Choice.

I was jolted out of my self-pitying daydream by the sound of the hospital door handle being turned from the outside. Whoever it was had paused mid-turn, making me wait eagerly to see who the visitor was and was torturing me.

"Hello," a voice breezed into my room like an unexpected gust of wind.

"Oh, hello," I smiled, begrudgingly, to the nurse.

"Well, I clearly wasn't who you had hoped would walk in the door! You have the same face my husband pulls when I come home from work," she laughed at her own joke. Or was it a joke?

"Sorry, I was kind of hoping my family would be here by now," I sulked.

"Oh, that won't happen, I'm afraid," she barely lifted her eyes from the clip board she was reading. "This is a private, government hospital that is not for public access. I understand how distressing this has all been for you, but for the sake of national security we don't allow the public in here."

"Do they even know where I am?" I almost shouted at her in exasperation.

"They do to a certain extent. They know where you are, as in, they know you are in a hospital receiving treatment. They don't know where you are physically, as in, the location. They have been kept updated on your condition and advised that you are now conscious."

"So, how are you planning on returning us home? With a bag over our head? Chloroform over the face? Will snipers be dropping us into our bed at the dead of night?"

The nurse raised her eyebrow at me, her face showed alarm mixed with what looked like surprise at my outburst, like I was the one being irrational.

"Look, sweetheart," she sighed, whilst lowering herself onto my hospital bed.

"You have passed all your checks; you are on the road to a full recovery to live a long, happy life. Just bear with us a little smidgen longer and you can leave and go back to your family," she soothed.

I tried to pull my hand away from her whilst agreeing with her, but she had an unexpected air about her. Her eyes were serious as she kept a firm hold of my hand, and I could sense that she was desperate for me to really listen to her words.

"I understand, completely," I replied, barely moving my lips.

"Great!" she exhaled with a look of relief that seemed to reduce her appearance by about ten years. "Glad that's all sorted. I will follow up with a doctor and hopefully we can release you both tomorrow."

"I appreciate everything you have all done for us here, I am aware of the repercussions that could incur if the location of the hospital or your offices were made known to the public."

I had adopted a monotonous, robotic tone to my voice that I never thought could possibly come from my body. I followed it up with a creepy, fake, Sarah smile.

"I'm pleased." She smiled back at me, watching like a proud mother as her baby takes its first steps.

"Wow," I breathed inwards almost inhaling the word.

It dawned on me that, that was probably the most intense and implied conversation I have ever had the displeasure of being involved in. I couldn't remember if I had taken a breath the whole time she was in the room. She clearly wanted us to survive this and move on with our lives, but why? Was it another test? Pretending I had an ally to see if I would slip up? It is a truly horrific feeling to question not only your own words and actions, but also your own thoughts.

I had just managed to drop off, when I was rudely awoken by Sonya bouncing into my room like a new spring lamb. All this terrible acting and constant fake smiling was draining my mind and my body. I longed to scream, throw something and cry for about a week or at the very least tell someone to piss off.

"We are getting out tomorrow," she sang to me and performed a dodgy dance, jabbing her forefingers towards me like a drunken uncle at a wedding.

Believe it or not, this was not her pretending, she really did act so cringe worthy when she was deliriously happy.

Seeing Sonya so happy made me a little calmer, I settled back into my plush pillows and allowed myself to unclench my knotted stomach for the first time since I woke up. I watched Sonya continue to dance. Oh, the running man she was now attempting. I couldn't help but notice she looked different. She had a glow about her, she had lost weight, shrunk, and her teeth looked sparkly white. Wow, what had they been brushing her teeth with when she was knocked out? I ran my tongue along my teeth and could feel plaque built up on them.

Comas obviously suited Sonya a lot more than they suited me, she looked fantastic.

She looked like crap, as did I, when we had been in the garden. Maybe she has been up and about whilst I lay here like I had already died.

"How are you feeling now after your tumble?" She continued to dance about like a prat, making me feel queasy. "The doctor said it was normal to feel a bit disorientated for a while. He said it was all a bit too soon, as you had just woken up from a coma."

"He has told you more than he has told me," I fumed. "And how come you were ok?"

"You took more of a beating than she did in the crash."

"She?" I scrunched my nose up.

"I," she laughed, and tutted at herself.

I bit my lip and could feel my throat tighten just a tiny bit, so much so that it made me gasp out loud. I rubbed my temple to imply that I had a sore head and that had caused my gasp.

"So, Transference, eh?" she stopped dancing and stared at me with intense eyes.

"Tran.... what?" I gulped. "Is that what they are calling us being discharged? Transference? Transferred home?" I put on my most genuinely dumb expression I could muster from the pit of my soul.

She stared at me without blinking for what felt like eternity and then laughed in my face.

"I know, how snobby is that, eh? The Transference of you will begin in approximately T-minus five minutes," she held her nose to produce a nasal voice.

Again, was I being paranoid? Here was my best friend in the whole world, who knew everything about me and yet she felt like a stranger. I shook my head hoping the negative thoughts would fall out and blinked more times than was socially required.

"Your mum and dad will be glad to have you home, my mum probably hasn't even noticed that I was away," she rolled her eyes and inspected her nails.

"You know what your mums like; she can't contain her fiercely independent daughter, so why try eh?" I stretched out my fingers.

"True, I had better be going back to my room. Let's rest a little before our big adventure home tomorrow, no, sorry our Transference home," she winked, whilst heading out the door.

"I bet Sarah has been beside herself with worry about you, she will be eager to have you home to cater to your every whim. You will be smothered to death by kisses from her and your mum. I wish I had a sister, but I suppose you are like my sister," she mused.

My heart had literally stopped beating as I willed myself to dissolve into my bed and go straight to hell.

"Love you, Lauren," she stopped half way out.
"Love you, too, whoever you are," I mouthed.

Chapter 18

I sat on the hospital bed, picking my nails and waiting for whatever else was going to be thrown at me today. I felt anxious to get out of this room, almost like when you are waiting to check out of a hotel.

I stank ferociously of body odour, mostly because of the panic sweats I keep breaking out in and I smelt vaginal. Every time I licked my lips I could taste the salty taste of perspiration. I looked like shit, I had gained a squeaky voice and my skin was all flaky. Basically, I would offend all senses of anyone that had the misfortune of being in my radius.

Despite being such a treat, I refused to shower, knowing full well I was being monitored by God knows who.

They would have particularly enjoyed my floor show last night, which consisted of but wasn't limited to: picking my pants out of my butt, flipping over from side to side like a pancake on speed, running my greasy hair between my fingers and then using my thumb to rub the grease on to my finger nails, farting like a sailor and sighing so much my lungs ached. I also attempted to count my eyelashes which would have added me straight into the curious creature's book of records. I had to distract myself whilst somehow acting normal (well, certainly act like you thought no one was watching) plus, I am a bit of a clatty mare at the best of times.

I kept running the whole situation through my mind, how the hell had I been caught up in such drama? I only looked out of my window to be beckoned over by the McNeil's and it all went downhill from there. I always said it, no good can come from being friends with your neighbours and we weren't even that friendly! I still called them Mr & Mrs McNeil for Christ sake.

I tried not to think of it in any kind of depth because a. there was a risk I would panic and crack beyond repair and b. I was still convinced they were in my mind.

"Are you not going to get dressed?" the nurse poked her head into my room.

"I don't much fancy dressing like the KKK," I held up my bedsheet and looked around the room to show there were no clothes in sight.

"Someone's humour has reawakened! That's a good sign, but if you look in the bathroom there are clothes folded on the shelf for you."

I padded into the bathroom as an automatic response to her instructions and did indeed see a pile of white cloth.

"Yikes, I thought that was a pile of towels," I grimaced.

"They will do you until you get home, dear," she followed me into the bathroom. "You and Sonya should probably talk this all through, like counselling. The most relaxing place for talking is in a sauna or a Jacuzzi." She was looking at me with her urgent eyes again. "Lots and lots of hot steam and noisy bubbles, very therapeutic," she smiled matter of fact.

"I understand. Thank you for taking care of me and for your advice, I will do exactly that."

"Well, talking in the house can be dangerous," she paused for effect, "I mean it leads to depression and flash backs which you don't need. At least in a spa you can talk things out and relax at the same time. It almost feels like you aren't talking at all, but it really does help to release all your pent-up emotions."

I softened my face and pulled her in for a hug, one of those grab on for dear life hugs that you never know the appropriate length of time to hold on for. I sensed she was desperate to prise me off her like a scabby plaster, but she let me cling to her for longer than she would normally permit.

She was my surrogate protector, looking out for me until I was reunited with my real mother. She wanted to keep me out of harm's way; why else would she risk her job and life to help me get out of here? I would heed her warnings and head for a Jacuzzi when we were far away from here. Her not so subtle hints were telling me our homes were likely bugged and not to breathe a word about Transference or what really happened in the car until we were somewhere warm or noisy, or preferably, both.

She lifted the pile of clothes and placed them in my arms, wrinkling up her nose as she did so.

"I think we will be burning your nightwear and undergarments, sweetie," she laughed a loud hearty laugh.

"Yeah, sorry, I know. I'm not usually so pongy, I just really want to go for a long soak in my own bath," I could feel my cheeks reddening.

"Don't sweat it," she patted my arm "you have more than sweated enough," she bellowed out another laugh.

"I kind of feel bullied by your harsh words!" I mock huffed.

"I'm half kidding on, sweetie, you almost died! Being a bit ripe is more than acceptable. Peel your clothes off and stick them into this bag, its heading straight to the incinerator, that's where we send all our problems," she deliberately kept her eyes away from mine with this statement.

"Jeez, Louise!" she exclaimed glancing at her watch fob. "I have many more patients I need to insult! I best be off, but remember what I said now," she cupped my chin with one hand.

"Oh," She walked backwards to enable her to continue our conversation. "I saw your friend today as well, you will be glad to know she is feeling more herself today," she winked at me.

"This woman is awesome," I thought to myself as she hummed her way out to the corridor.

I knew fine well that wasn't Sonya that visited me last night, but a really, dodgy, wax work museum double that had been sent in to test me out. I was rather offended by the fact they clearly must have low expectations of my intelligence if they thought I wouldn't recognise my own best friend. Or did they think because I was all over the place, doped up on barbiturates and painkillers and recovering from a supposed head trauma, that I would accept it was her without question?

I was so furious with the thought of how easily they thought I was to manipulate, that I had stripped out of my penicillin growing nightgown and into my new clean attire without being aware of doing so. It wasn't until I pulled on my bright white pumps, that I clicked on that I had dressed in rage.

"How can I not do this when I am late for work?" I asked out loud.

I was always late more often than not for everything in life, not because I wanted to be, but because I got easily distracted. My brain liked to take the total piss out of me and play a reverse game of word association at the most inopportune times. You know how it goes with word association, someone says cat and the next person says a word associated to cat, like fur or purr. Well the sensible part of my brain would say, "Oh no! You slept in for work, let's work on a plausible reason why and work out the quickest route there!" The asshole side of my brain would but in with, "Ah, but you really need to wear that pink top today that matches the pink in your tired eyes. And look out the window, there is a squirrel trying to bury a nut, let's stand and watch it for fifteen minutes," thus making me even more late.

Even thinking about all of the above has rendered me incapable of continuing to get ready to leave. The only good thing is, they will likely put my goofy and spaced out behaviour down to the trauma and distress I have encountered, not because I have tendencies to do this at every opportunity and have done since birth.

I have always run an inner monologue in my head as far back as I can remember and almost always at the worst possible times. I know babies can't do this sort of thing because they can't talk, but my mum often wondered where I went as a baby.

"You would disappear into your own mind for prolonged periods of time, we thought you had brain damage," my mum would often tell me.

Sarah hearing her say my name and brain damage in the same sentence, just once, was more than enough ammunition to bully me into oblivion more than she already did. Every argument or dispute would end in her spitting at me, "Shut up, brain dead Annie," much to the infuriation of mum. Her pleas to refrain from calling me that fell on deaf ears and even to this day she sniggers, "Oh, here we go, brain dead Annie is at it again," if I forget something.

I shudder at the thought of what she might call me when she hears I actually did damage my head in the car crash.

Sonya came hurtling into my room so fast, that I truly believed for a minute that she had been thrown in head first!

"Good grief!" I instinctively put my hands up in a surrender pose, awaiting being dragged to a well and thrown in for eternity.

"Sorry, sorry!" Sonya giggled with a slightly elevated hysterical tone to her voice.

"Can you tell I am excited to be getting home? I've missed my soaps! And you have evidently missed a bar of soap," she flared her nostrils like the Clyde Tunnel.

"Did that nurse put you up to saying that?" I grumbled.

"Erm. No. I didn't need them to show me what room you were in, I followed your pits and bits smell!" she folded over laughing at herself. This was definitely Sonya without a doubt.

"You look much better than last night," I lifted my chin as if I could smell something rotten.

"You, too," Sonya replied, eyeing me with suspicion.

We resembled a couple of scabby dogs trying to suss each other out; we circled each other slowly but stopped at sniffing each other's arses.

Without notice, she grabbed me by the wrist and spun me round, which did not sit well on my empty stomach.

"Please, don't make me any sicker than I have been, I do want to go home you know," I steadied myself on the edge of the bed.

"I'm just so excited we are going home, and come on, how many best friends can beat us? Now when we say we do everything together, we literally mean it! Comas together, Lauren, you can't get more BFF than that."

I honestly wanted her to tone it down a bit, we were skating on very thin ice here, but then this is how she would act in real life if we weren't caught up in this nightmare. My head was hurting from all the thinking I was doing.

"Your chariot awaits," a strong voice cut through Sonya's Oscar award winning performance. We turned to see a smartly dressed man standing in the doorway with his hands behind his back. The chauffer looking hat gave him away as being our driver.

A random doctor that I didn't recognise appeared alongside him with two grand looking gift bags.

"These are some strong painkillers for each of you," he handed us a gift bag each and continued. "You won't need follow-ups unless you start to feel unwell; you have both had extensive testing done to make sure you are unharmed. You may experience aches and pains, disorientation and confusion, but nothing to worry about. Please call our Matron on the number provided in your bag if you need any further assistance. Take care and have a nice life." With that, he turned without waiting on a reply and bounded down the corridor.

"Bye, then," Sonya shouted after him sarcastically, echoing down the long hallway.

We followed the driver down the twists and turns of the hospital and through the exquisite gardens in the grounds. Had someone told me we had died and were floating about in Eden, I would have believed them without any doubt. This place was astounding; my eyes glowed at being allowed to look at such beauty.

We were greeted by gardeners wishing us a good day and showering us with happy, smiley faces; I curiously looked down to see if there was a red carpet being unrolled as we walked.

The driver opened the limo door for us and provided his arm to allow us to balance on him when entering. Sonya must have used her remaining energy in her pretence that we knew nothing, because as soon as the door closed, her head flopped onto my shoulder and she cozied into me.

I was fed up being cooped up so I pressed the window open as we slowly drove down the luxurious driveway.

"I will need to put the window up in five minutes, love. The windows are tinted and you guys aren't allowed to see where this place is, otherwise you will need to be sedated," the driver informed us.

"Yes, National security," I replied "I just want some fresh air whilst we are still on the drive way, then you can roll it up," I begged. He nodded and put his eyes back on the road.

"So, how would one get oneself a job in here?" Sonya put on a posh voice and stuck her nose in the air.

"In here? Oh, you don't want a job in here, in Deafro," he snickered, but seeing our deadpan expression he continued unprompted.

"The professional staff are highly trained and head hunted within their profession. But those guys there, they are kept in here indefinitely. Like being on Death Row they will remain here until they die. We nicknamed it Deafro because we don't actually kill them, they die of natural causes or suicide, like most Death Row inmates these days, he looked quite proud of himself, nodding towards the garden and caretaker staff.

Once your eyes adjusted over the vast landscape, you could see hordes of staff tending to the foliage and general up keeping of the premises.

"Those poor souls are actually in patients, it calms them to let them think that they work here, but they are kept here indefinitely," he sounded genuinely solemn. "They are high risers and aristocrat's that are mentally unstable, no treatment can rehabilitate them back into society, so their families pay for them to live their days comfortably within their own world. Outside is too much for them, they can cause or come to harm and they are well protected in here."

I looked out the window enjoying the warm sun on my nose, when I suddenly saw a recognisable figure digging in the rose bush. "How would I possibly know someone in here?" I quizzed myself. I sat upright and squint my eyes until they hurt, which intrigued Sonya to do the same.

"It can't be!" I gasped looking at Sonya for reassurance that I hadn't lost the frigging plot.

"No!" Sonya disclaimed.

There in front of us was a gardener, loving life, ripping into weeds and delicately handling roses, wearing a name badge that bore the name of Steven.

We looked at each other in disbelief and whispered simultaneously "Jonathan!"

Chapter 19

We both stood outside my house like lost souls returning from war. The driver had handed us our gift bags containing hard-core painkillers and the remains of our handbags, which warranted a shopping trip for replacements.

"Take care of yourselves," the driver winked, before driving off in slow motion. He drove so slow that the hospital could potentially be around the corner and just felt miles away.

"I won't come in," Sonya yawned, looking frail and weary.

"Best not, unless you are prepared to hose me down out the back?"

I got a pity smile out of her and I knew from past experiences, that this was the best I was going to get from her at that moment in time.

We inter-mingled the tips of our fingers and headed in our own directions. Sonya, to her house and me, towards my bed, both physically and emotionally drained.

I had literally turned the key in my front door when my phone rang, it genuinely sounded like a pissed off ring, like it had been waiting for me to get home so it could go to sleep.

"Lauren?" my mum panted before I had even placed the phone on my ear. "She's answered, she's home, go get him!" she directed to, probably Sarah. "Hurry up!" she shouted, away from the phone. That confirmed it was Sarah, she was the only person who would dilly dally over such a request regarding her "missing" sister.

"Mum, can we tone it down to a dull roar please?" I rubbed my ear in pain from her screeching.

"I don't give a flying fig if I am too loud or not, the hospital told me hours ago, that you were being taken home, I have rung your number every ten minutes since, waiting to hear your voice!"

"Honestly, I am fine, mum."

"Fine? FINE? My daughter goes missing, told she has been in a crash, then a coma, and then I can't even visit? *I'LL* decide if you're fine or not!" she was hyperventilating into the receiver.

"Mum, calm down! I wasn't missing, I was in hospital. I was in a crash but it was mostly superficial, no one died and finally, it wasn't a real coma, it was more being drugged to let me recover."

"What are you talking about no one died? Jonathan McNeil died."

Crap, whoops, I had a momentary lapse and forgot that everyone had been told that Jonathan had died, when in fact; we saw him alive and well at the hospital.

"Sorry, mum, my heads a mess, yes Jonathan and Mary were killed, what I meant was Sonya and I were still here," I bit my lip and prayed both my mum and my professional ear wigs believed my slip up.

"We have been beside ourselves with worry, Lauren, I reported you missing to the police who at first were going to help us, then they came back and said that you were helping the government with an investigation into Mary and Jonathan and they were off the case. Next thing I know, Mary has gone wild with a gun, your car crashed and you were in a coma! My baby, in a coma! And I wasn't allowed to visit you; they promised you would be looked after." I could hear her sniffing into a hankie down the line.

"I don't know what else to say, mum, you pretty much know everything I know."

"I don't understand, Lauren. Did Mary and Jonathan murder Michelle? Why were you and Sonya helping?"

"Honestly? I have no idea, we were having an impromptu intervention for Mary because she was showing signs of a nervous breakdown over Michelle's death and she was blaming her GP for not picking up that Michelle was ill. The officers that were investigating her death had asked us to go with them to try and make some sense of her claims. She became hysterical and manic and had to be subdued, the last thing I remember was hearing her fire the gun and our car rear ending hers." I could almost feel them on the edge of their seat ready to disconnect the call if I strayed from the story.

"It's all so surreal, they should have let us visit you, I am going to write a letter to their head office and complain," she babbled.

"Mum, they did what they had to do; they work under the radar to protect the UK from infanticide. I was looked after very well with the best of care, please try and relax a bit now that I am home."

"Have they created this division because there is so much crime these days that the police can't cope?" she probed.

"It sounds like it, there are too many children being murdered these days like it's a new fashion. I suppose they need to get to the bottom of why and how to prevent it."

"Hmmm, it sounds all very American; I bet it was created by an American. They like to be so melodramatic about everything. Look at Halloween, Halloween was always low key, kids flung on bedspreads and adults hid behind their front doors, now it's like a bloody parade! People spend hundreds of pounds throwing parties, buying ridiculous costumes that aren't even scary and decorating their gardens like a movie set. And proms, don't start me on proms, what was wrong with a school disco?" she fumed.

"I really don't have the energy for one of your rants, mum," I had to cut her off before she turned racist and homophobic. I mean in normal settings my mum loved every human on the planet and wouldn't dream of uttering a bad word against anyone. Make her sleep deprived and anxious? She would morph into a crazy cat lady, with epic rants that spared no one, no matter race, religion, gender or creed.

"Sweetheart, can I come over and make you soup? Run you a bath? Snuggle with you until you fall asleep?"

"As wonderful and creepy as that all sounds, I would appreciate if you all let me settle home on my own. I swear I am fine. I need a bath and then I will be going straight to bed to sleep for a week."

"Please don't sleep for another week, you aren't sleeping flipping beauty," she laughed a nervous laugh.

"I love you, Mum, tell Dad I love him too."

"I love you, too, my little angel; remember we are only a phone call away if you need us."

"I know," I smiled, and hung up the phone.

I stood looking at the phone longer than I had anticipated, wondering if my version of events had appeased "the Gods" in some way.

My bath wasn't the luxurious treat that I had longed for, knowing that I was under surveillance kind of ruined it for me. I used my face cloth as a make shift bath duvet, alternating it between my breasts and my ladies garden, before giving up and draping it over my face. I stuck my tongue out under the cloth and stuck my fingers up at them behind the bubbles as my own little way of insolence.

I lay there allowing the warm water to envelope me, tempted to remain under the water and pass out just to see if they would burst in and save me. Of course, they wouldn't.

They weren't a protection detail placed to look after my well-being, they were assigned to watch me like a hawk and assassinate me if I became a problem to them.

I couldn't abide the dripping of my tap or the sound of my house creaking and settling any longer, it was like being bullied by an agitated ghost. I pulled myself out of the tub like a Kraken and went straight into my bed draped only in a towel.

If I thought for a minute that I was going to have difficulty in falling asleep due to my head spinning, I was very much mistaken. I jolted awake with the sound of my snoring and drooling onto the back of my hands. Nice, not. I wiped my face with the towel that had unravelled from all my tossing and turning and which now exposed my naked body in all its glory. I had to keep reminding myself that I was being watched and that I couldn't keep acting embarrassed and try to hide myself, I had to act like I would if I was truly alone. They would probably rue me deciding to go about my business as I had done beforehand.

I chuckled inward, as I thumped about my house bollock naked, fat jiggling, boobs swinging and even squeezing out a little fart for good measure. I could almost feel them gagging at such a sight and probably logging out for a much justified break.

I drew the line at having boiling water so close to my delicate body parts, so I grabbed my housecoat from the back of the sofa and slipped into its soft and cosy confines. The kettle must have been aware of my hostility towards waiting because it seemed to boil as soon as I switched it on.

As I gulped down the coffee, I welcomed the burning of my throat and gullet. It was almost as if feeling physical pain reminded me that all of this was not a dream. My throat however, was not as forgiving and repaid me by causing a coughing fit that could give an eighty a day smoker a run for their money.

The tears, snot and slabbers were running down my face rapidly. All I could think was how in a week, these poor guys have been subjected to every inch of my body, emotions, bodily functions and now, bodily fluids. As I tried to compose myself, I spotted Sonya walking up my path. Upon seeing me, she thought I was being killed off and tried to kick my front door in.

"It's ok, it's ok!" I reassured her in between gasps "I choked on my coffee, I'm just coming!" I walked shakily to the door and unlocked the chain.

"Don't do that to me!" Sonya's eyes were wide with panic.

"You go and sit yourself down; I'll go pack you a bag."

"Pack a bag for where?" I repeatedly tried to clear my nose and throat.

"I have booked us in for a spa day," she glared at me with a look of determination.

Chapter 20

Screaming. There was so much screaming, and wailing. She threw herself around the room so violently, that I began to question if I was witnessing a demonic possession of some kind. I didn't realise that the human body could provide such sounds, or such anger for that matter.

My eyes were wide with fright and I struggled to catch my breath as I clutched on to my seat for dear life. It almost felt like I was intruding on some personal emotional journey, should I stay? Or should I dissolve into the floor and seep out under the door seal?

I mean, I am literally the only person on the planet that can put my hand up and say that I 100% know exactly what she was going through. I too have felt her pain, her confusion, her sadness, her violation, but somehow, I just couldn't muster up the energy to reflect her justified reaction.

"How dare, they! HOW FUCKING DARE, THEY! They kill off my friends, kidnap me, violate me, drug me and stalk me! I mean how many fucking laws are they are planning to break?" she seethed. "And why are you so calm? Are you one of them?" she accused, stopping mid pace to growl at me.

"Seriously?" I sighed. "We have only just stepped into this steam room after days of having to watch what we do and say. I haven't been able to process any of this or think straight and you, you decided to go all hysterical on me. So, excuse me if I am not acting in an acceptable fashion, but there is only room for one banshee in here!" I pulled my knees up to my chin and rocked back and forth.

"We can't stay in here forever; we need to stick to places where they can't use bugs. So, anywhere noisy, wet and busy with witnesses, but not busy enough that they can mingle right beside us unnoticed," she nodded to herself, proud of her list.

"That wasn't you, was it?" I peeked over my knees. "That came into my room?"

"Nope. And I take it that skanky ass, cheap knock off that came into my room wasn't you either?" she enquired, already knowing the answer.

I shook my head slow and ominous.

"This crap just reached a whole other level of creepiness. I was hoping I was just out of my face on meds and it really was you that booty called me."

"That's what they were hoping for. Did I, she, it, try to quiz you about Transference?"

"Hmmm mmmm" she replied. "I told her bugger all, I hadn't come that far to be outsmarted by some cheap hair extensions and a bad dye job. Christ, for all the money they have invested in this you'd think they would have prepared better clones."

"Don't say clones!" I yelped.

"I know, sorry, anything is possible with them. What have they done to Jonathan? Steven, whatever the hell his new name is. He didn't look there against his will and they had no reason to have him cloned. Unless it was to trip us up? Oh, man, I don't know what to think anymore." She wept onto the steam room wall, pausing briefly to make swirls in the water droplets from the steam.

"Do you think that nurse was genuinely trying to help us?" I asked, hopefully.

"Yes, I do. I could see the empathy in her eyes, you can't fake that. I do think though that she was doing it to get us out of there alive, not to try and stop them. I mean, what can we do? We are nobodies, nothing, just people they can steal and manipulate."

I buried my face in my hands before uttering the next question.

"Mary didn't shoot herself, did she?"

She spun round on her heels and nearly slipped on top of me.

"There's no way. The only thing that is more powerful than the despair of a dead child, is the determination of revenge, Mary would have gone down kicking and screaming. I just know it in my gut."

I followed her hand with my eyes until it settled on her tummy.

"So, what's circulating? What version of events has the leaders of the illuminati punted out to the masses?" Sonya asked.

"For now, I am only aware of what my family know. Basically, the same lame ass story that they would like us to believe, possibly even less than that."

"Same on my side, I couldn't bear to look my family in the whites of their eyes and lie to them last night, so, I told them to stay away and let me rest. I ran over to yours before they had a chance to make a pilgrimage over to mine and give me the third degree. I personally thought the neighbours would have scrambled over to my house desperate for gossip, but they all believe it to be a series of tragic events and are staying away out of respect."

I couldn't stand the cloggy, warm, thick air of the steam room any longer, no matter how much respite it was providing me from our spies. Unannounced, I stood up and pushed the steam room door open, gulping in the fresh air like a new born lamb and headed for the Jacuzzi. I wasn't sure if we were being watched, listened to or both, so, I instructed Sonya to look happy as she vented in the bubbles, which let me tell you is a difficult task.

"We can't go on like this, Lauren. We can't come here every day just to have a conversation in private and even at that I am using the word private fast and loose." She gestured to the elderly couple that had made a beeline to join us.

If I thought murder, espionage and global conspiracy was the grossest thing to turn my stomach, this old wrinkly man in a speedo sure cleared that up for me.

"I'm done," I huffed, dragging myself out of the water at the sight of the old mans'... well, old man, that had been roaming free and bobbing about beside my leg in the water.

"I am not adding sexual assault to the list of offences that have been carried out against me!" I shrilled, almost inconsolable. After everything we had been through, that man's decrepit penis was what tipped me over. The straw that broke the camel's back as they say.

I could barely drink my coffee in the spa's cafeteria, due to the adrenaline making my hands as shaky as the tremble of an earthquake. It didn't stop me attempting to drink it though; it also didn't stop me spilling it all over myself like a deranged infant.

"Calm down," Sonya looked at me sternly.

"Oh, a thousand apologies, oh, Mrs suddenly queen of calm," I bitched back at her.

There was a couple of teenagers at the table next to us smirking and sniggering, I wasn't sure if it was because I was unable to drink coffee like a human adult, or because they assumed we were a lesbian couple having a public break up.

"You slept with my mother? How could you! I thought you loved me!" I feigned heartbreak in Sonya's direction.

"What the—" She was interrupted by the infantile and pathetic roar of laughter from the teenagers that were so engrossed in our conversation. One glare from Sonya and they hot footed it to the other end of the room.

"I was just checking," I slurped my finally steady cup of coffee. "Only childish brats would laugh at someone's dismay, not undercover assassins."

"Since we have never set foot in this place before today and our new friends surely can't have enough money to bug every building and room in the world, I will assume, for now, we are safe to talk albeit quietly."

I took solace in the fact that we could talk freely, to a certain point, but then I was crushed by the feeling that, come tomorrow, they will have been, bugged and gone. I decided then and there to have a little fun at their expense, if they want to bug our "local and frequent" hang outs, then I will run them ragged.

"I have a friend," Sonya cut through my thoughts, "he can detect if there are devices in the house, we can't remove any because that will make them suspicious however, he can make one room safe."

"Won't they click on though, if one room we constantly go into is silent? And how can you contact him without them knowing?"

"Na, he can install a loop to make it look like we are twittering away about random crap. He is so paranoid about everything, he would love all this," she looked solemn. "I met him in the library, not that you asked," she rolled her eyes. "Sneaking about the conspiracy section. I was bored and had popped in to use the computer one afternoon, but watching him was way more fun. Until he caught me and was convinced I was some Russian spy out to get him. After he calmed down, we started chatting and the rest, they say is history. And no, we are just friends. Man alive! Imagine being more. I couldn't live in his fantasy world, this is bad enough."

"1. Fantasy world, really? You are still preaching about paranoia after all this? 2. Why am I just hearing about you having a boyfriend? 3. Can we trust him?" I enquired.

"1. Yep, I know, but he thinks that celebrities don't really die and that they get shipped off to a secret country in the world that is unobtainable once they get fed up of the limelight. 2. I haven't told you because I keep him around to entertain me and you would have made me get shot of him after five minutes in his company. 3. We can 110 percent trust David, that's his name, getting him to believe and trust us with this information may prove difficult though. He might think I am creating this just to toy with him because he ends every rant with "I know you think I'm crazy". He once gave me a key to a safety deposit locker and said if I ever needed to contact him incognito I was to use the phone inside it. If he ever went missing, I was to take the envelope also in there, to the name and address on the front. By hand, not post," she informed me.

"He sounds really dodgy, Sonya, and you just happened to meet him right before all of this kicked off?"

"No, no, I met him last year," she shrugged.

"And I'm only hearing about him now? Christ, you must be really embarrassed by him!" I laughed.

She scrunched her nose up thinking about him.

"I am a little. He is an enigma, very unique. Not a lot of people can tolerate him, that's why we just hang at his house or the library."

It took every fibre of my being to dampen the suspicion I had started to feel towards Sonya. She was my best friend and I loved her dearly, but why was I now only hearing about a random, suspicious, spy-type friend of hers? I was getting myself into trouble in my own head for even considering that I could not trust her. This is what they wanted, us bickering amongst ourselves. Causing doubt and thwarting any attempt made at a revolt. I swallowed hard and pushed her for more information, but she interjected before I had a chance.

"Look, before you start accusing me of being a double agent here, the only reason I didn't tell you about him is because he is a weirdo. He is creepy, paranoid, dresses like a professor, intense and dare I say it, sometimes, boring."

"Sounds a treat," I grimaced.

"I'll ignore that," she tutted. "But amongst all of that he is also honest, to the point of insulting, it's quite refreshing. He is friendly, loyal and he educates me. I find him repulsive as equally as I do intriguing, if that even makes sense. And the main reason I have mentioned him now, is because he is the only person on this planet that I can trust right now, present company excluded."

"Does he know you are just friends?"

"Yeah, totally, compared to his level of intelligence/craziness, I am as thick as crusty bread. We are just kind of lonely and it's better to hang about with anyone if you have no one else."

"Hello! What am I? Chopped liver?" I felt suddenly unloved.

"Shut your face! I mean a significant other, the opposite sex, don't get me wrong we are completely platonic and I likely fill him with disgust at the thought of seeing me naked, as does he to me," she paused at this point to gag for effect.

"Oh. Righty then." I felt wholly un-needed in the role of best friend.

"I am not getting into a petty squabble over your dented feelings because I have another friend! There are bigger issues here, Lauren," her tone was serious and lower than a cat tap dancing under a snake's belly; wearing a top hat.

I sat in silence like a pupil that had received a rollicking from her teacher and Sonya just rapped her fingers on the table in a stubborn huff. As I swirled the remains of my coffee in my cup, someone pretending to read a newspaper caught my eye, just to my right, behind Sonya. She stopped rapping when she became aware of my posture and sat up straight as a dye and stiff as a board.

"Do we need to go?" she raised both eyebrows.

"I am so excited to finally meet Jason! But first let's go to my PO Box, before all of this, I had ordered some stuff online."

"Why didn't you just order them to your house?" Sonya asked, stilted.

"You know these companies, once you order from them they spam you with offers and all sorts of crap, these PO boxes don't allow circulars," I tried to sound as breezy as possible and prayed they fell for it.

Thankfully for us, the shop wasn't so far away from where we were. Double thankfully, David was smart and placed what we needed into a grey looking plastic bag, similar to online shopping parcels. The man behind the counter called us back over to him as we were leaving.

124

"Lady, I need that key back," he held out his hand.

"Um, how can I get access to my other stuff if I give you my key?"

"You can cut the crap with me, ok? The dude who owns the box paid us handsomely to action the following:

1 On the first visit that isn't him, the grey bag is the only item to be removed

2 We remove the key from the visitor's possession

3 We provide the visitor with a different key

4 We contact him to advise him of access

5 If we cannot locate him, we can allow access to remove the manila folder

6 He will contact you through whatever is in that bag

7 If he doesn't contact you within twenty four hours, you can return and remove the envelope."

"Ok," I said slowly, like I was addressing a child as he handed me a new key.

"You guys are sure as hell going an awful long winded way to cover up an affair. I don't think either of your spouses would care enough to follow up on any of this," he shrugged.

I shoved the parcel into my bag and linked arms with Sonya, we were painfully aware that whoever was in the café, was not far from us now. We had evolved into having a kind of sixth sense of our surroundings. It was a physical reaction, the hairs on the back of our necks stood on end whenever they were close to us.

We made a point of entering and spending at least ten minutes in every shop, café, bookies, flower shop and card shop on our long walk home. Even to the local petrol shop, just to piss them off. We were damned tooting if they thought we were going to make stalking and ruining our lives easy for them.

Eventually, boredom kicked in and the fun had been well and truly drained out of our antics, so we agreed to head on back to Sonya's house to open our secret parcel.

I headed straight into the bathroom and ripped open the parcel to find a mobile phone with a note attached telling me to switch it on; it was wrapped in a pink dress and black t shirt. I immediately switched it on and willed it to do something, anything; however, it lay in my lap like a brick.

After what felt like an eternity, I gave up and sauntered into the living room clutching both the phone and the dress.

"Oh, wow, is that the dress you ordered?" she snatched the dress and proceeded to dance around her window with it.

The penny dropped so quickly as to why the dress was in the parcel, I had to pretend I needed to run back into the bathroom to hide what the look on my face was really for.

Whilst I was in the bathroom, I could hear someone knock on the front door and Sonya run to open it. The voices were muffled, but raised and were heading towards me.

My lips went instantly dry as I had images of all the ways we were going to be killed, or lobotomised and kept in Deafro.

"Lauren, can you come out here?" an unknown voice boomed outside the door as he knocked it with his knuckles.

This was it, we had been caught out, why did we think we could get away with this? We were little children playing house in a cardboard box.

"I'M COMING IN TO GET YOU!" he shouted, as he kicked the door off its hinges.

Chapter 21

The metallic taste in my mouth was all too familiar. The warmth, the way it catches your taste buds and makes you instinctively gag. I lay perfectly still and used my tongue to see where the blood was coming from. Was it a tooth? Was it my gum? I was unsure. The only thing I was sure about was how fed up I was of being in pain, mentally and emotionally. I must have been a serial killer in a past life to go through this much nonsense.

The room was silent. A complete absence of any noise. It was eerie. I was torn between opening my eyes and facing whatever lay ahead or lie still, uncomfortable and sore. It would probably be obvious to all that I was faking anyway.

My over thinking of the many possible outcomes was moot, as I was prodded by the toe of someone's boot, making me squeal like a pig. I squeezed my eyes together as hard as I could in anticipation of a vicious beating. But the only noises I heard were my own rapid breath and my pulse ringing in my ears. I'd read once that when you are minutes away from shuffling off this mortal coil you have a feeling of impending doom? And *impending doom* must be sounded out in a slow, booming voice? Well, it is a very accurate description.

It took me longer than I should admit to realise that no beating was coming. No threats and no ominous voices. I opened one eye just a smidgen, but I couldn't see anything except the up-close image of my eyelashes clustered together.

"Fuck it," I sighed, opening both eyes and blinking uncontrollably.

Ok, quick assessment of the room done. I was on the bathroom floor, I seemed to be alone. The last thing I remembered was someone trying to get into the bathroom by force.

My hot breath on the bathroom floor tiles caused a collection of water droplets, which made my cheek stick to the floor. Also, and I can't stress this enough, I knew Sonya was not an avid fan of cleaning and this thought was disturbing me quite a bit. In fact, it was the thought of just what else was coating her bathroom floor that made me muster all my strength to push myself up until I was sitting on my hip and balancing on the palm of my hand.

"Gross," I wiped the condensation off my check with my sleeve.

I looked down and saw a piece of paper with the words "Shh. Don't talk. Go into the living room" scrawled onto to it by what looked like a child. I recognised it instantly as Sonya's writing. I peeled myself up off the floor, spat the remaining blood that was swirling in my mouth into the sink and headed for the living room as instructed.

I tip toed down the hallway and for the first time in a long time, my mind was blank. I couldn't think of anything, not even to ponder who or what the hell was waiting for me.

I pushed the living room door with one finger, to see Sonya and some random, strange looking, little guy. He was casually drinking from a glass. Sonya rushed her finger up to her mouth in a shushing motion and swung her other hand round in a circular motion. I took this to mean that we were being monitored. The weird guy gestured for me to sit in the chair beside him where he had an array of gadgets and notepads that had been scribbled in with what looked like random squiggles.

It was apparent that we were about to begin a three-way, in the conversational sense, on paper. The man went first, sliding me a piece of paper like it was an exam question and I was to prepare for an essay.

"Dear Lauren,

My name is David and I am a good friend of Sonya's. I am under advisement that she has briefly told you about me. We don't have a lot of time so; I'll cut the pleasantries and just get straight to the point. When you switched my phone on it caused an automatic GPS system to kick in and alert me via my stashed phone, both untraceable. I have only told and provided a limited amount of people with a key and details of this phone. I knew instantly it was life or death. What I didn't know was who Sonya was in trouble with or whether they had bugged her in audio, visually or both. I have done a full sweep and my understanding is that it is audio only, in every room, on a constant stream. I'm sorry about your face. I had to come in with full guns blazing and pretend to be Sonya's jealous boyfriend, to keep them off our tail. When I kicked the bathroom door open, you were closer to it than I thought and passed out on the floor. Sonya and I have had a fake argument and I guess they think that we are sitting in a mood with each other. The fact they have not made any attempt to investigate makes me assume this. When you finish reading this, nod your head and then speak out loud as if you have just come in the room. We will lead you into the conversation and then I will storm into the bedroom. Nod if you agree."

I nodded my head and shifted my glance between them both before starting my award-winning performance.

I tiptoed back to the bathroom and then stormed into the living room. "Sonya, what the hell is going on?"

"Lauren! Lauren, calm down. You know how David gets! He was just being ridiculously jealous; he didn't believe that it was you in the bathroom."

"You had buggered off for more than a week," his voice was high pitched.

"Yes. In a coma! You crazy, self-absorbed idiot!" I interjected.

"No one told me, you know, I am the boyfriend! I was left hanging on thinking she had run away with another man, or died. Look, I'm sorry. Can we start again?" He was shaking his head for me to say no.

"No way! Look at my face," I stuck my tongue out at him and smiled.

"Well, over my dead body will I be begging you," he stormed off into her bedroom as agreed.

Sonya gave me the thumbs up with both hands and picked up where David had left off.

"He will cool down in a while. Just leave him to get it out of his system. Wine?" She offered.

"I suppose, on both counts."

We carried on with the mindless chit chat for about half an hour or so before David came skulking back to join us. He was sporting a two hand thumbs up, then proceeded to give his forehead a wipe with the back of his hand.

"I'm going to head home. I have been an idiot and I think you should both get an early night."

"Well, at least one of those statements is true," I sniffed.

"I can't deal with YOU in particular," he glared at me. "Sonya, baby, I will speak to you tomorrow," he kissed her awkwardly on the cheek.

"Ok, baby?" She held in a giggle as he handed her more instructions he had written in a jotter.

No sooner had the front door closed behind him, Sonya sprang up and announced that I should stay with her and we should go to sleep, right then and there.

"I'm worried about you hitting your head because of *jealous David*, so, will you stay with me tonight? We should probably just head up now," she urged.

"Yes, Sure. I need time to build myself up for my mum's Spanish Inquisition anyway. Do you know that for someone that slept for a week, I am bloody shattered," I yawned, even though I was wide awake. Do you know how hard it is to yawn when you are energetic as hell and on the brink of being murdered? It's pretty hard.

We held hands like weirdo best friends do as we strolled to Sonya's bedroom. Not knowing what was awaiting us, we stopped just short of the room to finish our conversation.

"I am that disgusting rat that is falling into your bed sporting my clothes and furry teeth; do you accept this total babe into your bed?" I laughed.

"Why, ma'am, I do declare you are spoiling me with such delights," she fanned herself with her hand. "Sweetie, I am doing the exact same, I can barely keep my peepers open."

We hugged at the door and said our goodnights before entering her room. David had written in the jotter near enough exactly what we had just acted out. He told us once we were in the room, to text "done" to the number provided after twenty minutes and then to wait. We didn't need to wait very long before the phone vibrated into life. Vibrate. He had thought of everything.

"David?" She popped him on loudspeaker.

"Yes, I have not been followed; I am sitting a few streets away from you. When you texted I intercepted their technology and activated a loop that will continue to make rustling, coughing and light snoring sounds right through to seven am. We can talk freely in your room only and on these phones, but only at night when they think you are sleeping. It's only for the short term until I come up with a better solution. You must admit though, it's not bad for on the spot thinking."

"How many times have you accused me of not listening to you and I was!" Sonya laughed nervously.

"Their technology is top notch, but not impenetrable. I knew the government were up to all sorts, I just never dreamed I would actually be involved in it," he sounded almost turned on.

"Let's not forget that these guys mean business and will kill you in the blink of an eye. You have both stumbled into the rabbit hole here, girls. I had heard about Transference a while ago or certainly the premise of it. It's not a new concept; they have been waiting for "someone" to come along to try it out on. I just wasn't prepared for the "someone" to have been chosen already."

"That 'someone' had a name. *Michelle* was my little buddy," Sonya whimpered.

"What do you know?" I urged.

"A source has sent me an encrypted file with information about PODD and it is awesome." He must have sensed our repulsion at his excitement, as he followed up with a "sorry."

"Continue," I urged. He was hard work, no wonder she kept him quiet.

"Right, yes, so, PODD is basically a disease that has been infecting rich kids up to the age of six with no cure and a short timespan from initial infection to death. The cause is still unknown however, a cure, if you can call it that, has been found. The elite are part of a movement to ultimately use the little man, us, as their spare parts brigade. Keep us down and raise them high as they say. I must admit, when I first heard of this I thought it was a stretch, even for me."

"Honestly, David. You bore me with every conspiracy out there, you think they control the bloody weather," she scoffed. "But, this was too far-fetched?"

"I will ignore that outburst, Sonya, due to the pressure and distress you have endured. As I was saying, I will try and break this down for you both to understand. PODD is a living organism. I know all bacteria are alive, but this bad boy is like an actual creature. Once it's contracted it lives in the base of the spine. It's microscopic, but resembles an... an, octopus spreading through the body via the cardiovascular system. Are you guys with me?"

"Patronising much? Of course, we are," I replied, not actually understanding at all.

"The only way to survive this disease is to transfer it to another living human of the same age to complete the cycle. It's incredible! It's like it has a built-in Bluetooth system or cloning system." He was rambling a bit now.

"Don't get a hard on, David," I cut him off.

"Charming, excuse me for being dragged into the biggest conspiracy of all time, the biggest injustice, the most incredible finding of a living microbe ever and being a little bit excited. Excited and petrified."

"We are all tense and on edge and on the same side, so zip it, Lauren. Please continue, David," Sonya had gone all mummy on us kids.

"So, it needs to be extracted by a syringe and inserted into a new body to allow it to complete its cycle. This is where it gets complex. If it's removed and not housed into another host, the extracted bacterium dies and a new clone gets triggered and is born in the original host. Like it sends a Bluetooth to the original host that awakens a dormant, back up version, thus the death is still inevitable. Are you with me?" He double checked.

"Just," we replied, in unison.

"Rumours circulated that because we are already living in a spoon fed, manipulated society, escalating to actually killing us was a natural step in this world they are puppeteering. They refer to *them* on the dark web as the writers and we are all characters. I mean, I thought snuff films were horrific, but this is brutal. Somewhere along the line it was agreed that the remaining family of the selected child would be rewarded £1,000,000 as compensation. Oh, how kind of them."

"You seem to know an awful lot, David, why should we trust you?" I asked quite bluntly.

"*Some* of it comes from chat I've heard on the dark web, the majority of it I am reading out to you as I go, from my source. If you would rather I walk away and leave you both to it, just say the word. I don't take too kindly at being hauled into a potentially life threatening situation and called a traitor in the same breath," he raged.

"Oh, shut up, David, yes you do," Sonya rolled her eyes.

"Yeah, yeah, I do," you could almost feel his smile beaming through the phone.

"Anyway, the finger is currently pointing at the Government as being the ring leader.

They have set up a company called Transpodd that maintains and tracks all the information. The writers are on one list, we poor souls are on another. They link up and feed each other constant live information. Like a highly thought out dating application, skimming it for people that are a match. It starts to get more hi-tech and disturbing after a match is found," he sighed.

"How do your sources know so much about it yet we have just found out?" Sonya probed him.

"You refuse to believe half the stuff I tell you at the best of times, Sonya. The sources are men and women that were involved in the process at some point and have gone off the radar to try to organise a coup to stop it going further. They thought they had more time, but it looks like by taking it public with Michelle, the writers are powering on ahead of schedule. Likely before anyone tries to make the general population aware, because if their plans are foiled, the writers look like they are the enemy, killing us off. If they can sneak it in and then announce it, they'll come across as our saviour with the answer to our problem.

They are spinning it as painless and all for the greater good however, it is far from that. The new host dies a terrifying, painful death. Even though they are sedated, the clinical tests showed the test subjects present signs of distress and agony in the final stages of PODD. That's why they sedate them and the parents. It's all pretty grim," his tone dropped as he joined us in our dismay.

"I wish we didn't know anything about this," I wept.

"And, just how exactly did you both get caught up in this? You have no money nor children, I am a little perplexed."

"Mary went off the rails and blabbed her mouth to Lauren the nosey neighbour here," Sonya aimed her thumb at me as if he could see her. "And it all went downhill after that."

"Christ, you are both lucky they have permitted you to live. They have worked so hard to create this "miracle cure" taking down many, many people that have threatened to expose them. But then they have no proof so far that you know," he replied to himself.

"So, what do we do? Live like this forever? Like non-paid, boring celebrities being followed day in and day out?" I asked.

"For now, definitely. They will get bored after a while, once they are certain that you are no longer a threat and will move on to their next menace. They can't just go around killing people willy-nilly. Well, I mean, they can and do, but only as a last resort and if it is fully justified; in their minds. The question is what do *you* want from this? To move on and be shunted through life pretending you make your own decisions? Or to fight back with the masses to cut the tumour out of society's body?' He almost sounded like he was making a speech to a crowd.

"Erm, I'd like to bloody live," I sneered.

"But, is it really living? And think about future generations, YOUR possible future kids, can we turn a blind eye and let them be slaughtered like cheap market meat so as to not inconvenience some jumped up, conceited, narcissistic bigwig?" He retorted.

"I'm in, David, all the way in. I'd rather die for the right reasons than live for the wrong ones. If we lose our integrity, our empathy and our humanity, we are no better than them," Sonya declared.

Damn. She was right, she was almost always right, except, when I was. If someone had stood up to Hitler sooner, opened the world's eyes to his atrocities just that little bit earlier, they could have prevented the abomination that he had stirred up, saving millions of innocent souls from genocide.

"Ok, if we can't win a home run, we may as well go down swinging like a maniac," I finally confirmed.

"Fantastic, now I need you to tell me everything you remember about the hospital, the people, the names, anything at all because it is not something my sources are aware of. We only have until morning to do this and hatch a sketchy plan. You can't keep staying at Sonya's or they will become suspicious. I suggest you return home after tonight's slumber party."

"Let's do this," Sonya yawned.

It was to become one of the longest and most soul-destroying nights of our lives.

Chapter 22

I struggled to breathe as she covered my mouth and nose with her warm, sweaty skin, holding me tight until I fell in and out of consciousness. I coughed and spluttered as I begged her to get off me, but she was grabbing at me and shouting at the top of her voice. My lungs were failing to expand with the constriction and the dull ache was making me feel sick. I prayed someone would grab her from me before she killed me.

"Jesus Christ, Mum, her face is scarlet! Will you put her down before you put her back in hospital!" Sarah was unclenching my mum's fingers from what felt like inside my bones.

"My baby! I was so scared we had lost you!" she screeched, finally releasing me from her grasp.

"Not as scared as I was thinking you were going to smother me to death with your cleavage," I recoiled, wiping her breast sweat off my face.

"Don't mind your mother, Lauren," my dad shook his head, "she was planning your funeral the whole time you were in hospital. Let her fuss over you another ten minutes."

"I know, but remember I am still fragile you know. You almost crumpled me up like a piece of paper."

"I wish! If I could crumple you up into a little ball, I'd carry you around with me like a keying," she huffed. The truly scary thing was, she wasn't kidding.

"This is all your fault," I glared at Sarah and Nathan. "Because you both have the emotions of a stone and the empathy of a serial killer, I get this ridiculousness at every opportunity!"

"You bloody love it. Drama queen," Sarah snipped at me.

I told them everything that had happened so far, not the truth of course, the fake version that the writers thought we were believing. I most certainly was not going to drag more innocent people into this than necessary. They believed it, every word, although more questions were conjured up than I cared for and I had to keep pretending I felt queasy to put them off.

"It all sounds so far-fetched, that's why I stopped watching the news, it was like watching previews to films," my mum was sounding incredulous. "Almost, like it's all paid actors they have on the news. There probably is no war going on in the Middle East."

After staying an acceptable amount of time, giving them all the gossip they required and fulfilling all my mother/daughter pandering duties, I said my goodbyes. Just as I thought I was home free, Sarah came galloping down the hall behind me and followed me out the front door.

"I don't know what you're involved in, Lauren, but I know when my sister is lying. I have known your covering-up face since you were old enough to do it for me."

She was right, I had covered up for her. Like the time she jumped on my leg and broke it and I had to convince my dubious parents that I had fallen from my bunk bed. Or the time she cut off my hair because I used hoi brush. I told my mum I had done it because I thought I had nits. I ran my fingers through my hair as I remembered.

"Is it drugs? Do you owe someone money? Or is it gambling?" She queried, like a badly trained interrogator.

"Who's far-fetched now? Drugs and gambling! I'm a bit fat to be a junkie, Sarah," I jiggled my bingo wing at her.

"Well, whatever it is, you just tell them that no one messes with my little sister. No one harms a hair on your head. No one," she pointed at me ominously.

Don't get all gooey thinking she was an awesome tiger sister looking after her tiny cub sibling. She ended the conversation with, "When you finally die, it will be by God's hands, or mine."

I rode a jiggly bus home, with my head against the window despite it being banged more times than a prostitute's bedpost. I wondered to myself if I should tell Sarah about Transference. Not because I wanted to confide in my sister, or because I trusted her, purely because she would hunt them all down like a deranged vampire hunter killing off the blood sucking beasts. One by one she would turn up at their place of business or abode and take them all out. Okay, maybe a tad over exaggeration on my part, but she would give it a bloody good go.

How do you take down an empire when you have no idea who your enemy is and who they are allied with? We basically had three choices:

1 *The Trojan Horse. We join their kingdom and accept them as our liege, renouncing all modern-day laws and social values. Then, when they least expect it, betray them at the most critical moment and bring them all to*

their knees. We become heroes and we are carried on the shoulders of our comrades, with the possibility of having statues made of us.

2 Full-frontal Assault. Recruit and build an army to infiltrate their core and very existence. We plough at them in full force taking absolutely no prisoners and kicking the stool from under them, allowing them to hang for their crimes. We'd die in the battle, but we are given a hero's funeral, with the possibility of having statues made of us.

3 Blankets Over Our Heads. We do nothing, ride out this surveillance intrusion, and when it all comes out into the public domain, we go along with the brain-washed population. We smile and nod and live our lives taking drastic action that will render us barren. Life as we know it will be a distant memory in the libraries until a few are consumed by hate and lead a revolution. They will become heroes and be carried on the shoulders of their admirers, with the possibility of having statues made of them.

No flipping way was I allowing some other cocky insurgent to swoop in, grab all the glory and have a statue made of them instead of me. Right, I know I keep banging on about the statue, I am kidding. Well, half kidding. Well. Anyway, I do feel a pang of guilt in my daydreams in the scenarios where we didn't try to prevent this.

I was jolted back to reality just in time to see my stop approaching. Scrambling for my belongings I wobbled my way to the front of the bus. The bus driver was trudging along at a snail's pace and I had barely even acknowledged his existence before he started whistling the familiar tune of 'I'll be watching you'. I was taken aback and did a double take to see if he was looking at me. He wasn't, but that didn't stop the palpitations drumming in my chest.

I jumped off the bus before it had come to a complete stop, almost spraining my ankle and ran into a newsagent for a bottle of water. The shopkeeper didn't look up from his phone as I chucked my money at him and almost water boarded myself drinking from the bottle.

As I turned and headed shakily towards the door, the silence of the shop was filled with the ever so soft whistle of the shop keeper, whistling the same tune as the bus driver. It couldn't have been a coincidence. Sarah once told me that coincidences were intentional actions perpetrated to look like a dazzling series of spooky events. I kept my pace fast and nervously continued along the street. Once the local coffee shop came into view I upped my pace to a power walk and hustled right through the little café's open double doors.

"Can I please use your bathroom?" I asked a young barista that I didn't recognise.

"It's meant to be for customers, but yes, sure, on you go," he blushed.

"Trust me, I am a regular customer, I'll grab a latte to go on my way out," I smiled, awkwardly.

"Okay doke then, I'll be watching you."

It was the last straw. My face went as white as a sheet; I dropped my water and ran out of the café with the boy shouting behind me "Hey! I was only joking!"

I ran as fast as my chaffing legs would carry me. Through cars beeping their horns at me, women congregating on the pavement with prams, dog walkers with stretched leads and a gaggle of pensioners on what could have been their last walk on earth.

I became increasingly aware that I was being followed and prayed for the first time that it was death itself that was following me, because it had to be better than what the writers had in store. I furiously looked around trying to catch a glimpse of my tormentors, but alas, they were hiding in plain sight.

I was almost home when my phone came to life flashing an unknown number; I hesitated before I answered it.

"To hell with you! To hell with all of you! Leave me alone!" I screamed into the handset before launching it into a nearby hedge. Suddenly a car approached at full speed flashing it's headlights at me. I sat down onto the pavement crossed my legs and awaited my fate.

"GET IN!" David demanded, looking at me in annoyance.

"Oh, I might have known you're one of them, you ugly, strange little cretin," I spat as I slithered begrudgingly into the car.

"What the hell, man? One of who? Are you having some kind of episode?" His voice was high pitched and shaky.

He did not care for my accusing tone as I ranted and raved about the spate of incidents in the build-up to my "episode" as he called it. I told him about the bus and the tune and the whistling newsagent, all of it. I returned his look of traitorous disbelief, when he burst out laughing at my perception of what had taken place.

"Lauren, I get it, I do. You are in a very delicate place and the world seems very dark and lonely, but please listen to reason. I am the one that has been following you all day, wait…" he just managed to bring his arms up in defence as I threw a punch.

"You scumbag!" I continued to lash at him with increasingly weak arms.

144

"Will you bloody stop!" he pleaded. I slowly stopped and held my face in my hands.

"I have been following you all day because I wanted to check for myself if anyone else was following you. I was going to give it another hour and move on to Sonya. I swear to you, as I was tailing the bus the radio played that song by what's his face... about basically stalking someone, I remember because I found it so ironic. The driver must have been listening to it and the shop keeper too, as for the café boy? I think he was trying to be funny and possibly flirting with you."

We sat in silence as I tried to absorb his story and weighed up whether it was a lie, or in fact the truth.

"Why did you phone me, Mr Undercover and risk it all then?" I asked.

"I used a jammer, I can call anyone undetected and speak for no more than thirty seconds, but I didn't even get five seconds on the line before you hung up anyway. FYI no one has been following you, but a few places you passed flagged an audio bug. They obviously see you and Sonya as a low threat, which is a good thing." He said.

"I can't do this," I breathed heavily "I am a wreck; I can't think straight. I can't bring them down. WE can't. We are nobodies."

"You're right, we are nobodies and we can't do anything to stop this."

I twisted my head round so quick to look at him, I almost gave myself whiplash. I expected him to have more fight in him that that, this was his wet dream coming true and he was waking himself up before he climaxed.

"Not right now," he added, raising one smug, ominous eyebrow.

Chapter 23

Fourteen months later.

Fourteen months. You can do an awful lot in fourteen months. You can get married, start a new job, move back to your childhood home, and even have a baby. What you can't do is find a specific, unknown address. We had assembled a small army in our plan to stop the writers from rolling out Transference, but we needed the address of the hospital Sonya and I were held captive in. It was crucial because it contained answers to questions we had stock piled and we needed solid proof that Transference was not as non-evasive to people's lives as they made it out to be.

Our people had been working around the clock to try and pin point the hospital coordinates with the limited information we could provide, but to no avail. All we knew was that it was approximately an hour and a half away from our homes, but they had to factor in speed, diversions and the possibility it could have been longer, or less. They had punched in the details and were provided thousands of possible routes with even more destinations, but none that had a secret hospital at the end of it.

On some days, it felt like we were making progress to try and waken the characters up from the dystopian novel we were living. But most days it felt like a big, fat, waste of time. It was beginning to feel like a frivolous hobby, something to pass the time, but with no actual intention of completing the task at hand. I think we would have had more success if we had been trying to roll water up a hill with a fork or throw a Frisbee to the moon.

That day, fourteen months ago, when I had my "episode" as David referred to it, changed the course of our plans to what they are now. We (just me, but Sonya says we, to make me feel less of a flake) were too emotional and physically exhausted to walk the length of ourselves, never mind plot against these murderers. We were a couple of grains of sand, lying on a beach trying to get the attention of a child to put us into its bucket.

Back then, even with David adding to our numbers, it was essentially the three of us and we knew it was only a matter of time before they cottoned on to what we were up to. We naively assumed we had years before Transference would be a regular occurrence in our lives, but we were wrong. So very wrong. David's sources kept us updated with the writer's strategies which showed they were speeding up the big reveal at an alarming rate.

The writers quickly decided that Sonya and I were as much a threat to them as cranberry juice was to fighting an infection that had advanced to kidney failure. After only a few short weeks, they had removed all audio surveillance from our homes, and everywhere public that we frequented followed shortly after. The Government gangsters had visited us to advise that statements may be required for what had happened in the lead up to the crash. Due to the fact, that we remained uncertain about anything other than waking up in hospital, they didn't come back for those either.

We tried to slot back into our lives as if nothing had happened and our friends, neighbours, families and co-workers all seemed to accept our version of events without question. Except Sarah. She had such a stick up her butt that someone out there had tried to harm me, without her permission or authorisation.

Sonya and David realised that they were unlikely to find anyone else in the world that they could trust more than each other and got married, although; he still hates to this day my implying that she married him out of desperation. She totally did. But who am I to slate their relationship? I had unwittingly become a nun, without believing in God, or wearing a penguin outfit. Ok maybe not a nun, just as celibate as one, but by choice may I add. David and Sonya went to extraordinary lengths to make sure that Sonya never fell pregnant, I shan't go into too much detail as it genuinely became excessive, bordering on fetish and was way more than what was required. I reckon they just got their kicks from it all.

It was hard not to feel jealous of their relationship and sometimes I would daydream that I had made a move on David first. Not because I fancied him in any way, shape or form. God, no. He was as attractive as he was interesting, which wasn't very much. He had a nervous kind of tick in his left eye, he stuttered when trying to get his points across and he wore brown, a lot, like he got commission for doing so. But he was the only man in our life that was a constant that we could trust and I only really wanted him because there was no one else. And because Sonya had him. If she had remained celibate like me, I would have been fine, but she didn't and I was like a child that wants a rubbish toy because another kid is playing with it.

I often wondered if when the truth about Transference all came tumbling out, would Sonya dump David like a ton of bricks and go skipping down the street looking for a better replacement? Or, would she keep him like an old musty blanket because it was her only comfort when she was cold? Loneliness and jealousy of your best friend is an absolute ball kicker.

No sooner had the writers removed us from their watch list, they moved into the next phase of their operation *screwusover*. Reports were trickling in from all over the globe about possible attempts at Transference. People were disappearing and vast amounts of money were appearing in less than desirable's bank accounts. It was all pure speculation, as nothing had at that time been officially reported in the news.

It was a cold and miserable Sunday night when the world as we knew it changed. People would have been having evening cups of tea, drying their hair by the fire, checking computers for last minute deadlines and just generally plodding about, as that's what Sundays are for. In the middle of their routine, the news must have shocked to their core. It had only been two months since we were deemed unimportant and so we too were caught completely off-guard by their bold move.

Flashbulb memories. It's when humans remember learning about dramatic events so vividly, they almost get flashed back to the exact moment. We recall the experience of learning about an event, not just the factual details of the event itself. Princess Diana's death, 9/11, Transference. Ask anyone alive for those events and I guarantee they will remember exactly what they were doing, where they were and above all the emotions they felt.

All news stations began simultaneously reporting about this horrifying disease that had the power to kill estimated millions. Of course, the writers' played their hand well and their spokespeople played their parts to

149

perfection. I almost threw my cup of tea at the television in a rage at the smugness of the news reporters. They were in on it, they were involved in every major scandal since the dawn of reporting, pretending to be a voice of the people, bringing us news, being one of us. They were in cahoots with the Government and they made me want to vomit.

Were any wars real? I genuinely did not know what to believe anymore. We only had the newsreader's say so and footage that, to be quite blunt, could have been created in a studio like action movies on the big screen.

The point is, these bastards could not be trusted with their smoke and mirrors. They released enough information to let panic seep in, but not too much to generate suspicion.

They pulled on the public heart strings by playing the dead baby card they had stashed up their sleeves. They confirmed the following: That it was terminal, infected children, there was, as yet, no known cure; it was called PODD, some of the symptoms (generic enough to cause mass hysteria) and how the government was working tirelessly to figure out the cause and contain it. They omitted the following: That they had known about it since the start, that only rich kids were affected, that they were planning on murdering our children, they had been unable to link a cause and how they were uninterested in finding a cure as they had already found a solution that was suitable to them.

That night, immediately following the announcement and when the breaking news banner flashed across the top of the screen continuously, you could feel the general mood of the population shift into panic. The news outlets were advising people with children showing symptoms to go straight to A&E or call emergency services. They were intentionally winding up the hornets' nest by implying there was help out there, they were contradicting themselves so much and people didn't know whether they were coming or going. The fuse had been lit. Parents were waking up their small children and associating anything they could to being infected with PODD. Bleary eyed kids were being awoken from their slumber by parents that were usually the only constant calm in their lives, but had now become frenzied unrecognisable states. Parents were confusing their kids alarm and distress to being on the brink of death as opposed to the fear of being startled awake.

The streets were littered with pregnant women being ushered to maternity wards, young children being bundled into cars and sped off into a game of extreme racing with other parents. People argued and fought over how their child was more important than everyone else's, symptoms that hadn't been announced were being invented by adamant mothers and fathers that *proved* PODD was escalating.

Phone lines and internet connections practically burned out due to the amount of calls that were being made to family members, friends, priests, 999, NHS 24, police stations, private hospitals and even local vets!

Hospitals were forced to barricade their front doors and ambulance bays, only allowing admittance via direct communication from ambulance drivers. Ambulance drivers that were being targeted by insane men and woman alike to transport their dying children, pharmacies were being overrun and raided for antibiotics in the vain hope that it would kill off the disease.

I have never been more genuinely scared for my life and everyone else's around me, than that night. That night, they triggered the crazy switch. I closed my eyes in anger at the needlessness of it all. The people who were wrecking our much-loved cities, were the ones that had no need to. There was no way their children were infected. They didn't need any help at all, their actions were moot and all just part of the game the writers were playing.

I could almost see them sitting, smirking, tapping their greedy, fat fingers together joyful with the outcome.

That night and the few thereafter was etched into your flashbulb memory bank. They must have felt some remorse, or guilt as they reined it all in after a few days. Probably because if they didn't, there would be no one left to manipulate.

The death toll was quickly in its thousands, not from PODD, but from the fights, carelessness and opportunists. The damage caused was widespread and massive. With it and the fatalities, once everyone stopped and took a good look around, we were shell shocked to the core.

A public health announcement was finally made by all Government authorities that there was a world-wide lock down. Everyone was to remain in their homes until further notice, anyone needing medical assistance was to call 999 and follow instructions, be it to remain inside, or venture to their local hospital. They insisted that further investigations had revealed that a sure-fire symptom was a red rash around the torso area and unless this was evident on the child, they did not have PODD. Anyone seen outside engaging in any kind of riotous behaviour, or blocking up emergency assistance for others, would be arrested.

They caused this, they caused it all and were then making the people feel guilty like they had engineered some terrorist acts amongst themselves and everyone was falling for it. People slowly calmed down once they saw that their offspring weren't sporting fictional red rings, but the intended fear and control had been instigated. Our overseers had our best interests at heart and had warned us of imminent danger, they had soothed us when we needed it most. It was inevitable that we would lap up any kind of solution from them without question.

And so, this led to our next Flashbulb memory, the memory of the day they offered murder and bribery as an acceptable form of cure and no one batted an eyelid.

Stockholm syndrome

Noun

Feelings of trust or affection felt in many cases of kidnapping or hostage taking by a victim towards a captor.

Chapter 24

Stockholm syndrome may feel to some, too strong a description of what was beginning to evolve around the world, but it's a description that sits well with me. It's a psychological phenomenon first described in 1973 in which hostages in Stockholm, Sweden, expressed empathy and sympathy and showed positive feelings towards their captors, sometimes to the point of defending and identifying with the captors.

Okay, so, there was no physical similitude, but the premise was the same and could be transferred (pardon the pun) to many situations. The writers had dragged us into their problem, created the situation we were in, fed us false hopes and empty promises. It was never about helping the human race to try and overcome this terrible disease, it was all centred around helping themselves. We were purely a means to an end, disposable, collateral damage, exploited to the brink of destruction and then handed a life line, a way out.

I fail to see how it could be called anything but Stockholm syndrome.

As far as the characters were aware, we were all in it together. The disease would take any child it fancied without warning and without prejudice. However, that wasn't true. It only took rich children. Naturally, this vital piece of information was kept so close to the writer's chest, it was almost beating in time with their own cold hearts. It was imperative that the real facts were not revealed. Or at least not revealed too early; *we* were never part of the pandemic, only part of the cure.

PODD was discovered and publicised in this order:

- Children were dying from this new, brutal disease

- Mass hysteria was created to have us believe that the problem was everyone's

- Sob stories and continuous pictures of dying children to pull on the heartstrings were shown twenty-four hours a day

- It was suspected that it was only wealthy children that were affected

- Confirmation that only wealthy were affected followed soon after by...

- Sob stories and continuous reasons why it was for the greater good that these potential doctors/rockets scientists and future heroes had to be saved

- Constant streaming of how the rest of us were struggling to live in the economic climate

- The cure was announced to the public, followed swiftly by the announcement of the compensation

- Transference was "created" to transfer the disease to the poor and working class

It reminded me of a time when Sarah decided to become an entrepreneur and I was her target, I mean, first customer. I was nine when I started noticing little black beetles with crusty shells crawling about my underwear drawer. In my young mind, I assumed it was because I smelled, even though quite clearly, my knicker drawer was full of clean, washed knickers. I was so embarrassed and had convinced myself that my mum would be super angry with me for not wiping myself properly.

Sarah would often cosy up and ask me if everything was alright, which freaked me out even more than I was already.

"I can tell something is going on. Tell me what's wrong?" She would ask me with a genuine look of concern.

"It's nothing," I would lie.

"Uh huh, what does mum always say to us?" She would tease.

"We never tell lies in this house," I'd reply.

I hated it when she used mums house rules against me, especially since she never bloody followed them herself.

I could feel my face blushing crimson at the thought of her knowing that my knickers were literally crawling about in my drawer. I had tried to remove the bugs myself by flushing them down the toilet. I then had it in my head that sprinkling salt in my drawer would work, courtesy of watching some gardening show on dealing with slugs. No matter what I did the little buggers kept reappearing, in some cases even bigger than before. Naturally because kids are dumb, I thought it was the same ones that kept coming back time and time again.

I felt as if I was being targeted by beetles, they were silently picking on me and making my life a living hell. Every night I would sneak into my room, tip toe across to my drawers and peer inside, holding my breath, only to be heartbroken all over again. I even named one of them Bert.

Eventually I opened up to Sarah about my beetle problem and how much it was making me miserable.

"Sarah, have you ever had, erm, things in your, erm, drawers before?" I asked nervously.

"Well, yes, doofus brain, that is what drawers are for, to put things in."

"No, I mean, like bugs and things in them. Live bugs?"

"Bugs!" she crinkled her nose up in disgust.

"Aw, man, I knew it was just me," I crumpled to the floor and whimpered.

She placed a big sisterly arm over my shoulder and told me not to worry, my secret was safe with her and she would help me out. For days, she was by my side, step by step as we tried all the concoctions and crazy ideas that she had to scare the creatures out of my life. Forever. Nothing worked. Every night we would check and there the little shits would be, mocking me, taunting me.

The only good thing to come from it all was how nice Sarah had been to me. I knew she had difficulty showing me she cared so this turn of events was a silver lining.

After nearly a week of watching her jump around like a shaman, cast spells, remove them by hand and spray them with water, we knew it was time to get professional help.

"You know, if you tell mum she will be furious with you, because you aren't wiping properly and these things might spread," she confirmed my fears.

"I know," I hung my head in shame. "But what else can we do? Nothing is working."

"Well, there is one last thing we could try, it's not cheap, but I have a friend who mentioned a cure and I know for a fact that it will work," she enticed me.

"How much are we talking about here?" I gulped.

"He told me about £3."

"I have £3 in my piggy bank!" I squealed, running over to get it from the window ledge.

"Oh, wow, do you? What a coincidence," she smiled.

I gratefully handed over the cash and eagerly waited on her coming back from her friend's house with the magic powder. She returned a few hours later with the powder, a bottle of juice, an ice cream lolly, packet of crisps and a chocolate bar. How lucky was she that her friend's mum had treated her in the shop to all those sweets and juice!

She made me sit safely in the living room as she risked her life to sprinkle the toxic powder into my drawers. We waited an age and then returned to the scene of the crime. There was nothing there, but I would need to wait until night time to see if they had returned.

"Should I worry about the powder that's left behind?" I asked her.

"Nah, it's only toxic when you are sprinkling it, it's settled now so it's safe," she reassured me.

When night time rolled around I headed straight to my drawer to see if I had been released from this hell, or were they waiting on me, judging me with their beady eyes. There was nothing inside, no beetles, just a little residue from the powder that I shook from my knickers to the floor.

"Thank you! Thank you! Thank you!" I tried to hug Sarah.

"You're welcome, glad I could help my favourite sister," she resisted my hug with her usual evasive moves.

I went to bed that night content. I was the happiest I had been in a long time not just because I had got rid of the nasty beetles, but my sister was my best friend. She was there for me through the whole ordeal, supported me. I trusted her completely and accepted her help gracefully. I fell into a deep sleep that night only slightly stirring to the muffled sound of my mother angrily saying random words.

"Mrs Green saw you…shop…sweets…tell me now…talcum? How cou…disgrace."

I didn't find out about how Sarah had instigated the whole thing and had been putting the beetles into my drawer every night until years after. She found them in the cellar, knew I had £3 in my bank and came up with the idea to con me out of my cash. The toxic powder was my mum's talcum powder. Her demeanour when she finally admitted it was pure evil, no shame, no regrets, she laughed in my face about how she played me like a fiddle. I told you she was a complete cow.

I thought of that story often because it was like déjà vu to what was happening now. Slimy, horrid, scumbags were causing situations to create a false sense of security to help only them. Every time I thought about it I got so angry at the world and I mentally stuck yet another pin into my voodoo doll of Sarah.

They did an announcement before the announcement, to announce that they would be broadcasting an important announcement and warned us not to miss it. It was pathetic. They were pathetic.

Sonvid and I (my new name for Sonya and David, who were two creepy people now merged into one, yuck) braced ourselves for the announcement with baited breath, interested to see where they were taking this now.

The screen of the TV went blank, before gradually revealing a serious-looking Prime Minster. Her hair neatly coifed, make-up perfectly applied to make her appear manicured and polished. Refined, concerned, empathetic. It was pathetic.

"Hello, thank you to everyone that has taken the time to tune in to this announcement. Following our first statement regarding the outbreak of the disease PODD, we have joined forces across the globe, come together in peace and discussed at length what we can do to eradicate this pandemic. That was what was happening behind our governing doors however, what was happening outside, in your streets, amongst all of you, was not such a haven.

"We have witnessed riots, thefts, murders, violations, gross negligence and in such a short period. We, as humans, cannot carry on in this panic ridden state, for we will eventually all turn on each other until there is nothing left but dust."

"Oh, she's good with the bullshit," Sonya jumped in quickly between a rehearsed pause.

"I and leaders around the world, have been tasked, nay forced, to come up with a solution that may fare better than the situation we are immersed in, in the long run.

"This disease is, for reasons still unknown, only affecting the affluent at this moment in time. Now before you turn your backs on these people, ask yourself this... if the current generation and those generations thereafter are to continue to decline, who will perform the surgery on your families? Who will defend your family when in peril? Who will create rockets to take us to another planet, when we finally destroy this one? Who

161

will continue to come up with cures to save millions of lives? Even possibly a cure for this?

"They have pooled their resources over the years to fund water, food, helping hands, medication, adoptions, you name it and these people have provided without question or delay.

"We must remove from our heads the thought that a cure is only for their benefit, it is for the benefit of humankind. The greater good must be at the forefront of our drive to continue making earth as miraculous as it is.

"We must swallow our selfishness right now or there will no longer be a right now for anyone."

She stopped long enough for the crowd to cheer her on like she had just invented fire.

"We have found a temporary solution to PODD." Everyone cheered wildly. *"However, it comes at a cost,"* she warned ominously.

"Scientists have confirmed that there is a way to remove the disease from the inflicted and have it transferred to another host. A like for like.

"It can be done without the new host being aware, it is painless and there will be compensation to the sum of £1,000,000."

The crowd gasped, before continuing with their brainwashed approval.

"Foodbanks will be no more, debts will melt away and the elderly will no longer need to work past sixty to then choose whether to eat or be warm. Joining forces means that the human race will NOT disappear into the ground with the dinosaurs, we will NOT be a forgotten race, and we WILL rise up from the ashes, a new, improved breed."

They were lapping this bullshit up like eager puppies tasting water for the first time. She hit the poor with fables of a future without being destitute, without feeling like a failure, without the feeling of dread in the pit of their stomach that their families may need to go without food another day. You can't really blame them. If we hadn't know all of this beforehand, we would have been swept up in this fantasy future as well, but we did and we weren't and we were boiling with hatred.

She didn't hang around for questions, for the hype to die down, or for people to realise the exact meaning of what new law she had just passed. She skipped away almost delirious and proud at how she had managed to dazzle and confuse the poor, uneducated hillbillies into signing away their children's lives.

All the world leaders spewed out this steaming pile of crap speech at the same time, it was all captured on video and it was used against the people any time a revolt was attempted. It was like a live, legally binding contract that was signed by the people's cheers and initialled by the lack of disagreement.

May God have mercy on our souls.

Chapter 25

As the dust settled and the characters thought long and hard about how this solution may or may not benefit them, there was an unnerving feeling around the world.

Emotions swung like a pendulum on acid. From feelings of self-assured collectivism, doing your part for the greater good, which of course came with a generous helping of cash to keep you just on their side of righteousness. Then it would swing across to animosity and hatred. Hatred mainly for being made to feel that everyone else's problem was yours as well.

Humans are in fact selfish in nature. Kill or be killed, fight or flight. Feelings of oppression and domination are not generally well received. And why should they be? Why should humans be at the top of the food chain to dictate and be in charge of every other living thing's fate? I understand that we are the boss in nature, simply because we have the means, necessity and the brains that evolution has generously graced us with over the years.

This kind of manipulation has been coded into us right from the very start. By accepting that it was ok to murder and sell animals not solely to survive, but to fulfil our greed and very curious taste buds. Why are animal's lives and purpose here on earth decided for them by us? Why is it okay for us to kidnap and hold cats and dogs hostage in our homes? We force names on them; check those when they don't behave to our liking and punish them for behaving like, well, wild animals.

Then we moved on ever so slowly to wars, who decided here in the West that the practices of tribes and other societies in other countries were no longer acceptable? Who decided that we, the west, have more right to their own natural resources than they did?

We started wars as distractions to the fact we merely wanted the toys they were playing with to be our own. We drained them of every resource we could pilfer, killed them in their droves, destroyed whatever will they had left to live and rubbed our hands in glee at how rich we had become.

Is it any wonder we convinced ourselves that this was the way forward? Those in power already took what did not belong to them, so as to remain the top dogs, living in their ivory towers, showering us all with lies.

The thing is, the top dog always looks after his pack, and seeks to isolate anyone that is not remotely part of it. Take a good look around, who is openly and publicly begging the average Joe Bloggs for money to send and help every cause known to man? The writers. Who could eradicate 99% of the world's issues if they pooled together their vast and obscene wealth with their pals? The writers.

Now look again, who are the ones walking the streets at ridiculous times and temperatures with no regard for own personal safety, just to provide the homeless with food, clothes, and a friendly face? The characters. Who are the ones barley scraping enough money together to pay their bills, but stop to give a few pence to an unfortunate man with no fixed abode? The characters. Who struggles to buy enough food for their family, but buys a few extra tins to hand into the local food bank because they know that the bottom rung can get lower? The characters.

So, you see, the writers delude themselves, or certainly remove any moral obligations to help because they can see us all pulling together. We go out of our way to try and help each other and they think that is more help than is warranted.

Characters WANT to help, so they plead to us on national television to part with the minuscule sums of cash we have so they don't have to. They believe that by keeping their own money for their own people, but gracing us with their time and unloading guilt onto us, it is a win-win situation.

"I helped with some missionary work," they will boast to their peers at parties filled with endangered animal carcasses, whilst downing champagne that has been through the urinary tract of a unicorn. If the perfectly polished shoe was on the other manicured foot, the reactions and outcome would be on a completely different scale.

If a writer was to fall on hard times, they would be frozen out and removed from any social interactions quicker than a bird in the wrong nest. Invitations would dwindle, calls would never get returned and doors would be closed in faces as if they were salesmen carrying around carpet samples.

The gossip drums are viciously beaten to share the news of their downfall and to warn everyone to don their best shunning outfit should they approach them for help. It becomes irrelevant how far up the social ladder they climbed together, what ties they have in common, or even if they are family, once you have fallen, you fall alone and hard.

Like a wounded bird, they assess their new surroundings to see if there is anywhere that could offer shelter, only to see a stark, empty world.

What is the most fascinating is not only how quick the doors get swung open for their imminent arrival once their money woes have passed, but how rapidly they run back into the fold of acceptance. Skipping gleefully, already forgiving and forgetting the fact they were shunned and ready to inflict the same harshness to the next unfortunate. That's even if they do manage to regain their failed empire. A few have since become worse off than even the poorest of natives, yet still manage to isolate themselves by looking down on others as they are a better class of hobo.

It's almost as if their DNA has been pre-coded to alienate, judge and be superior in any given situation they find themselves in, they can't help but follow their integrated paths.

That is the true differential between the characters and the writers. Writers are a breed that fends only for themselves come hell or high water. Even if they are wrong they will fight till the death to be perceived as superior.

The characters however, in general, will help anyone in a crisis, even if they are knee deep in one of their own. They will source and exhaust every avenue to try and offer a solution to the predicament, whether they know you or not. Characters will never sit back and be comfortable watching another person struggle or be in danger if they can help them. And what if they truly can't help them? They will surely offer an ear to listen, a shoulder to cry on, and a cup of tea if available.

The dark contrast between the characters and the writers ran deeper than just a superficial need to look better than everyone, but in fact, it was a blood thirsty hunger to BE better than everyone by any means necessary. Please understand, on each side there were people that surprised us i.e. characters that had attitudes and behaviours like writers and vice versa, but they were rare.

After the announcement, the characters subconsciously shifted into four groups:

1 The ones that were 100% against Transference being injected into our society with every fibre, but their voices were too small to be heard

2 The ones that weren't entirely happy about it, but thought that the chances were minimal for their child to be chosen for subjection

3 The ones that were overjoyed about it, purely as a money-making scheme and a way to start a business

4 The ones that swallowed every bit of propaganda thrown at them in a state of mass manipulation and believed that this really was the way forward for world peace.

As much as everyone tries to deny it, money does indeed make the world go round. If they had dared to utter a word about Transference without the guise of money to sweeten the deal, it would not have been as welcomed as it was.

Parents have a love for their offspring like no other love in the universe and sometimes that love provokes them to make some difficult choices. If you were struggling at every opportunity to provide your child with adequate food/water/clothing/a roof over their head, would it be fair to keep doing it until they died of some illness caused by their upbringing? Or would putting them out of their misery be kinder to them?

What if there was a tiny chance that you could save them from this fate without it being your choice? The child is saved from a tragic death, you are saved from the guilt of allowing them to die from your inability to provide for them, and the greater good gets another saved soul. Or what about the same situation if you have more than one child suffering? What if the same outcome as above is applied, but with the prospect of having £1,000,000 to support your other children in a comfortable setting. Are the futures of your remaining children and their well-being worth the sacrifice of one?

These are the kind of thought patterns that were forming in the heads of the very people the writers were hoping to guilt trip into accepting their proposition. There were vague deliberations of holding a referendum for an official count of who was for and who was against, but it was agreed upon that the lack of rioting and uproar was the people's way of showing that they had agreed to play Russian roulette with their children's lives.

You know the old saying that in Scotland we suffer four seasons on one day? Well after Transference had been passed as the new "cure" for PODD, the world seemed to suffer four *emotions* in one day. One stroll down the road to get your lunch could expose you to a range, from normal everyday people going about their day, to someone quoting passages from the bible about how the end is nigh. You needed your wits about you for writers were creeping around wanting a sniff from the fountain of youth (being around young characters) and you were in a constant state of high anxiety. Continually waiting on someone that had lost the plot from losing their child, screaming down the streets wielding some sort of weapon.

The latter were few and far between, due to the writers keeping close tabs on them so as to not scare the public into thinking it was the wrong move. They were generally plucked from their very existence and locked away into hidden accommodations to rock back and forth for eternity.

Myself and our team, oh, get me, eh? I sound like we were some kind of superhero clan! Anyway, we were working hard in the background at collating information to put a stop to Transference. Or we were at the very least, opening everyone's eyes that it was morally and legally wrong. Many warriors for our cause had gone rogue and attempted to bring the regime down in one very public fell swoop, but this did not go unnoticed nor was it tolerated by the writers in the slightest. They had answers for everything, they were masters of distraction, never sweated a brow over any situation or scrutiny they were subjected to. They were one step ahead of the game from every angle and used every ounce of energy into presenting themselves as the utmost picture of honesty.

Missing posters plagued nearly every wall surface, a mix of people that had become an annoyance to the writers, people who couldn't cope with the death of an infant family member, people that just didn't want to live amongst other humans anymore, and genuine missing people that had fallen through the cracks of proper investigations.

We had been as careful, as we had been selective, over whom we entrusted into our, as we called it, circle of hope. Our very lives depended on the ability to welcome like-minded folk into our fold, hell; *all* lives depended on us having the right team of revolutionaries by our side. Up to that point we had been successful in our plight to free the shackles that the writers had forced around our ankles, we couldn't let it all crumble around us like a wet ginger bread house.

I remember vividly the moment that the hospital had been traced and found by one of our scouts. It was yet another lead that was expected to turn up zilch, but to everyone's shock and amazement, it turned out to be the headquarters for Transference.

"Is that… I gasped, at the phone.

"It bloody can't be!" Sonya almost choked on her own tongue.

We were both standing staring at the solitary, un-traceable, burn phone that was almost dancing as it shrilled into life. It was reserved for THE phone call to tell us when they had found the hospital, nothing else, not even a life or death situation. It was programmed to have a full stadium standing ovation blare out from it, then stop. Then Bluetooth across the coordinates of the hospital in an encrypted message embedded into a picture of the local A&E. It was all very hi-tech, super impressive, and highly recommended by still our most paranoid member, David.

Of course, the team and I were still not clued up with all this secret agent technical nonsense, we just knew from the ring that it had been found. The downside was that we had to wait on David to come and decipher the message and reveal where our next stop was going to be.

"This might take a little longer than I anticipated," David advised, upon opening the picture on the phone.

"I need to - ,"

"Just, do whatever you need to do and tell us the outcome, honey," Sonya interrupted him with a gentle kiss on the head. I was grateful that she had saved us from another near-death experience caused by overshar-ing in the form of public affection.

"Harrumph," David stuck his bottom lip out so far that pigeons were circling it to perch on.

As he started straining out the information from the cyber gunk, a few unprofessionally angled photographs popped up, presumably taken from inside, or certainly of close proximity to the hospital.

"That's us locked onto the address of the hospital now," David sighed, as we whooped and danced around him ungracefully.

"This hospital is the spine of this creature, once we get in there we can start pulling at the threads to unpick all of this craziness," Sonya laughed, almost hysterical.

"But, you do realise that you two can never go back there?" David wagged his finger at Sonya and I. "They know who you both are, they will kill you without so much as asking why you are there. It's not safe; we will take our time to assign the right people to this."

We were both angry that we weren't allowed to go back and get the answers we were so rightfully owed, but we knew he was right. They would clock us in an instant.

"They said that these pictures show the main ring leaders that are involved in the hospital, this one in particular seems to be in charge," he said tapping the screen with an accusing finger. It was the back of a tall, blonde woman. I don't know why, but I felt as if I knew her from somewhere. The slight stooping was not the stoop of a tall person, but a forced stoop to intimidate whoever they were speaking to. They had instinctively reacted to the intimidation by never looking the person directly in the face and playing nervously with their thumbnail.

"I'm surprised it's a woman, I would have bet good money on the callousness stemming from a man," Sonya looked genuinely thrown off scent.

"That ponytail, is it bonkers that I recognise the back of someone?" I quizzed David.

"Not at all, animals in the wild can tell their pack from the back, and from afar, not just by smell. We are but animals after all."

I racked my brain. I sat back onto the edge of the table and drummed my fingers, much to the annoyance of the other two.

"It helps me think," I stuck my tongue out at them.

Was it someone from when we were in hospital? Was it a random politician I had seen on the news? I closed my eyes as my head begun to hurt trying to force a memory to appear.

It reminded me of the time that Sarah was trying to get me to remember what Michael had said about her at the school disco. I had the briefest of conversations with him about random crap like, where I had got my leather jacket from or if I had any cigarettes, but Sarah had convinced herself that some the conversation was him really, secretly, asking about her. I was smiling to myself remembering how pathetic she was around him, or even at the mere mention of his name.

"Sarah," Sonya whispered, in such a small voice I almost didn't hear her.

"Yeah, I'm thinking about Sarah," I smiled back.

"No, Lauren, that's Sarah," she pointed to the stooping head honcho in the surveillance picture from the hospital.

Chapter 26

My heart literally stopped in mid-beat. My blood ran cold, and the colour had drained from my face. For the briefest moment in time, I had turned into a vampire. When it decided to start beating again, the thudding sounded like a creaky house whose door was being knocked on by an old frail hand. Slow, innocuous, weary knocks. It frightened me and kick started my startle reflex. When Sonya placed a worried hand on my shoulder, I almost jumped through the ceiling.

"It can't be her," mouthing the words was all I could muster.

No one replied to me and the room remained deathly silent. The only sound that could be heard was my ragged breath against the cold air. In reality, it wasn't actually that cold, but I certainly had shivers running up and down my spine like a loose ferret.

"I…," I tried to speak again, but the words just wouldn't form in my mouth, they seemed to get lost in my throat on the way up.

"It must be a mistake, or someone similar, I mean you can't even see her full face," I tried desperately to reason with the team. It was a futile effort, I already knew fine well it was Sarah in the pictures.

"Err, yeah exactly. We can't jump to any conclusions just yet, there might even be a perfectly good reason why she is there," Sonya replied, sounding unconvinced by her own words.

"I'm sure there are a number of reasons why your sister is in a highly secured, unknown to anyone, possible source centre of a deadly disease," David rolled his eyes at my inability to believe she was one of the bad guys.

"David!" Sonya slapped him with the back of her hand, and gestured for him and the team to leave us alone.

I racked my brain to remember any kind of clue, anything that would either clear Sarah's name or confirm her betrayal. My eyeballs were so dry due to my lack of blinking but I just couldn't muster up the strength to speak due to my humiliation, and her treachery.

"Lauren, no one here thinks that you are involved in Transference with your sister, so get that thought out of your head," Sonya's sympathetic tone made it hurt all the more.

They always say betrayal is like a stab in the heart, a punch in the gut, winds you and all sorts of other melodramatic metaphors however, they are not melodramatic at all. I felt so ill and achy all over, like I had been at the gym, with the flu, drunk. I couldn't bear it. All I wanted to do was curl up into a tight ball, pull my duvet over my head and fall asleep until this was all over. I was abundantly aware that this was not an option, but my actual options were not ones I sought to follow up on.

Did I let Sarah know that she had been found out and risk not only being killed myself, but have all our hard work be for nothing? Or did I keep quiet and bring her tumbling down when we out the writers for what they are? I didn't have much time to absorb this information. I left the others and figured I would go for a drive to clear my head. I had to decide what to do when the initial shock had worn off and I was more rational, but before I calmed down too much and followed my heart. The fact she was my sister was making this the hardest decision to make and being surrounded by people that didn't give two hoots about that didn't help. I was arguing with myself out loud in my car like a demented animal.

"She has betrayed me! Our family and our country! How could she? The sneaky little bitch!" I ranted. "But then, she had probably saved us? They for sure would have wanted us dead and she saved us," I reasoned. "Ack, she probably chose us and the McNeil's to mess around with because we were close to her and to fulfil her need to torment me," I was back to ranting. The worst part of it all was, I was answering myself back and that was never a good place to be in. I reached home, still confused and angry.

It took me drinking two straight whisky's, smoking a stray cigarette I found in my kitchen drawer from God knows when, and a flick through some family pictures, before I summoned up the courage to call Sarah.

"What?" She asked without any hello or acknowledgment.

She quickly followed up with, "Hello?" after I refused to answer.

"Oh, so you can say hello?" my sarcasm and rage were spilling out and down the line without my approval.

"Is everything ok? You sound more brattish than normal," she poked at me in such an obnoxious way, I swear I am going to jump through the phone and slap her so hard in the face.

"Where are you right now?" I asked, through gritted teeth.

"Right this second? I am eating a sandwich in the park, well I say eating it, I am mostly feeding the pigeons because it is –"

"Feeding the pigeons?" I interrupted her false and boring version of events. I have never seen or heard of Sarah being nice to any living thing on earth and now she wants me to believe she is acting out some kind of lunch hour from the movies. I think not.

"Look, my day has been crap enough without you phoning to quiz me and interrupting me, may I add, on the only hour of peace I get a day."

"I'm terribly sorry to be inconveniencing you, your highness; I would have thought your minions would have been treating you to the finest eatery in the land. Are you sure it's not golden geese you are feeding instead of pigeons?" my voice was raising at an alarming rate.

"What the f… Are you drunk or something? Is this a wind-up call from the radio? I don't have time for this nonsense. Call me back when you have found your marbles." She slammed down the phone.

Well in this day and age she just pressed a button to hang up on me, but I could feel it was executed with hate and contempt.

At the corner of my eye I noticed the ever so subtle flash of a blue light on my mobile that I hadn't seen for a long time. Someone had activated a tracker on my phone. David had all of our phones, homes and cars fitted with a sweeper that would flash a blue light whenever someone had triggered a tracker or listening device on us. I stared sadly at the phone as it winked its blue sheepish light at me, almost feeling the pity it emitted in my direction. Sarah was tracking me, or one

177

of her goons were. I had never felt so depressed in my entire life.

I ignored the flashing that was coming from my phone, along with the umpteen voicemails, texts, missed calls, emails, and various other attempts to contact me. I was not in any mood to be trifled with by either my stalking, murderous, backstabbing sister or my scared, confused, genuinely worried, but also paranoid, best friend.

I ran my whole life through my head in rapid rewind and fast forward modes, desperately trying to pinpoint the moment in my life when I subconsciously realised that Sarah was more than just a weirdo sister. I must have seen something, SOMETHING other than her blinding genius, her outstanding intellect and her coldness.

My head was bursting from the mixture of grief that my sister had died (she was officially dead to me) and anger from her leading me to believe my life was more than her lies. Were mum and dad involved? And Nathan? God, Nathan! He was like her twin brother, they mimicked each other in every way possible. You could almost have believed they were clones.

The blue light on my mobile flicked off. Sarah must have given up on trying to figure out what my ramblings were about, and chalked them up to me being drunk. That kind of hurt as well; the fact that she could believe I was a mid-day drinker, one that was capable of calling people up to shout abuse at. I conveniently turned away from my empty glass that had recently contained whisky.

I left all forms of communication on my living room table and headed to the kitchen to rummage around and clear my head, comfort food is always a winner in these situations. As I switched the light on, someone's reflection on my window froze me in panic, which refused to let me move an inch or even breathe.

"David!" I was finally able to shout as I turned around to punch him.

"I had to know for sure that you weren't in cahoots with Sarah, Lauren," he tried to protect himself from my pathetic attempt at a punch, but it didn't take very much energy to avoid.

"And creeping about in my kitchen like some kind of rapey, murderer is going to quash that thought for you?" I growled, at him.

"Granted, I gave you a fright and entered your house without your permission, but I think under the circumstances I am allowed to be concerned. There was a distinct possibility that our hard work was deliberately sabotaged or has all been for nothing."

"I take it Sonya has no idea that you are trespassing in her best friend's home?" I tilted my head already knowing the answer.

"That would be a flat-out no. Look, I get that you're angry, but Sarah is just a small fish in a big pond. The fact you are still alive after so long proves she is not interested in you," he tried to reason.

"I know," I sighed. "I just have so many questions for her, but I can't form them properly in my head. I mean, where would I even start? She tracked my phone for a bit but I think she thinks I'm just drunk, because she switched it off not too long after."

"I know, all of your communications are linked to me. I get notifications of any devices that are being tracked or monitored. That's good that you told me though, proves you're on our side." He smirked, half kidding.

I shook my head at David and threw my dish towel at him, which he pitifully avoided by dancing like an Irish jigger.

"Give me strength," I laughed.

"On a serious note, we all have your back. We need you to remain calm and focused, we have a mission to complete."

"I know, but what do you do when the enemy you have been chasing for so long is your own flesh and blood? What if it's her I come face to face with in the final battle?" I asked.

"You look her square in the eyes, pull out your sword and chop her head off. Victory will be ours," he nodded.

Chapter 27

Standing in the reception area of the hospital was the most nerve racking and surrealist moment of my life to date. The team and I had very lengthy discussions, debates, arguments, and an actual physical fight regarding who was going to infiltrate the hospital.

Seeing as I had already been there once before and my sister is seemingly the queen of all the soldiers, the safest option was for me to wiggle my way back in armed with surveillance.

I had to build up to it by making numerous appointments with my GP with complaints of headaches and night terrors, which then led him to refer me for a scan, and some counselling. Somewhere along the line, this information had managed to catch the attention of the writers.

They were equally as suave as I was. They waited until exactly a year and a half had passed, but before any appointments could be made with outside professionals.

***

"May I speak with Lauren?" an over friendly voice chirped into my ear.

"Speaking," I announced, without a follow up of who was asking.

"Hi, Lauren, my name is Louise calling on behalf of HCT, you will recall you briefly spent some time with us after an unfortunate car crash?"

"Yes, of course I remember. What is this regarding?" I tried to keep my voice breezy.

"Well, okay. You may not be aware, but we offer an eighteen-month courtesy call with the option to return for a little MOT. Patients with injuries such as the ones you were subjected to, often find that they are plagued with secondary conditions. In these instances, we offer the patients to come back into the hospital for a checkup to make sure your health is/has returned to normal. How would you say you have been since the crash, Lauren?"

"Funny you should mention it, lately I have been suffering from extreme headaches and night terrors. I didn't think to associate it with the crash because it was so long ago."

"Hmmm, have you reached out to your doctor about these symptoms?" She was polite, but obviously trained in interrogation.

"I have, he is sending me for a scan of some sort and some counselling, he obviously thinks I have some kind of delayed stress or something."

"Okay, well in this instance I think it would be wise to arrange for you to come back to the hospital. I feel we would be doing you a disservice if we didn't follow up on your well-being." She almost sounded sincerely interested.

"Great! What perfect timing," I genuinely tried to keep the sound of sarcasm out of my voice.

"I shall book you in with one of our in-house specialists. Once this has been arranged, we will send a car to pick you up and to take you home again. I'm sure you understand that for the protection of the company we will require you to remain in the car and not open any windows or doors."

"Yes, I remember from when we were taken home. Will you be contacting Sonya as well?" I quizzed her.

"Sonya? But of course, we call all of our patients to check on their well-being. Can I ask if you will be pursuing your appointments with your GP?"

"Oh, no. You guys are obviously better than private health care! I will call him today and cancel." I bit my lip hoping she was falling for this tripe.

"Perfect. Yes we do hold ourselves to a great stand-ard of healthcare, we would hate to feel that other resources are being utilised when they really don't have to be. Whatever you are suffering from I am 100 percent confident that we will get to the bottom of it. We will be in touch in due course, take care."

"Thank you, speak soon." I let her hang up first.

The call was swimming around my head as I tried to work out who had been spewing the most fake niceties out of the two of us.

***

I was dragged back to reality when the chirpy hospital receptionist asked me if I was ok.

"Erm, yeah," I replied, slightly dazed. This helped my performance of looking unwell.

"My name is... "

"Lauren!" she interrupted. "We have been expecting you back, please take a seat. Doctor Morrison will be with you momentarily," she gestured, to the most luscious looking sofa I have ever seen.

I did what she asked and poured myself into the sofa, groaning with delight as every inch of my body melted into the welcoming fabric, like being hugged by melted chocolate. I resigned myself to the fact that I may need to live in the sofa forever and imagined myself having food brought to me like an emperor.

"Lauren, hi! Sorry we have to meet again under the circumstances," another over friendly voice approached me. He extended his hand far earlier than was necessary. He noticed my confused face immediately as he followed it up with, "I shan't be offended that you don't remember me, you took quite a beating from that crash."

"Do you believe your own bullshit? Does it make it easier at night to think that this is not the working of your bosses?" I was desperate to shout out to him. Instead, I managed a weak smile.

"Please, follow me." He demanded.

Before I had a chance to reply, he turned on his heel and marched towards, what I presume was his office.

As much as I wanted to hate the hospital, knowing what it was built for, you had to give them credit for the amount of money and detail that was thrown at the place. If you didn't know any better, you would think that you were on another planet, a filthy rich planet.

We had breezed through the pleasantries and were half way through my in-depth description of "symptoms" that were ailing me, when the door was opened gently, catching us both off guard.

"Doctor Morr-" the nurse started, before closing her mouth and gulping.

It was the nurse that had saved Sonya and I when we were here the first time, with her subtle clues and tit bits on how to leave, alive.

"Can't you see I am with a patient?" He asked, remaining calm, but noticeably a tad miffed.

"I am terribly sorry, Doctor Morrison, I came in to ask if you would like the patient to have her basics checked? Mr Sal is having an issue that he needs you to assist with, I thought it would save the patient having to wait," she smiled, sweetly.

"You're absolutely right," he sighed.

"You go now and assist Mr Sal, I will take good care of Lauren, until you return," she shooed him out the door.

The door had barely closed when, Nurse Attitude, turned and glared at me like an angry mother trying not to lose her cool in the supermarket. She put one finger on her lips whilst miming a phone to me with the other.

"I'm going to remain silent for a few minutes whilst I take your blood pressure and temperature, I feel sometimes chatting elevates these things to give a false reading," she finally said.

I stared at her blankly and nodded, to which she gestured again with one finger, doing a circular motion round the room, and tapping her ear with the other.

"Oh, yes, that's fine, carry on," I sniffed.

She manhandled me and started patting me down like an overzealous member of airport security, pulling out my mobile phone. I was unsure at this point whether she was still an ally, if she was now the enemy or if she even knew herself.

Taking a deep breath, I focused on what she was trying to achieve. I could see that she was typing into my phone like she was sending a text message.

"We dnt hve much tme they r listening but not watching. I can type in your phne but not send so clear this to txt bk. What the fk r u doin bk here u need to go"

She was glancing between me and the door and hoping from one foot to the other as I read her message.

"I am here to bring them down, I need ur help"

I passed the phone back.

"R u crazy? They hv killed so many people for less tell them wot they need 2 hear & go"
"I cant they need 2 b stoped, evry1 needs 2 no the truth think of the chldrn"

She was rubbing her temples with her now sweaty hands and breathing harder than a porn star at the end of a scene.

"Ok, Lauren, everything is looking good here. Just a few more checks and then Doctor Morrison will be back for your evaluation," she spoke again, startling me.

"No problem. I love how quiet and serene it is here, it makes a nice change of pace," I replied.

"My frnds r watching this place I am wearin a camera in a contct lens & a scrambler in my watch help us"

"ok complain of lady pain I will take u whr u need 2 go let ur frend see this they must scramble as we walk or we die"

I nodded to show my agreement and looked at the phone long enough for David and the team to see the message. This had better work.

"Lauren, I am terribly sorry about the delay. I trust you have been well looked after?" Doctor Morrison burst in the door in high spirits.

"Very looked after, but I'm afraid I will need to re-schedule," I attempted to put my jacket on.

"Wh- why is that?" Doctor Morrison sounded slightly panicked.

"I am too embarrassed to say."

"We are all adults here, Lauren. What's going on?" His eyes were bulging.

"Well, I, I think I have had a ladies' accident and leaked through my clothes," I stammered. "I would really feel more comfortable going home, showering and changing."

"Not to worry, this is one of my rare quiet days. Nurse Camille can take care of your issues. Nurse Camille, could you kindly take Lauren to one of the private showers and provide her with a change of clothes?"

"Why, yes, of course I can, Doctor Morrison. Right this way." Nurse Attitude, or Camille as I now knew, guided me towards the door.

"Take your time, we take care of our patients and want everyone to feel right at home here. If we reschedule I may not see you for months and we will never get to the bottom of your headaches and terrors."

"Thank you so much, Doctor Morrison. I truly do appreciate your help and discretion," I smiled at him.

As we walked along the labyrinth of corridors in silence, it dawned on me that I might bump into Sarah. I was more scared of that than anything these guys could do to me. It's one thing for strangers to wish harm on you, but your more than capable sister? That's a whole other world of terror.

My heart was galloping like a runaway stallion. I glanced at my watch anxiously waiting for it to flicker that the scramble was activated. I was sure I was going to get caught as we walked what felt like twenty miles.

At one point, I questioned Nurse Camille's loyalty to me and if she was in fact leading me to a permanent room, or death.

Nurse Camille sensed my hesitation and scooped her arm through my arm like we were high school BFFs.

"It happens to the best of us women you know, please don't be ashamed."

"Thank you, I ju- right, show me what I need to see," I demanded, aware that my watch was indicating the scramble was activated.

Nurse Camille's breathing went from calm and rested, to shallow and raspy within a couple of seconds of the scramble kicking in; so much so, she had to steady herself against the wall.

"When I walked into that room and saw you, I almost had heart failure," she spoke through her breathy pants like she was in labour.

"I'm sorry, Nurse Camille, but you need to pull yourself together, and we don't have much time."

"I know, I know. And please call me Cammy, I think we go well beyond the pleasantries."

"The scramble alters the feed so it shows twenty minutes of the previous twenty minutes on visual and sound, if that makes sense. Our only risk is being physically seen," I looked up and down the corridor.

"We should be ok, there isn't much wandering around in this hospital. You know, since it isn't an actual hospital. Everyone is usually in the rooms they are assigned, the windows can be looked in for observation, but not out. Stay by my side at all times and if anyone does come, follow my lead. Okay?" Cammy waited until I nodded in agreement.

We hurried along the longest corridor I have ever seen, it felt never ending and I was positive we were going to get caught.

Have you ever had that flutter in the back of your throat? Mixed in with the double vision from holding your breath too long? That is what I was experiencing in nauseating waves.

Before long we were standing in front of a darkened room, my eyes were struggling to adjust to an outline within. What were we looking at? My question was soon answered as Cammy turned the volume up a little on the intercom at the side of the window. There were four small babies, around less than a year old, in individual cot beds, sleeping soundly.

"You will struggle with this," Cammy informed me.

"Is this, is this a transfer about to take place?" I gulped. Hard.

"Yip. They have told the world that it is painless because when they do it, the children are always sedated. This is not exactly true. Yes, they are sedated, but they are able to feel every inch of what is happening to them, the sedation is only for the benefit of the person performing the transfer. It's used to ease their guilt; it has jot all to do with the comfort of the little innocent souls." A few stray tears slipped down her cheeks. "They do these tests once a month to see if they have managed to find a sedative strong enough to numb the pain, but keep you awake at the same time. There is no such cure for the pain of literally having your life ripped out of your body and your soul being left in limbo.

"The two babies on the left have been sedated, this is what they sell to the public as painless. The two babies on the right, only the original infected baby is sedated, the receiving baby is not."

"So, they basically have locked in syndrome?" I asked.

"Yes. Not only will they feel the pain, but they will be questioning why no one is helping. Their little lives flashing before them. They die thinking they are completely on their own, with no love or affection as they take their last breath. They feel complete abandonment that you wouldn't wish on your worst enemy."

Two doctors entered the room with faces as stony as concrete, carrying an array of syringes and clipboards. One doctor went to each set of babies and busied themselves arranging the syringes that they would be harrowingly forcing upon them.

"You do realise that in these tests the transferee can hear what is being inflicted on to the transfer baby? The remaining transfer baby is not only going through its own demise, but listening to another suffer the same fate. Although the transferee is perfectly safe from harm, it doesn't know that. We don't know what physiological damage we are inflicting on them by making them lie and hear such turmoil, wondering if they are next. There are no winners in this process."

"Why do sedatives not work?" I asked, confused.

"It's difficult to explain in detail," she sighed.

"Ok, give it to me in laymen's terms," I urged, pointing to the camera in my eye.

"The PODD disease needs to be awake for the transfer to be completed correctly. If they use a full anaesthetic then the host becomes unconscious, so does PODD and this triggers it to hold on to the host for dear life. Like a built-in safety mechanism. If it isn't aware of what is going on around it, it locks in to the host to prevent any attempts to kill it. They basically have to sedate the children enough to cause paralysis, but not full unconsciousness."

"What the hell are we dealing with here? It sounds like an alien living in their body!" I panicked.

"In some ways that's exactly what it is. It's so sophisticated, there has never been anything like it before in this life time, but you will see more on that shortly," she raised an eyebrow.

I watched intently as the doctors concentrated on the task of sedating both transfer babies and making sure they were comfortable before moving on to the transferee babies. The doctor of baby one began whilst doctor two stood over baby two with an ominous look in his eyes. Once the doctor of baby one was satisfied that his guinea pig was not likely to cause him any hassle, he turned and gave a nod to doctor two.

They flipped over the transfer baby with such care; you would think it was a bag of precious stones they were upturning. Doctor two held the baby boy's neck as he delicately pierced the skin, inserting a syringe into the base of his spine, drawing out a clear liquid with blue strands of what looked like hair. Satisfied that they had removed whatever they were fishing about for, they lay the baby back down to recover from his ordeal in peace.

Both doctors moved across to baby one, placed the syringe down on the cot bed and flipped the baby over with no regard for his life at all; well, they were killing him anyway, I suppose was their thought. They haphazardly stabbed at his spine and injected the liquid straight in, lying him flat on his back like he was sleeping. Doctor one attached a heart monitor to him that suddenly started beeping rapidly. He was in obvious internal distress, but outside he looked the picture of contentment.

"The monitor tells us that he is in incredible pain. The sedative hides this for videos to the public and to make the transfer team feel better about what they are doing," Cammy spoke up.

Doctor one shifted brazenly across the room to the remaining babies and performed the same delicacy to the transfer baby as he had done with the first one. Once the liquid was removed, he injected it into the transferee baby as before however, this time the baby was not sedated. He was instantly awoken by being manhandled onto his front by two strangers and then stabbed in the spine with a syringe. He was so disorientated from being dragged out of slumber and having sharp objects forced into his delicate little body. He writhed around trying to rub off the pain, like when you jam or stave your finger and you try to blow it or shake it off. His cries were so upsetting to hear, he wanted to be picked up and reassured that everything was going to be okay. He wanted his mummy to rock him gently and kiss his sweet forehead, promising to protect him from all evils in the world.

It was utter, utter crap to watch, but it really was just the beginning of his long, painful journey.

As he settled down into little gurgles, I sighed a little that it was over, even though it had only been a few minutes. I couldn't watch anymore. As I turned to walk away, I did a double take as I heard a low grunting noise coming from the baby.

"This, this is Transference," Cammy poignantly touched the window.

Transferee baby two was grunting like a wild animal and his little chest was puffing out and sinking in like he was being deflated and blown back up again with a hand pump. His once sleepy eyes were now wide with fear as pain rippled through his tiny body in waves. His cries were deafening, soul destroying howls of desperation. He squirmed and convulsed as his tiny body was turning purple and sweating so much liquid, he was soaking the cot bed.

I looked away in disgust and despair that I couldn't run in and pick him up. I couldn't stop what they were doing to him. Nothing so small should feel pain so large.

"You need to see this, THEY, need to see this!"
Cammy grabbed my face by the chin, turning my head
back to the heart wrenching scene that was unfolding.

The baby's cries had turned into unearthly screeches
and I was positive they were going to shatter the glass
that stood between us.

As this was happening, sedated baby number one's
heart rate was becoming erratic; obviously reacting to
what was happening around him as well as what was
happening in his own little built-in nightmare.

It was breaking my heart to watch and yet, I couldn't
stop watching as his little body flailed around, desperately trying to find an end to his pain. I was willing him
to pull through, even though I knew that wasn't feasible
and I was also half praying for him to die. Death was
surely a much better end than the torture he was being
subjected to. Again, I had only witnessed a few minutes,
this was to go on for another hour.

His cries had already begun to grow hoarse, he was
choking on his own tears, vomit and saliva, his tired
body was ready to surrender. But he was needed alive
for the transfer to compete in full. Keeping him alive to
endure more of this hell was the only time the doctors
had any physical contact with him.

I was trying desperately to hold in my tears and anguish so we wouldn't get caught, but my body gave up
and I involuntary vomited all over myself.

"Please, I can't take anymore!" I wept to Cammy.

"Hold it together!" she hissed at me, dragging me
away down another corridor.

I was inconsolable as she frog-marched me into a
large open spaced bathroom which housed showers and
changing rooms.

"Clean yourself up as quick as you can, wet all of your hair and I will fetch you some clean clothes," Cammy looked at me with such sorrow.

I pitifully threw myself under the water wishing I could either wash off the stench of what I had just witnessed or I could dissolve in the water and wash myself away down the plug hole and into the sea.

"Put these on quickly, we need to make our way back before Doctor Morrison gets suspicious and comes looking for you," she panicked.

"I can't talk to him, I need to go home," I shook my head like a child.

"Look, he just wants to assess if you are likely to get counselling for your terrors and get flashbacks to what really happened. Tell him the terrors are about something random and opposite of the crash, your headaches are when you are on a PC or something, anything to throw him off."

"Ok," I shivered, as I dressed myself.

As we hurried back along a different corridor this time, I was unsure if this was actually some cruel and wicked nightmare that I was eager to wake up from and laugh about in work.

"That over there, that is where it was created," Cammy pointed, to two huge metal doors that spanned about thirty feet wide and stretched from ceiling to floor.

"What was?" I asked, confused.

"PODD," she whispered.

I whipped my head round and tried to adjust my eyes on her face.

"You mean, it actually was created, by them?"

"Come on, you believed them when they said that a mystery disease made its way over here from Japan and affected only wealthy children?" She actually laughed at me, to my face.

"Well, we have toyed with the idea that the writers may have deliberately infected everyone for some kicks, but that was half paranoia and half joking. We never dreamed in a month of Sundays it was genetically engineered by them for this sole purpose. But why?" I begged.

"Money, sweetheart, money. The government want money and control, the same as the wealthy do, but the government only let them think they are the top of the chain. They still control this whole world honey, they are the magicians that distract the audience with the beautiful assistants. They knew the rich would pay any cost to save their children, not out of love, but for status, *look at me I saved my child with my greed and wealth.*

"It's all a bank account lottery, just as Transference is done without anyone being aware of it, PODD is injected by the same process. The only difference being is, when they are infecting the child, they are fully sedated and immediately reversed on completion.

"Fuck," was all I could muster.

"This is much bigger than any of us anticipated, there is no way we can bring them down," I was totally crestfallen.

"Don't you dare, Lauren. Don't you dare come this far just to give up and walk away! These babies need you, future babies need you. I need you."

"Ok, I need to get out of here. Let's make our way back and get this over with," I sighed.

As we turned to make the long journey back with not much time to do it in, we were stopped in our tracks by the echo of an opening door.

"Stop right where you are, Lauren. I think we need to chat," a voice boomed behind us.

Chapter 28

They'd forecast the warmest day that I was ever to witness, or even imagine. There was no way I was going into school!

Back then, no one had mobile phones, social media or anything remotely exciting to communicate with. With the exception of a dial up internet connection that took two hours to load and no one really knew how to work.

To enable me to skip school successfully, I had to trust that Maria had the same thoughts that I did and pray that she hadn't already left when I popped in for her on the way there.

I picked up my school bag, foraged around for some lunch to take that didn't resemble a homemade feast made by mum, and skipped off down the street imagining all the things we could do on our day off.

As I approached Maria's house, I could see she had already sensed that a plan had been forming in my mind much similar to hers. Her face was practically absorbed into the window looking out for me.

Her expression of excitement when she saw me was not too dissimilar to that of a dog happy to see its owner, that and her tongue was wagging about; I was more surprised a tail hadn't sprouted out of her bum.

"Look how sunny it is today!" she sang at me, nearly ripping the front door off its hinges.

"I know, isn't it such a shame we will be stuck indoors at school," I replied, thinking my sarcasm would have been evident.

"What?!" Maria burrowed her eyebrows into each other like they were having a passionate love affair. "No way, are we…"

"Joke!" I butted in before she started foaming at the mouth.

"Have a good day at school, you guys," Maria's mum shouted to us from the kitchen.

"We will!" we replied in unison, quickly followed by a hushed "not" once we were a safe distance from being heard.

"This is super exciting; I have so many plans with things for us to do. Today is going to be written about in the future as the day that the word fun is based on," Maria rambled on confidently as she danced around me like an annoying fly.

I can confirm wholeheartedly that the only thing that was written about that day in our 'not so far away' future was in fact, a punishment exercise, along with the sorest arse I had ever encountered.

It didn't take us long to realise that the world was *not* our oyster. We weren't free to do whatever we liked, fun is not inexpensive and whatever other childhood clichés we could cram into one breath. The truth of the matter was, we couldn't walk about anywhere local for fear of being seen, we didn't have any money to go gallivanting into Glasgow city centre and the sun had buggered off within minutes of us being reported as absent from school.

We pooled what little cash we had and treated ourselves to a can of juice and a packet of chewing gum between us. We instantly regretted this decision when the realisation that we had no bathroom to use, and the sweets had done nothing to curb our growing hunger, kicked in.

We got swept up in the excitement of dodging school, but the reality couldn't have been any further if it had lassoed itself onto the back on a jumbo jet.

"Man, this is boring," I whined, more to myself than anything else.

We were huddled in the bottom of old Mad Joe's alley, using our jackets as a make shift invisibility cloak in case any family members, or friends of family members, came past us. There was no skipping about the place gleefully and no wild adventures to be recounted to future generations as we tucked them into bed. So far, the only interesting thing that had happened was finding a cigarette butt and match, which we toyed with smoking, me having to pee at the back door of one of the houses like some kind of tramp and Maria nodding off and hitting her head on the wall.

The streets were deserted as if we were in the midst of a zombie apocalypse. Everyone was either at work, in school or up to no good in the privacy of their own homes. The only people to be seen were the local lollipop man, the bin men pretending to empty the bins, and a few other undesirables that were also dodging school.

They were fun to watch because they were pretending to each other that they didn't care if they were caught. However, they were walking about with such a petrified look on their face; I thought they might physically burst a brain vessel.

Before long, we were desperate for the comfort of the wobbly chairs in Mr Drumander's English class. Ah, to be swayed like an old sailor's ship tied up at the docks as Mr Drumander recalled tales of his youth. To be so cold, that when Mrs Kingston asked you how to say hello in German, your response included seeing your own breath; that made you question whether you had died and are haunting the place.

"It's a bad day, when I actually miss school," I blurted out.

"I know. Me too, this is so rubbish," Maria agreed.

"Look, Mrs Fletcher is in charge of registration all week, if we sneak into our next class they won't question why we are there. She is as mad as a box of cats, thinks no one knows she is drinking in that filing cupboard," I snorted.

"That's true. She misses out half the class all the time," Maria confirmed.

I helped Maria up off the filthy floor and we both stretched out like we were preparing for the Olympics, just as cramp started to ripple its way through her calf.

"ARGHHHH! Holy bloody hell!" she screamed at the top of her lungs.

"Stand on your tippy toes and pull your feet down, slowly," I ordered her, but it fell on deaf ears.

"Ouch! Ouch! Argh! Don't touch me. DO NOT TOUCH ME. Don't leave me, please help!" she whimpered.

As she continued to hop around, wailing in a fashion that an Italian mobster's widow would be proud of, I tried my best to catch her from falling. I failed. Miserably. Her jaw bounced off the wall in super slow motion, all I could do was watch and laugh. Man, did I laugh. When she remained motionless on the floor, my laughter soon stopped.

"Maria?" I poked her with my finger and jumped back expecting her to punch me. Nothing.

"Crap," I cried out loud.

Do I go get help? Do I run like hell, leave her here and deny all knowledge of this? Do I drag her into the woods and cover her with brambles and hope she is never found? Ah, the craziness of a scared witless teenager's mind.

"Boo!" Maria jumped up causing me to tumble over my own feet and onto the ground beside her.

"What the hell, Lauren! You didn't even ask me if I was ok, or go and get help. Did you think I was dead?" She laughed.

"No way! I was wondering how to bury your dead body," I stuck my tongue out at her.

"Seriously, though, that was proper agony," she rubbed her jaw and calf at the same time with frantic hands.

"Right, come on," I pulled her up onto her feet yet again. "We need to get into school within the next twenty three minutes," I checked my cheap market stall watch.

"Aye, aye, captain!" she saluted me.

Approaching the school, we could see that the main gate and our only means of access, was closed. We both knew our only choice now was to climb it and hope that none of the teachers were too bored on that particular day to look out the window and catch us.

"Get your bloody, fat arse out of my face!" Maria shouted at me as I failed to try and hoist myself with my belt.

We were on our way to victory, just another thirty seconds and no one need know how rubbish our day had been and no one w...

"How do you solve a problem like Lauren and Maria?" a voice boomed behind us, causing us both to slip back down the fence.

We were too petrified to turn around and face our captor. We closed our eyes and prayed that gulping would somehow make them disappear into the marshy ground, it didn't. It was our head teacher, Mr Andrew who had caught us whilst he was having his sneaky cigarette. His gloating moustachey, yellow, pointy toothed smile of smugness said he had not only caught us, but would shame walk us through the school like dead men walking.

That memory flew into my head as I stood unable to move in the hospital corridor with Cammy glancing at me like a terrified rabbit in the headlights. We had come this far, only to be caught red handed and probably murdered on the very spot where we stood.

The only good thing to come of it, was the characters would be getting to see the horrors I witnessed and watch in repulsion at our pre-emptive deaths.

Cammy and I refused to turn around and face our fate and whoever was standing behind us remained silent to the point that I almost thought he had slipped away without us noticing.

The air was thick and I could just about make out his subtle breathing and nervous shuffling from foot to foot.

"Friend or foe?" He finally spoke up.

"Well, erm, a little bit of both," I stammered. "Friend to the people, foe to you and your disgusting group of conceited, narcissistic, 'out for all you-can get' scumbags," I hissed.

Cammy shot me a look of, "Well, thanks for that, we are completely done for now."

"Nice to see they haven't managed to penetrate that feisty attitude of yours, Lauren," the voice suddenly became familiar to me.

"Jon… Jonathan?" I involuntarily spun round holding my hands up in a surrender pose. "But how?"

201

"We don't have time for specifics now; they killed my Mary because she was too much of a loose cannon. I had the pleasure of them performing a number of brain washing techniques on me, but I decided to stop fighting before they finally lobotomised me. That's what most of the patients that are in here have had done, if you're not careful you will be next," he warned.

"No, no, it's ok, don't worry, we have a plan. We are bringing these guys down," I informed him, without much conviction in my voice.

"We can join forces. I am allowed to roam about free because they think I have been emotionally destroyed by them. They are cocky and over confident, they believe they are invincible. Sometimes I wish they had killed me so I can be at rest with my girls. I can't rattle around here anymore like their pet, watching and hearing all the things they subject onto innocent lives, all the horrors," he shook his head.

"I hate to interrupt this truly touching reunion, but we need to head back or Doctor Morrison will have a search party out for us," Cammy was trying to remain calm, but was sounding far from it.

We all walked together, with me wedged in between Jonathan and Cammy like an unwanted sandwich filling. As we headed towards a single, larger door, Jonathan ushered us to one side.

"You have immediate contact with the outside? A camera or audio?" He asked me.

"Yes," I replied.

"Tell them to let you both walk through the doors and switch themselves off after five seconds. Act normal, both of you," he nodded at us both and then shoved us away from him towards the door.

We hesitated at the door handle, took a deep breath, and then walked through the doors. Silence, silence, silence, silence, silence.

"And I told her at the time, I said she shouldn't have worn fake tan with a white dress, but you know what sisters are like, they can't take a telling!" Cammy was laughing at her own impromptu story.

"You know what's good for getting fake tan stains out? T…"

"Who are you!?" Jonathan had kicked the door open that we had just waltzed through and lunged at me.

"Steven, calm down. Security!" Cammy shouted.

"Tell me who you are!" he demanded, grabbing me by my shoulders.

It all happened in a split second, I couldn't take my eyes off Cammy and my mouth had lost its ability to remain closed.

I heard a commotion behind me and as I turned to glance over my shoulder, I felt a sharp pain shoot through my cheekbone making me stumble backwards into a heap. Three security guards rugby tackled Jonathan to the ground and Cammy was checking my pulse on the floor beside me.

I put my hand up to my face and felt warm blood dance between my fingers. I then clocked Jonathan's flailing knuckles covered in blood. My blood. He hit me! The crazy idiot had sucker punched me square in the face!

If he was after the authentic look of this being a real unwarranted attack, then he had succeeded in every possible way. From my potential broken cheekbone, my unnerving swelling eyeball, right down to the genuine shock that I was teetering on the verge of.

Doctor Morrison appeared by my side and helped Cammy pull me up onto my deer-like unsteady feet.

"What happened? Who was that?" I asked as innocently as I could muster.

"Never mind that for now, let's get you checked over, Lauren. I am desperately worried about that eye of yours," Doctor Morrison announced.

Back in Doctor Morrison's office, I was plied with water, tea, coffee and blankets. I wasn't far off resembling a refugee that had been saved from death's door.

Doctor Morrison made sure he covered his ass by performing every check he could think of, my blood pressure, heart rate, breathing, pulse, temperature, hearing, everything but a colonoscopy.

"Now, I know it is painful, but I need you to look into the light that I am going to shine in your eyes, ok?" He asked me whilst trying to prise my swollen eye open.

"Erm, no thanks, I'm ok," I panicked, realising the contact containing the camera was in that eye. Cammy clicked on to why I was so frightened and tried to hide her rising alarm.

"Lauren, as a respected member of the medical profession, I cannot in good faith let you walk out of here with an array of possible injuries, especially ones caused by another patient of mine."

I gulped so hard, that my tonsils ached. I developed a little bit of a coughing fit, which led to me vomiting all over myself, again.

"See, that itself is not a good sign after a head trauma, if you don't let me inspect your eye and cheekbone to a degree in which I am satisfied, I will have to ask Nurse Camille to restrain you," he sighed.

I looked to Cammy, who put her hand on my arm and looked at me in way that made me shiver. We have no way out of this.

"Ok, I'm sorry. I'm just a little rattled by the whole incident," I squeaked.

Doctor Morrison wheeled his chair closer to me and began inspecting my cheekbone like he was admiring a recently discovered, rare painting.

"Hmm, you are extremely lucky, Lauren. I don't think it's broken."

"Bloody feels like it," I laughed, touching it gingerly.

As he attempted to open my now welded shut eye with his right hand, his left remained tight around the back of my neck. I knew that within the next few seconds, once he saw the contact lens, that hand would grow tighter round my neck until it snapped it. The contact was barely visible to the naked eye, but under scrutiny and by a trained government spy, it was pretty obvious that it was some super highly advanced technology.

He was rooting about in there for more than three minutes, I counted in my head, in complete silence. His breathing didn't quicken, his grip didn't tighten. Nothing.

"Again, you are really lucky, Lauren. I mean you should probably buy a lottery ticket." He finally broke the awkward silence.

"Are you sure? It kind of feels like my eyeball is on the verge of falling out," I laughed, out of nerves.

"I know it feels like that, but I have had a really good look and poked about your cheekbone, there is nothing serious, no long-lasting damage done. I do want to flush the eye if that's ok? It looks a little red and irritated, could be something transferred into it from the patients knuckle."

"Flush away, if you think it will help."

He rolled himself away on his chair to a cabinet by the door, was he getting a gun? Pressing a button for back up? I honestly didn't know how much more I could handle the anxious waiting.

"Nurse Camille, could you please flush Lauren's eye for me? I want to follow up on what exactly happened today," he announced, standing up, not really waiting on an answer.

"Yes, of course, Doctor Morrison," Cammy busied herself collecting the necessary items to complete her task.

As the door clicked shut, we began speaking to each other in dodgy sign language which involved a lot of pointing and shrugging. I was relieved when she showed an interest in actually flushing my eye, but it was more like having a one-sided water fight with a blind person.

To make it sound good, I restarted the fake conversation in the good doctor's absence.

"Who was that man that attacked me? I didn't even see him coming; did I upset him in some way?" I rolled my unharmed eye.

"Steven is one of our in-patients; he is usually docile and harmless. He regularly walks around the hospital to stretch his legs. I am positive you were just unlucky. It could be a number of things like your perfume, he might not have taken his medication and sometimes our in-patients have little episodes. I'm sure when he calms down he will feel just awful about it all," she reassured me.

"I really want to go home and forget about it. Oh and take some strong painkillers!"

"Don't you worry; Doctor Morrison won't keep you too long. He is a fabulous doctor. Once he asks you a few questions about your headaches and stuff, he will send you home with some high quality drugs."

"What about Steven? What will happen to him?" I genuinely queried his safety.

"Well, that depends on you, honey. Do you want to press charges on a mentally challenged man who won't fully understand why he will be punished? Move him from here into to a prison?"

"Oh, goodness no!" I gasped, at her (fake) tactics.

"He won't know why he attacked you, we will just need to keep him from wandering about where outpatients may be and reiterate the rules."

Doctor Morrison came breezing back as if he had left the room for a quick pee break.

"Is everything done here, Nurse Camille?" He asked.

"Yes, I was just tidying up," she patted the remaining water from the corner of my eye.

"Good stuff, now why don't we discuss why you are really here, eh?" He gripped my shoulders like a bird of prey carrying its young back to the nest. He slowly walked me over to a chair opposite his desk and plopped me down. He lowered himself down into his big comfy seat, crossed his legs, and let out an almighty sigh.

"Now, let's go back to the start, shall we? Tell me everything."

Chapter 29

I squirmed in my chair with every question fired at me. I was like a child being interrogated by her mother; after spending the weekend with her estranged dad and his new girlfriend.

"Tell me everything, Lauren, what have you found out about Transference? What happened when you and Nurse Camille went on your little jaunt?" the questions were making me feel dizzy.

Before I could answer one, he was asking me another and it was making me feel queasy. My eye and cheek were throbbing like a horny frat boy in a strip club, and the sweat was somehow coming out of me like a spraying fountain. I was not looking my best.

"Leave her alone for a few minutes to catch her breath, she isn't going anywhere; you will get your answers," a protective voice came from beside me.

"Stay out of it, I am already wondering if you are more on her side than ours, can we trust YOU?" He spat back in reply.

"David!" I tutted, and shot a look of annoyance in his direction. "How can you even say that to Sonya."

Sonya was standing with her arms crossed across her chest so tight, that her cleavage was holding her jawbone up.

"I was out of order, I know. I'm just tired and desperate to know what happened in that hospital. We didn't know if you were dead or alive after that psychopath attacked you and the camera wouldn't switch back on."

"Is it broken? Was everything deleted? Has this all been for nothing?" I pointed to my eye with an unintentional pouting lip.

"Well no, definitely not for nothing. We recorded everything that you saw in there but, we have since tried the camera a few times and there is nothing but blackness. We will keep trying, intermittently," he reassured me.

"When Jonathan hit me, it must have fell out my eye and got stepped on or something. I honestly thought it was still in there until I came here."

You see, what Doctor Morrison was ominously referring to in the hospital about, "Let's go back to why you are really here," was in fact, why I was there, the headaches and night terrors. Thankfully my inability to reply to him swiftly, due to the fear of being brutally murdered, allowed him to follow up with, "So, when do you notice the headaches more," preventing me from jumping in and confessing our whole plan.

After an hour of lying through my back teeth about how the headaches were almost always when I was watching television/using a computer/reading and that the terrors were possibly me being a tad melodramatic, it was diagnosed as nightmares after caffeine fuelled days.

He reassured me that I was more than likely in desperate need of a pair of glasses and I was to lay off the eight cups of coffee I was guzzling down like a possessed coffeeholic.

He showed more interest in whether I had seen the man that attacked me or not, probably to ascertain if I recognised Jonathan, who was "dead". He showed no sign of knowing or even suspecting that I had a secret camera wedged into my eyeball.

I explained to him that Nurse Camille and I were too engrossed in our conversation to be aware of any situations building up round about us; I only became aware of "Steven" when I heard a shout, and his fist became a close acquaintance of my cheek. After that, I was in far too much shock and pain to even recite my own name, never mind soak in the fine details of my attacker. I wouldn't have had a chance to see him anyway as he was covered in security guards like a rugby scrum.

He seemed genuinely satisfied with each answer that I provided, even laughing at my humour because, well let's face it; even under the threat of imminent death, I am hilarious.

Camille was such a natural at whatever situation she found herself in, whatever side she had to pretend to be supporting, that it was hard to trust her intentions sometimes. I couldn't help but wonder if she would consider a career in Hollywood once this whole thing was out in the open and a thing of the past.

I reassured the doctor that I would not be pressing any charges. It was just an unfortunate incident that happened due to me being in the wrong place at the wrong time. I wasn't seriously hurt and could milk it for at least a week off work, if he would be so kind as to provide me with some kind of letter to back it up.

I said my polite goodbyes and left with the following:

- A prescription for strong ass medications for my eye and cheek

- A prescription for antibiotic eye drops

- A sick note detailing my attack and injuries

- A bag with my clothes that I had changed out of for my shower

- A promise to switch to decaffeinated coffee

- A promise to go and see an optician

- A promise to call if I had any other questions or problems

I tried with all my might to contain my excitement at being able to leave the hospital in one piece. Cammy's sentiments were exactly the same as mine, I could see it in the glint in her eye. My sincere appreciation for being alive was obviously being interpreted as innocence and of no threat to them.

The driver dropped me off at my house after yet another silent and blackened window drive home and I went straight to my living room chair. I waited an appropriate length of time for any of my alerts to show I was being monitored before sending a cryptic text to Sonya. She replied that I was to go full emissary, which meant I was to mix up my journey back to the gang by taxi, train, bus and foot. Making sure I swapped and turned back on myself a few times like a mad woman.

It was here that I found myself being interrogated by David before I had the chance to remove my jacket or let the past few hours of my life actually sink in.

"You, my dear, will be making up for that ridiculous outburst," Sonya finally spoke in David's direction.

"I can't believe Jonathan is still alive," David ignored her.

"I know. I thought he would have been dead by now," Sonya agreed.

"Well, I think he certainly will be dead after today. I really don't understand why he hit me, maybe he really is unhinged from what they have done to him," I shrugged.

"Lauren, what you witnessed, it must have been harrowing for you. There wasn't a dry eye or an un-churned stomach in the room as we watched through the lens," Sonya was sympathetically rubbing my back.

I lifted my head and looked round the gang thoroughly for the first time since I entered the room. I could see the mix of expressions from petrified, angry and scared all the way to determined and disgusted.

"I am not denying it was brutal however, it needed to be seen. It's needed to be shown, the people must see the truth," David was sounding all speech like again.

"Guys, you need to see this," Liam, one of our minions, was beckoning us over to his screen.

"Tell, Lauren, I'm so sorry. I could see this thing ten miles away in her eye and I needed to cause a distraction and get it from her at the same time," Jonathan was clearly holding my lens camera and talking into it.

"How does he know w…?" I tried to ask.

"He doesn't, he has already said he kept it in his fist this whole time and he was hoping we were watching," Liam was shushing me.

"I needed to get her out alive, I drummed her up some sympathy and her real shock gained her bonus points. I also needed to let you see what they do to patients in here, they will be back for me soon. Please do not try to save me; I have nothing left to live for. Please, save the world from these bastards."

The screen continued to show Jonathan attempting to place the lens into his eye and then staring at the wall, with only the sound of him gently weeping and praying to be heard.

No one uttered a word, we all pulled chairs around the screen in slow motion, positioning ourselves to watch a real live snuff film. It felt wrong, it felt sombre. We were united in our sorrow however; we knew that we owed it to him to see exactly how his fate panned out.

I wished there was some subtle way we could let him know that we were there with him, for him, in his final hours. Did he know we were? He was humming away to himself and chuckling, not in a maniacal way, more like in a smug/acceptance kind of way. We glanced at each other every few minutes to reassure ourselves that we were definitely going to follow through witnessing his murder and not just switch the monitor off.

"Look, no one is going to judge you if you decide this is too much to watch, we are all still a bit delicate from watching the Transference with the babies," David spoke up with such authority; it almost sounded like an order to leave.

No one spoke. And no one moved either. We all remained huddled round waiting for Jonathan to be forced to his fate.

It made me question why family members or friends would go to executions of their loved ones, was it the final act of goodbye? Was it the closure they needed to help them move on? I can understand the victims or families of victims attending, hoping that watching the light flicker out from the cold, murdering eyes would provide them with the feeling of vengeance and comfort they needed to appease themselves.

I didn't have to ponder on that thought for too long as we followed Jonathan's shaky view from sitting on the floor to being dragged to his feet and then finally escorted down a few corridors in silence.

There were two of them, one at each side with a good enough grip on his upper arm and wrists to let him know it wasn't worth trying to cause them trouble. He made sure to casually glance around him to show us what they looked like, how they held him and in what direction he was headed.

The corridors were quite dark and eerily quiet with only a dim light up ahead, like the light emitted from a candle, but it wasn't flickering. You could see there was a few people in the room, but not how many or what sex they were.

"Ah, Steven, do come in," an unfamiliar doctor extended his arm out to welcome him into the room.

"What's going to happen to me?" He asked, sounding slightly panicked.

The doctor sighed and looked around his three other medical-looking companions, with a shifty, menacing look.

"Come on now, Steven, you know what we need to do. You have been very naughty today and I need to ascertain why you attacked that pretty looking lady."

I was disgusted in myself that I felt the tiniest flicker of happiness that he called me pretty. This was followed by an even tinier flicker of annoyance that he called me lady, and finally enveloped in a wave of guilt for even thinking about any of that in this situation.

"Please get him ready for interrogation," the doctor ordered one of his henchmen.

Steven didn't fight as he was strapped down to the hospital bed with his head put into a restraint that prevented him from moving it. Still glancing from side to side and up and down, we could catch glimpses of what was happening. An electrical pad was secured onto each of his temples, which were then hooked up to what looked like a fancy battery.

214

"Now just relax, Stephen, I am going to ask you a few questions and I would like you to tell me the truth. If I think you are lying, I will shock your brain which will convert your lie to the truth. Don't try and fight it, you would much rather live than die, wouldn't you?"

Unfortunately for Jonathan, but fortunately for us, he didn't give two fucks whether he lived or died. In fact, death was welcomed by him and that meant his determination was about to overcome any pain they inflicted onto him. We hoped.

"Do you know the lady's name you attacked today?" the doctor asked.

"No," Jonathan replied.

"Why did you attack her?"

"I thought I knew her from somewhere."

"Where?"

"I don't know. I thought I knew her and I had this feeling of hatred towards her."

"Do it," he nodded, to the female henchman to switch on the machine.

"ARGHH!" Jonathan's body seized and his eyes rolled into the back of his head.

"Let's try that again, shall we? Why did you attack her and what is her name?" the doctor urged.

"I don't know her name and I don't know why I attacked her," Jonathan panted.

This went on for about ten minutes, each time the machine was switched off you could see Jonathan's life was slipping away bit by bit. He was groggy for longer, more confused and his answers were getting shorter.

"Dunno… feeling… door," he slurred after the latest zap.

"Shall we tell her that he knows nothing? That it was just a random attack?" the second henchman queried the doctor.

"Hmm, I'm not sure, something doesn't sit well with me about it all. Do it again for a bit longer and we shall see what he says."

The henchmen switched the machine on and left it longer than the other blasts, this one for some reason caused a sort of convulsion that jerked Jonathan around. When it stopped, he was foaming at the mouth, but very much still alive.

"What the hell is this?" the doctor pushed the henchmen's arms away from Jonathan's body. "Jonathan? Are you still alive? Are you in pain?"

"Yes," he croaked.

We all gasped as he replied to his real name. We also became aware that the angle of the lens wasn't were it should be.

"Well, hello there," the doctor wiggled his fingers to the lens as he picked it up from where it had fallen out of Jonathan's eye.

"Shit," David jumped up like a skittish cat.

"How adoringly ruthless and elaborate! I don't quite know who you are, but it won't take us very long to find out," the doctor smirked.

The henchmen all looked at each other with satisfied looks on their faces that they had done a good job getting to the bottom of the problem.

"And you wanted me to tell the boss he knew nothing," the doctor was now twirling a scalpel between his fingers.

Before we had time to take another breath, the doctor turned to the henchman and slit his throat in one fell swoop. He then aimed the lens at Jonathan as he stabbed the scalpel right into the centre of his forehead.

He smiled into the lens as he sang, "Ready or not, here we come."

Chapter 30

We were growing very tired of each other at a very fast pace and considering there was about thirty of us cooped up together, it did not bode well.

It had been less than twenty-four hours since Jonathan was murdered. My phone had lit up like a Christmas tree as it monitored me. We made a collective decision to disable and ditch all forms of communication and go underground. Quite literally.

The writers had obviously put two and two together and come up with the explanation of Jonathan receiving his camera lens from me, the poor innocent girl he had attacked earlier that day. I was the only person from the outside that he had physical contact with and I was already under suspicion, hence me being there in the first place.

My head was scrambled with images of poor Cammy being subjected to the same fate as Jonathan. She was with me the whole time and so will be treated in accordance to traitor's law. I hoped Doctor Morrison didn't fall short of punishment. I can just see him trying to worm his way out of his incompetence with excuses for why he should be spared.

Did I now have a bounty on my head? Did Sonya? Did David? How far would they stretch the net out on death by association? We had been careful with all our communications to each other, so the thirty of us hiding away was probably a bit of an extreme panic, or was it? These people were capable of the most heinous crimes, I was confident that we had only scratched the surface of how far they would go for world dominance.

Thoughts of Sarah pretending she was worried for me and enquiring about my whereabouts to our family, my workmates, and my neighbours in her quest to hunt me down and turn me over to her chums, was making me feel violated and sick to the pit of my stomach.

I was jolted out of the grey and depressing image of me being buried in a shallow grave somewhere, by Sonya and David attempting to bicker under their breaths and failing miserably.

"This wasn't part of the plan! What the hell are we going to do now, David? We are sitting ducks, just counting down the days until they find us," Sonya was whispering with a trembling voice.

"You need to stay calm, I have the recordings with me they are untraceable," he added, seeing the panic in her eyes. "I still have means of communication with some contacts, I just need to come up with a plan of action. We are in a game of chess here, a real life game, we just need to have all possible moves covered," he soothed.

No one spoke. It was almost as if we subconsciously thought that if we spoke, an alarm would ring and pinpoint our exact location to the writers. I know, even that was a stretch for them but, being so scared and exhausted is a dangerous state of mind to be in; especially when you add paranoia into the mix.

We were in an old war shelter that David had found and declared as his own although, by the state it was in when he found it; it clearly didn't have an owner. It was fifty feet underground and about the size of a football pitch, it sounds quite big, but believe me, when there are thirty people anxiously pacing, it really isn't that spacious.

He had thankfully been expecting an impending war/invasion/divorce, because he had it fully stocked up with supplies that would enable us all to live here for at least four months without starving or dehydrating to death. Great, the party can rock on for four months, although that length of time together may be a fate worse than what the writers had planned for us.

"They won't know about any of you guys, you can probably all go and live your lives perfectly safely," David was trying to reassure the remainder of the team.

"He's right you know?" Sonya agreed. "The only sure fire connection will be Lauren, David and me. I'm sure Sarah will confirm that your family are none the wiser," she nodded to me.

"Yip, thanks for reminding me that Sarah also wants me dead, I mean, more than she usually does."

"There is no way in hell I am taking the chance. They are animals and will eliminate us by any means possible, on the smallest of hunches about us," Liam interrupted.

"So, what do we do then? Stay here for a few months? The only difference to the outcome is that we will be smellier and weaker, making us easier to kill," Sam, one of our younger gang members piped up.

We all attempted a subtle smell of our underarms, before sitting back in silence to collect our thoughts.

"I'll do it," Liam stood up like a proud soldier offering to be executed to save the masses.

"Do…what exactly?" David asked, confused.

"Oh, yeah right. I kind of thought it out in my head and not out loud," he sat back down sheepishly. "I will venture outside and take copies of the video from inside the hospital to the press/government/police etc."

"Right into the hands of the enemy? You do realise that no one can be trusted, well, no one that we know," I scoffed.

"Hold on, hold on, Lauren. My contacts had managed to locate a few people who are not in the loop. There are not many I grant you but, they do still exist. I need to try and make contact with them first to see how we can expose this to the characters. We can't just light this fuse and expect there to be no fireworks," David replied.

"How many copies can you make from down here?" Sonya asked with her palms pointing to heaven.

"About fifty," David confirmed.

"Ok, we need to narrow the list down to only absolute trusted acquaintances. Then we need to fan out, try and reach who we can, wherever we can. Let's not keep this limited to Scotland or even the UK; this is the world's problem. Let the world do what it can to fix it," Sonya replied.

"I don't think we will be protected by any whistle-blower clauses and until this is out in every newspaper and television network, we cannot trust anyone. You're right though, we need as far a reach as possible," Liam had jumped back into the conversation.

We needed the perfect plan to execute this as smoothly as we could. David and some of the other gang members had squirreled themselves away into a corner to perform a step by step process of elimination of the who's who in the wheel of corruption.

Sonya and I had elected ourselves head of the remaining group to brain storm how we could get the Intel to our chosen few without being caught, or leaving any trace that would lead back to us. We had toyed with the idea that the best form of disguise would be for everyone to don a niqab. A niqab isn't quite the full Muslim attire, it essentially covers the face and shoulders only, however, the public's perception of Muslim's was already on a shaky nail thanks to the writers using all news outlets to fuel their hatred and propaganda. We felt that this may bring us more unwarranted attention than we desired, along with the fact that it would be something else for the writers to use against them if our plan failed. They had enough troubles and daily battles to fit in and be left alone in peace without us adding fuel to the fire.

It made more sense for us to deliver the parcels in plain sight, with the exception of Sonya, David and I, who were currently the writers conjoined number one enemy. We weren't 100% sure that the others had been linked to us yet, or if they ever would be at all. They would each take a parcel and spread out to a different post office across the city to post to their designated contact. Due to it being sent secure delivery with signature confirmation, they needed to use a local business right beside their designated post office as the sender address; in an attempt to have the writers running about chasing their tail and exhausting their man power.

Considering we had no true grasp of the scale of their resources or indeed how far up the chain the corruption went, we had pretty much covered all the bases we could think of at that time. We appreciated that our efforts may have been fruitless and that if they were caught, well, we would endeavour to make their deaths to have not been in vain. They were making the ultimate sacrifice for OUR greater good, for everyone's greater good, for the whole human race; not just for a select few.

The writers had given us a bitter pill to swallow, wrapped in good intentions, but they had forgotten that even the most subjugated society will eventually rise to fight back.

It was about time that we stood up for ourselves again and not let the bullies get away with our lunch money every day. The bullies would allow us to stand beside them and inhale the second-hand smoke from the cigarettes that they bought with their stolen money. It didn't sit well with me at all that every one of our little group was going to be out there risking their lives, and all I could do was sit back and pray. I would feel like the Ant Queen sitting waiting on her colony of scout ants to come back unharmed from their mission of keeping me well fed and fanned. Unlike her, I would much prefer to join my fellow comrades, to get out there and trample over anything that stood in my way.

David had stayed up all night, buzzed out of his head on highlighters and magic markers, with paper cut and rope burned hands, little blisters forming on the tips of his thumbs. It sounds like he had been up having an enormous night of fetish fun with Sonya, but no, his injuries were from pushing pins and attaching post-it notes to maps.

His hard work had paid off, they all finally agreed to the whittled down shortlist and it only took eighteen hours, two hundred cups of coffee, three very vocal arguments and one near carnal fight. Emotions had been running higher than helium balloons that had been let go by an innocent child's grasp at the circus. It was bound to kick off at some point.

"You have all looked over your lists of targets, or hopeful newfound allies. You have all been briefed on exactly how to execute this, covering all eventualities, including being caught. Just remain calm and nonchalant at all times. Do not speak with anyone unless absolutely necessary," David was trying his best to sound in charge.

"It's cool, we've got this. Try not to over think it," Liam reassured him.

"You know the drill, Liam. Recite back to me your every step from leaving this place for us all to hear."

"Okay…

1   Walk to the nearest train station two at a time, ten feet apart in twenty minute intervals

2   Take a train to two stops away from our designated post office

3   Use the underground to get us one stop closer

4   Use a bus to get us as close as we can

5   Find a coffee house or café and have a cup of tea/coffee and wait for ten minutes

6   Go to the post office and send the parcel special delivery to our designated target

7   Use a local company name and address with the name of Jason Bondage as the sender

8   He paused briefly to scoff at the name Jason Bondage and then continued.

9   Jump a taxi to our designated partners post office - in my case, Paul's

10 Find a local coffee house or café and have a cup of tea/coffee and wait for thirty minutes

11 Use a bus to get to the underground

12 Use the underground one stop

13 Take a train to the nearest station from here

"Being vigilant the whole time," David added.

"No, I was going to tap dance the whole way whilst wearing a sign saying 'Transference' in large font," Liam couldn't contain his sarcasm.

David didn't reply to Liam. He just shot him a look of contempt which turned into a look of unease and then finally it turned into a look of "fair enough".

They all huddled into the middle of the room, patting each other's backs and wishing each other well on their mission ahead. They were upbeat and looking positive about the predicted outcome however, the air was still a little tense and strained.

We all tried to have a good sleep in preparation for the gang's upcoming assignment, but the amount of tossing and turning that night would have you believe that we had kangaroos held hostage under a flipping tarp.

The following morning everyone was well rested, well fed and well briefed before we all hugged awkwardly, genuinely trying to convince ourselves that we would all be eating dinner together that night and clinking champagne glasses.

We stood and watched as everyone slowly left in two's, until there was only David, Sonya and I left in the shelter. I waved them all off and stood like a proud but scared mother, watching her babies walk to school on their own for the first time. That is, if the mothers feel petrified to the point of hyperventilating, wondering if they're kids are going to come home that night, or if she will ever see them again. Alive.

Chapter 31

"Tell us who you are working for," the voice demanded.

"I'm not working for anyone. I don't know what or who you are talking about!" Liam sounded genuinely convincing.

He had been caught by the writers as he sat outside his chosen café, drinking his coffee and contemplating life. He didn't struggle as they approached him and indicated that they would very much like to speak with him. Speak with him inside their car, without any witnesses around. The innocents around him were unaware that his following them to the car was actually a subtle hostage situation taking place under their very noses.

To the untrained eye, they hadn't physically forced him, shown any signs of aggression or even raised their voices. They barely uttered more than a few words to him, but he obediently followed them into the back of the vehicle. It didn't speed away nor did Liam look under any duress as he stared out the window, petrified of his likely demise.

The atmosphere was calm and silent as they drove for miles away from civilisation, presumably to allow an interrogation to take place without interruption.

Finally, the car door was opened gently, as a big burly man gestured for Liam to vacate the vehicle and head over to a small red door that was also being held open. He walked as slowly as his legs would allow, without looking too much like he was stalling his imminent future.

"You've been a hard man to track down lately, Liam. Please, follow me, we have been expecting you," a small grey haired man smiled at him wryly.

"I don't understand what is going on here," Liam protested.

"Oh, you know," winked the grey haired man.

They continued in silence along corridors that appeared to be going in a downward slope. Enough to make Liam's body hunch forward, but not enough to be 100% positive he was indeed going further under the earth.

Ducking to enter what appeared to be his destination, Liam's face could not contain his confusion and he was internally questioning if he had been abducted by the tiny man brigade. He looked around puzzled as to why he had to duck; he wasn't exactly the tallest man in the world and could fit through most modern doorways with ease.

Suddenly, he was brought round from his temporary daydream about doorframes, when a few other associates of the grey-haired man ominously entered the room.

Liam sat down without being invited to, cleared his throat and remained silent, staring between the three men.

"Look, we know why you are here, you know why you're here, so let's drop the cute act and get down to business," Mr Grey bit right to the bone.

"I really do…," Liam began to protest his innocence, but Mr Grey was having none of it.

226

"You would not have followed my esteemed colleagues out here without questioning them, putting up a fight or otherwise showing us you indeed had no idea who we were," Mr Grey banged the table with his tiny fist.

After he regained his composure, he fixed his tie and begun circling Liam like a starved shark circling an unwitting victim in the sea.

"If this is how you wish to do this, I shall just get right to it and stop wasting both of our time," he gestured to his friends to carry out whatever they had pre-planned.

"Let's talk about this," Liam pleaded, as the two men heavy-handedly dragged him by his underarms to the next room.

This space wasn't as cosy and professional looking as the previous one. It had a bed in the middle with restraints and a large table with medical tools all laid out. Liam's shoulders dropped as he quickly realised what was going to happen to him. There was no point in fighting it and he definitely wasn't going to survive it.

"We know that you are working with Lauren, Liam. We have been tracking her communications and we also have a note of every one of you little geek techs from your pathetic little group. Did you really think you could outsmart us? Even if you don't tell us where the others are, we will find them. This all is just a little bit of foreplay for me."

His two associates roughly picked up and positioned Liam onto the bed, strapping his fragile body down as tight as they could. He was brave and showed no signs of fear, except for his chest raising and falling a little too quickly. His attempts to regulate his breathing were failing miserably.

"Your insignificant friends would do well just to remain in hiding for you see; they are little tiny grains of sand in an ocean of power. They will never achieve in ten lifetimes what we have achieved in less than half of one. They are nobodies; they *will* be stopped. And anyway, who is going to care about what they have to say. We are untouchable, we control the strings of the world and they dance to our tune," Mr Grey had a delirious smile etched across his face.

The two associates left the room leaving Mr Grey alone to hum tunelessly as he prepared a syringe to go into Liam's right arm. Once he was satisfied, he plunged the needle in without so much as a flicker of emotion in his eyes.

"This is just to keep you still whilst I cut every limb from your body and if you are unlucky enough to survive that, I will the remove your organs one by one. You won't be able to move, but you will feel every slice and you will question every decision in your sad, pathetic little life," he seethed, into Liam's face.

"But, why?" Liam whispered.

"Why not?" He laughed.

As the concoction of drugs hit his bloodstream and Mr Grey cut into his arm, Liam lay with a blank look on his face. A single solidary tear rolled off his cheek.

"Lauren?" Sonya was shaking me awake, like I was a new tin of paint.

I wiped the collection of saliva off my chin and sat up dazed and confused. Then I remembered, that everyone had come home from their mission, except Liam. No one had heard from him and no one had any clues as to where he could be. I must have dozed off; my dreams were being invaded by thoughts of Liam being taken by the writers.

"I dreamt Liam had been taken, it all felt so real, so life like," I shuddered.

"We can't think like that!" David interrupted, it was clear he hadn't slept in a while.

It had taken hours, but the gang had all managed to come back in dribs and drabs and in one piece. None of them had a sniff of anything dodgy going on, no one cared what they were doing and they managed to complete their mission uninterrupted. It was easy, or was it too easy? Were they leading us into a false sense of security? But, why take Liam? Was his contact not in the loop and could have helped us? Had we hit a nerve?

"I can't stand this," I shook my whole body as I stood up. "All of this waiting."

"Even if they have Liam, he knew the risks, we all did. He wouldn't throw us under a bus, he knew this was all for the greater good. His death won't have been for nothing," David replied.

"Now you sound like them," I scoffed"

"Fuck you, Lauren!"

"No f…"

"Hey. HEY! We are all on the same side here, if we lose our trust between us we may as well give up now," Sonya tried to keep the peace.

Just as I was about to flick David's glasses off his face, just to be childish, Liam shuffled into the shelter with a cast on his arm and hangdog look upon his face.

"Liam!" I ran over to him but thought better of it and stopped myself from hugging him.

"Before you all start on me, at least let me lie down first," Liam proceeded to lie flat out on the sofa bed.

We all clambered round him unsure whether we could still trust him, but eager to hear of his whereabouts for the past twelve hours.

"So, it was all going to plan. There I was heading out of the post office and on my way back when bam! This blonde chick bloody hits me with her car. I'm telling you, woman shouldn't be allowed on the effing road."

Sonya, Paul and I all managed to slap him simultaneously on the back of the head before he continued.

"Anyway, she helped me up and was babbling about how sorry she was and how she should take me to the hospital. The thought did cross my mind that she was a writer, but she took me straight there and waited with me until I was seen and x-rayed. She barely touched me, just bored me to death with chat about her neighbours and her cat."

"And you're positive it was just bad timing? She wasn't following you, planted anything on you?" David pushed for more information.

"No, seriously man, this chick was definitely nothing to do with Transference. She was clumsy as hell and kind of hot, but she isn't a government spy," he laughed at the thought.

"We were all so worried, Liam. I had crazy dreams about you and everything, we were sure they were going to storm in here and shoot us all," I replied.

"Really? You have dreams about me?" He raised an eyebrow.

"You wish," I tutted, secretly relieved he was finally home and safe.

"So, anyway, this chick says she was so happy I was ok and how much she would have hated for me to have died at her hand."

I stopped in my track as I was walking away to get him some water. My blood ran cold and I nearly passed out. I ran over to my bag and pulled out my purse, dropping everything everywhere in the process.

"Is this the woman that knocked you down?" I asked, thrusting a picture in his face.

"Erm… yeah that's her, why do you have a picture of her?" He asked, confused.

"That's Sarah, my sister," I gulped.

As sure as fate would have it, the mere mention of her name caused an erratic beeping noise to come from David's laptop. He flew over to Liam and patted him down like he was on a diet and Liam was harbouring a chocolate bar. Ripping Liam's phone out of his pocket, David threw it into a nearby bucket, which I swear I hadn't seen until that moment.

We all stood in shocked silence, staring at David and waiting for an explanation as to why Liam's phone was literally melting in a bucket.

"I put that bucket of acid there as soon as you guys all left, I bloody knew someone would be tracked," David answered our unasked question.

"Sarah must have been waiting for you to resurface, staged the accident and placed a tracker on your phone. The beeping was my sweeper alerting me that a tracker had been activated, thankfully it wasn't on long enough to trace back to here."

"But she didn't touch me at all," Liam was beside himself with exasperation.

"She's looking for me, her henchmen will have told her about my connection to Jonathan; she will haunt us down and kill us all. We are a thorn in her side, Transference is her baby and she will protect it to the death, of everyone," I informed them.

"I'm not going to lie, Lauren. A part of me thought it was all a bit far-fetched for Sarah to be in charge of the writers. The video never really showed her face and her name never popped up anywhere else in our searches. I mean, sure she is the creepiest person I have ever met, but I never really believed she could kill anyone. But this, this is proof that she is just evil and nasty and that we are basically all doomed. Well, you certainly are, sweetheart. She always said you will die at her hand and now she is fulfilling her warped destiny," Sonya looked broken.

"That's what made me realise it was her, those words 'to die at her hand' who actually says that except Sarah?" I sighed.

"Well, I tell you one thing she deserves, a bloody Oscar," Liam shook his head in disbelief.

I think he was probably more gutted because he had hoped he was in with a chance with the strange blonde woman once this had all blown over.

I was absolutely livid with Sarah and looked forward to killing her myself as soon as I clapped eyes on her. No one was really speaking to me on account of either crapping themselves that I was also part of the conspiracy or feeling sorry for me that my sister was a psychopath. Actually, it was probably both of those reasons. It suited me anyway, I was so angry with her continual betrayal and the fact she would be traipsing about out there pretending to be worried about my whereabouts.

For reasons that are unknown to me, I still loved her. But, if she thought I was going to roll over and let her kill me, she had another thing coming. I would sooner hang myself right then and there with my knicker elastic before I let her watch me take my last breath.

"Everyone, gather round," David summoned us like a nursery teacher at story book time. "The packages have all been sent, everyone made it back successfully, more some than others," he glanced at poor Liam. "I have our outside source's looking everywhere for any leak or outbreak of the story stemming from our footage.

I also have alerts set up to notify me if anything pops up within parameters I've set. We have released the cats amongst the pigeons, people, we just need to lay low a little while longer and hope that someone has received, and will follow up, on our distress call."

"Once the truth is out in the open, they can't kill us, the world will be looking for us like some protected endangered species," Sonya added in. "It will all be over."

We all half smiled at each other out of tiredness and out of sheer scepticism that any of us were ever going to see the light of day again.

"Goodnight," rung out through the shelter like a vocal set of dominos as we all attempted to get some sleep, knowing full well that it was unlikely to happen any time soon. It was better to pretend to be asleep than face the reality that we all had the same nightmares and thoughts keeping us from closing our eyes for more than two minutes.

It was going to be a long night for thirty people lying on a floor, imagining who was going to kill them and using what methods. The sighs were as synchronised as the tossing and turning and the inability to contain the sound of dismay was as heart breaking as the situation we faced.

Should we just give in? Were we fighting a losing battle and just dragging out the inevitable like a poor horse that just won't lay down and die? I made a deal with myself that if I slept right through till the morning, I would get up unnoticed and go surrender myself to Sarah.

"That's what I'll do," I yawned out loud to myself before I slipped into a dark, deep sleep.

Chapter 32

Man, I had the worst hangover ever! My head was thumping, my mouth was bone dry and I felt like I had been run over twice by a train.

I started to come around a little bit more and gather my thoughts, and then I remembered through my haziness about the shelter.

As I tried to sit up, it quickly became apparent that I was tied up and my arms were bound behind my back like I was a kidnap victim. Wait, was I kidnapped? My head was fuzzy and I was positive I was going to throw up. I lay back down onto my side and tried to recall my last clear thought before going to sleep.

Sarah! She had somehow found me, and now she had me hidden away to torture like a cat with a new-found mouse. I stopped my crazy thoughts for a minute to realise that I was still lying in my, using the term quite loosely here, bed in the shelter. What the hell was going on?

"Sonya?" I croaked, out to the empty room.

I could hear footsteps walking around behind me, but I was too groggy and stiff to try and manoeuvre my aching body to see who it was.

"Why am I tied up?" I asked the figure looming in the room.

There was nothing but silence.

"I swear, when I get free, I will kill you," I shouted.

"Ever the drama queen," David's voice boomed as he sat down beside me.

"Oh, I'm sorry. I am tied up and have presumably been drugged by my friends as I slept, but I am being a tad dramatic. Um, if this isn't the perfect example of a time when I can be dramatic, I don't know what is," I spat at my new found enemy.

"Can you at least let me explain?" David pleaded.

"Nope. No way. Negative. I knew I couldn't trust you, not with my best friend, not with my life and especially not with the lives of thousands. You are pond scum David, I never did like you, but you know what? You can't account for bad taste. I bit my tongue when she shacked up with creepy Dave, that's what I call you by the way, Sonya always could do better, but for some reason she gravitated towards you. So, what are your plans? Are they to kill me? Or maybe sell me to the writers? Where are the others? Are they in on it too or have you killed them all?" I stopped my rant briefly to catch my breath.

"Oh, wow. Ok. Firstly, you are a sleep talker. We all heard you muttering your plans to hand yourself over to Sarah first thing. Sonya suggested that we should sedate you in order for us to tie you up, to prevent you from making the biggest mistake of your life. Secondly, we saw you coming round from sedation and sent everyone outside to stretch their legs, the sedative can sometimes cause vomiting and we wanted to save you the embarrassment; I stayed to make sure you didn't choke and to explain what had happened."

"So, you saved me from handing myself to my sister because she wants me dead? We are still on the same team?" I cringed.

"Yes, and yes," David cut my hands free and then stormed out of the shelter.

"Crap," I muttered to myself.

I gave David enough time to go outside and fill Sonya in on how much of a bitch I had been before I attempted to stand up, and adjust myself, ready for a rollicking.

"You really don't make it easy for folk to like you, do you, Lauren?" I could hear the rage in her voice as Sonya slowly walked towards me with her arms folded.

"It was the drugs?" I scrunched my nose up and shrugged my shoulders.

"You told him you called him creepy Dave!?"

"You didn't tell him I called him creepy Dave?" I counter asked.

"I am going to let you away with this because we are all on edge and well, we did drug you and tie you up. But, please be nice! No more silly ideas to hand yourself over to Sarah, we need you, Lauren, we need you to stop her."

I tried my best to blend into the wallpaper whilst adopting the shamefaced look of a dog that had been caught eating from the bin. It wasn't made particularly easy by a select few that continued to giggle at me every time I looked in their direction. It was like being back at school all over again. Everyone was always sniggering to my face and whispering behind my back after I got drunk at the Valentine's Day ball.

I had always fancied Andy for as far back as I could remember, but I never once uttered how I felt to a single soul. Not even Maria, especially not Maria! The mixture of nerves and alcohol did not go down well in my young, adolescent digestive tract, particularly not so when I had also drunk almost a pint of milkshake beforehand.

Anyway, after a good few swigs and a good old shoogle on the dance floor, I was feeling amazingly full of confidence. I sauntered right up to Andy, tapped his shoulder and introduced myself in an over joyous slurred voice.

"Andy! I pure fancy you, by the way!" I hiccupped, adhering to the Scottish laws of declaring feelings to someone.

You see, in Scotland, no feelings were ever deemed passionate if you didn't add "by the way" to the end of it. It was like a Scottish, dramatic, vocalised full stop. It was true love if it had "fucking" in there as well. Let me give you an example of each, feel free to say it out loud as you read: I fancy you, Meh, feels like you may have a small kindling of emotion going on but it may just be desperation and boredom. I fancy you, by the way! Oh, my God. They have sealed it with a by the way. They really like me and I feel so special. I fucking fancy you, by the way! Well stick a ring on my finger and get me some cystitis cream because they have such strong feelings for me. I feel so overwhelmed at how much they want me right now, they are my soul mate. The same goes in any situation where emotions are being shared, add on a by the way or throw a fucking in there and it could be the difference between life and death.

"Oh, right. Ok…I think," he looked positively startled. "Lauren, am I right?"

"Yes! That is totally my name! I'm going to kiss you now," I informed him.

"Please don't," he pleaded, quietly.

As I lunged at him like some kind of teenager predator, I took a sharp intake of breath and started choking on the copious amounts of his cheap aftershave.

Naturally, my coughing fit lead to a choking fit, which led to the full contents of my stomach bouncing about like an overzealous kid on a pogo stick. The tears were streaming down my face, the snot was congealing at a rapid pace around my top lip and my gullet was determined to find respite from all the heaving it was enduring. In a matter of seconds, I threw up onto poor Andy. His face was aghast as I then proceeded to try and apologise to him and say how sorry I was by hugging him. Because he was fighting me off like a desperate antelope trying to escape the clutches of a lion, it ended with me rubbing the bodily fluids from my eyes, nose, mouth and stomach straight onto his horrified self.

This caused him to throw up, which then caused a few of our spectators to throw up and before we knew it, the whole hall had turned into pandemonium. It was like something from a sketch show. For years, I was referred to as *Spewtina* and was avoided like the plague at any social gathering that involved alcohol.

That feeling of social embarrassment was exactly what I was feeling now, even though it was not my fault and it was nowhere near as disconcerting as the dance hall incident.

My embarrassment and equally everyone's opinion of me were soon forgotten about, as we huddled round the computer screens like they do in the films, when the president is making a speech.

Except, this time there was no speech, no reports, no big exposé of the writers and all they stood for, nothing. It was highly anticlimactic and sorely depressing; even though we hadn't truly expected anything to come from this whole exercise.

We were all unable to hide our feelings of frustration with full throttled sighs echoing round the room as every channel known to man was scanned for something, anything that would make us feel vindicated and less sequestered. David was taking it harder than anyone, almost as if he was taking it as a personal slur against his name.

"So, no one is going to speak up for the people," he growled, whilst rubbing his forehead like he was expecting a genie to jump out.

"Give it time, David; they can't just pop footage like that out to the public without verifying if it has been tampered with. Look at how amazing some of the special effects are these days, can you imagine if they ran this and then it was a hoax? Have faith, darling, someone out there is going to help us," Sonya tried her best to appease David's growing feeling of despair.

"I know, I know," he exhaled, long and hard. "Just some form of acknowledgment would be sufficient, a code, a subtle doff of their hat just to let us know not to give in," he whined.

It was hard sometimes to accept him as our "leader" when he partook in these uncontrollable toddler-esque little breakdowns. I suppose even the most highly intelligent amongst us have a weakness of some sort. When you think about it, all super heroes have vulnerabilities so why shouldn't us mere humans.

You know that way when you really want a party or a bonus at work, but you protest out loud at every opportunity that you don't? You scoff and wave it off saying nonsense like, "What will be will be," and "I couldn't be bothered with a party I'd much rather sit in drinking tea," whilst secretly wishing for it? You even manage to convince your face and your whole demeanour that you couldn't care less, but deep down inside you can't stop that little voice from internally screaming, "Please throw me a party!"

That is pretty much how I was feeling inside the shelter and inside my mind. Trying to pretend that I knew no one would help us whilst furtively praying someone did. It is human nature to try to protect ourselves from heartache and hurt despite the fact that we allow ourselves to get hurt anyway because, well, because we never truly believed anything but our inner voice. We act like we know the outcome even though it is no more predictable than a football score of a team we have never watched before. We could drive ourselves insane with the unbalanced and unexplainable way that we think:

We truly want something to happen i.e. a job. So, we convince ourselves out loud and by our manner that we won't get the job.

Your inside voice is still saying, "There's a chance!" and "I hope I get the job."

You tell anyone with a set of ears that you didn't really want the job anyway, so you won't be too upset if you didn't get it.

Inside you're picturing all the things you can buy with your new wages and how much life would be better with the opportunity.

You don't get the job, you shrug and say, "See, I told you I wouldn't get it," thinking you have saved face. But inside you are crushed because you still had that tiny shred of hope.

You did get the job, you jump up and down and say, "I knew all along I got the job, I just didn't want to jinx it." Whilst inside you are breathing a huge sigh of relief because you still had that tiny shred of doubt.

It seems we lack the ability to realise that everyone knows all of the above when this situation arises and that you are fooling no one. When someone else is displaying these actions, you know straight off the cuff that they are at it, but when it's yourself? You seem to be oblivious to the fact of what you are doing and of being aware of everyone's pity from knowing the truth.

This situation was a little different, we were all gathered together dithering about how we would never get help and focusing on all the doom and gloom of the day. We were vaguely aware of our little glimmer of hope that was taking the form of a butterfly in our tummies, but oblivious to the fact each other had it. Every time we looked at each other our tang of hope was confused as a kick in the guts by the desperation and weariness etched on their faces.

Our hope was merely a candle whose wick had all but burned out, whose light was so subtle that we had forgotten its presence and had started using our hands and our ears to guide us around the room.

The silence amongst us was strangely deafening, I felt trapped in the shelter and unable to take anything other than shallow breaths. The realisation that this was where we were likely to spend the rest of our days, which wouldn't be for very long, was causing me mild anxiety attacks. I was jumping at the slightest noises. Not because I thought it was the writers or that we were caught or anything, it just seemed that anything other than silence was startling me like a skittish horse.

My change of character did not go unnoticed nor did it gain any kind of sympathy from my dear friends and acquaintances. It felt like I was grating on their last nerve, a nerve that they were so desperate to cling onto at any cost.

"I will cut your fucking legs off, Lauren, if you don't stop that stupid, fucking, pacing about!" Liam seethed at me.

Everyone looked away or down at the ground, they shared his very valid opinion and they were glad he had voiced it however; they didn't want to look like the bad guys by agreeing with him.

"I'm sorry," my voice shook with genuine hopelessness. "I feel like my heart is going to jump out of my chest, I can't shake this feeling of looming disaster," I croaked, in between sobs.

Sonya gasped, as she quickly realised I wasn't handling any of this very well at all, my mental health was teetering on the edge of destruction and we were both frightened that if I broke down, I wouldn't come back.

"Sweetheart," Sonya pounced to my aid as I fell to my knees and wept in slow, painfully loud sobs. I knew I must have looked appalling, I wasn't the most attractive crier at the best of times and I sounded like a harpooned seal.

"This isn't fair to Lauren or to any of us. She needs professional help, David," Sonya warned her silent audience.

Heads were hung in defeat, breathing was short and rapid and feet were shuffling about in sadness. It was time to go out into the big bad world and face our fate.

There was a faint tapping noise in the corner of the room that had caught our attention, not enough to show any enthusiasm or worry, but enough to make us all turn and face its direction.

"We hear you. They must be stopped. Repeat. We hear you. They must be stopped," David was speaking in a robotic voice.

"Christ, not you as well," Sonya cried.

"No, no, listen," David urged. "The tapping, it's Morse code. Someone has reached out to us. Can't you see? We have help!" He punched the air and then spun Sonya round until she almost vomited.

"I hope the light at the end of the tunnel, isn't a train," I cautioned. But my worries were drowned out by the laughter and whoops of an overjoyed gang of desperate souls.

Chapter 33

I was sat outside a moderately upmarket coffee house with a cup in one hand and that morning's newspaper in the other. I was kitted out with the obligatory oversized dark sunglasses and sun hat that must be worn at all times when you're involved in a secret rendezvous. Audrey Hepburn would have been chuffed to her wee cotton socks had she seen me, even though I was more three am snack in a chippie than Breakfast at Tiffany's.

After the initial raucous happiness due to someone contacting us had subsided, the paranoia of a set-up had slowly crept in and over taken every single thought in our heads.

Who was reaching out to us? Were they a friend or the enemy? What were they going to offer as support? My head was spinning with the countless questions and the grip of fear that had stopped for a rest in the centre of my chest.

The suspicion didn't get any less once we had deciphered the next message. Our new-found saviour had requested to meet me alone, had used *my* name, and issued a set of instructions on how we would identify each other at our rendezvous.

"Hell, to the no!" Sonya retorted, in her usual subtle way.

I looked around the sea of desperate faces that were staring back at me, like anxious little puppies waiting on their mummy providing them an answer to where their next meal was going to come from.

"It's more than obvious that Sarah is the one sending this message or at the very least, standing behind the person sending it making veiled threats. She is trying to flush me out and if I don't give her what she wants, she will come after all of us," I used my finger to point at everyone dramatically.

"She's right," piped up Caroline, one of the quieter gang members.

"Erm, thanks," I was pleased with her agreeing that I was right, but not so happy at her responding so quickly to me, basically, committing suicide.

Looking solemn, she nonetheless continued, "We are in a lose-lose situation here, Lauren. *If* they don't know about all of us, you meet with them and they kill you…it might give us a chance. *If* they do know about us and you don't meet them…you might lead them right to us, we all perish and it has all been for nothing."

"This is the worst choice I have been presented with since that time I was offered horseradish or mustard with my chips. Do you remember the poor guy that had run out of any decent condiments?" I gagged to Sonya.

"Stay and die with us, or go and die alone? Hmm, still not as unappealing as that guy's chips," Sonya was trying her best to be droll.

I was stuck between a shelter and a hard place. I didn't want to take part in either scenario, but I didn't want to not take part, if that makes sense? This had to end somehow and I wasn't sure how much more I could physically and mentally cope with. I was already as fragile as a bone china cup at a bull's family reunion.

I wasn't certain if the gang were too tired and fed up to talk me out of my decision to go or if they just couldn't care less that they might never see me again. I chose to believe the first option; it was slightly heart-breaking to believe the latter.

Sonya refused to say goodbye, so I was subjected to an elongated ramble about what she was making for dinner that night and asking me, if I could bring back some magazines to quench her thirst for celebrity gossip.

A couple of realists within us gave me a hug and kiss, whilst reminding me that I would never be forgotten, I would be remembered as the hero that died a heroes death. The rest were more optimistic that they would clap eyes on the vision of my beautiful self once again and settled for a, "Good luck! See you later".

To be honest, the whole departure was unsettling. Do I leave positive and have them think I was a poor soul for believing I will live to see another day? Or, do I leave with my face tripping me and have them think that I was destined to fail? I settled for a fake smile. The one where you show every tooth that lived in your mouth, but your eyes blinked away any possibility of being believed.

I had the directions of where I was to meet my mysterious lunch companion clutched in my ever so slightly shaking hand and trotted out the door to await my fate.

I shan't bore you with my travel itinerary, so here I was sitting outside the chosen coffee house, very much aware that I had an invisible target tattooed onto my head. The coffee house was a strange abode, it wasn't fancy enough that I would look out of place perched outside on a warm day, but it wasn't common looking enough to draw any attention to the fancy ass luncheon date that would soon be accompanying me.

The world is a strange and frightening place when you are mindful that your every move is being watched and monitored by an unknown fleet of adversaries. I desperately tried my best to emit the perception of elegance and decorum, basically that I was the pinnacle of high society, just as they were.

As each new customer entered the premises I received some sideways glances and not so subtle double takes. It was either, the dodgy get up making me look like an incognito super star, they were impressed at a single gal soaking up some rays on her lonesome or they were pitying me for being stood up. I might have also just been a tad suspicious and they were just turning their head as they pulled open the door.

I sighed, so forcefully that the napkin wrapped round my coffee cup like a little shawl flew off the table in a bid to escape.

"No, you don't, you little bugger," I laughed, at the napkin as it danced on the pavement, mocking me. Suddenly a well-polished leather brogue positioned itself onto my coffee cup shawl as I reached out to snatch it back.

"Yours, I believe?" a voice spoke as smooth as caramel.

"Yes," I gulped, too petrified to look up past the man's knees.

He bent down and retrieved the napkin and tried to catch my gaze by squatting down in front of me. I shot up, mortified, that I was chasing a piece of glorified toilet paper around the street like a savage animal.

"I have a nicer one you can have," he smiled at me, reaching into a little pocket hidden inside his suit.

"No, it's ok, thank you," I declined, blushing.

"It's of no imposition to me," the man smiled sweetly, as he handed me a neatly folded handkerchief with cute little roses on it.

"Thank you," I smiled, taken aback.

"You're welcome, Lauren," his eyes glistened a little at his startling introduction.

My defences were well and truly up. I couldn't believe I had allowed myself to get caught out so early on in my mission. My smile faded as I subconsciously stepped back and I deliberately let the handkerchief dramatically fall from my grasp.

"I am only responsible for what I say," I recited to him, as per his instruction.

"Not for what you hear," he replied, sitting himself down.

Neither of us made any attempt to pick the handkerchief back up from the ground. I positioned myself in front of him and resumed drinking my coffee as nonchalantly as I could.

"So, who are you?" I asked.

"Straight to the point, I can already tell I am going to like you, Lauren."

I rolled my eyes at his pathetic attempt to flatter me whilst trying to deflect the question.

"Look, neither of us can afford to pussyfoot about here, I am risking everything I am and have, speaking with you," he glanced around us without moving his head. "David approached one of my esteemed associates with some quite disturbing material. We were aware that something of this nature was going on behind the scenes, but not to this extent," his face could not hide his repulsion.

"That is all very well and wonderful, but how did you get *my* name? Why did you not ask to meet with David?"

"Let's just say we have a mutual acquaintance, they have approved you as a trusted source. Plus, when I probed a little more into Transference, your name it seems, is well known."

"Yes, well, that doesn't provide me with any comfort over my safety," I scoffed. "Jesse James was also well known in his time."

"Lauren," he placed his soft hand on top of mine. "If I wanted to harm you it would have been done by now, and I certainly wouldn't execute it myself."

"So, what do you want?" I could feel myself getting irater.

"You truly are as sprightly as she told me you were, I can understand why she adores you so much," he chuckled lightly.

"Who are you referring to?" I asked, sceptical.

"It's irrelevant. Just know that I was asked to meet with you on her behalf to make sure you were ok. She has been looking for you for a long time. You can rest assured that I am your new ally, Lauren. Just because I am of a privileged background does not mean I condone this sort of antediluvian behaviour," he sniffed.

"Is our mutual friend my sister?" I squeaked, panicking that she had indeed set me up.

"No, it is indeed not your sister." He blinked, slowly.

"And, how do you know that you can trust me?" I tried my best to sound sinister.

"Darling, I have seen the footage of what you witnessed, no one would subject themselves to that just for jollies. I also saw your reaction, your empathy. That harrowing look you had engraved on your face? No one is that credible an actor. I really believe that this is our chance to remove the social wedge that has been violating our freedom of thought for a long time. People need to see the truth and understand what is happening right under their noses."

My shoulders sagged at the memory of those poor babies and my eyes filled up like water balloons in the hands of eager teenagers.

"So, what do we do?" I took the deepest breath for the first time in days.

"Well, we need to be positive that everything is co-pacetic before we continue to the next step. Has anyone else made contact or shown any signs of assisting you?"

"Not that we have picked up on."

"I prayed that somebody would, but everyone is almost definitely in someone else's pocket, there is a lot of back scratching going on."

"And whose pocket are you in?" I pushed.

"My involvement, as I have already reiterated, has transpired from our mutual connection and a serious of peculiar events."

"Well, I suppose we don't really have any other options at this moment in time, do we?" I sighed.

"Have I to assume that our shared feeling of conten-tion placates your harboured thoughts of doubt?" He asked cheerily.

"Christ's sake! I wish you people would speak nor-mal," I quipped. "If you mean do I feel a bit better that you are on my side because we both hate the bastards, then yes, yes I do."

"Well, on that note, I shall bid you farewell for now. I have things to do and people to scrutinise to allow us to move forward. Hi, guys," he waved into my left eye.

"I needed some back up," I shrugged.

"As did I, Lauren, as did I," he saluted me with his forefinger at his left eye.

Before I had twigged on to what had just happene he had swiftly removed himself from my company strode down the street with his arms clasped behind his back.

"What the hell had just happened? Who was he? Who was our mutual acquaintance? And most importantly, could he be trusted?"

Chapter 34

It had been all hands-on deck at the Transference takedown bunker since my unexpected, unscathed return.

I was welcomed back into the arms of my gang to a champion's reception, but without anyone lifting me onto their shoulders. I shan't lie, that did disappoint me a little, but they did throw me a victorious, celebratory party, I am playing fast and loose with the word party here.

Seeing via my replaced contact lens camera that I had not been stolen to the realms of beyond, Sonya ran to the nearest shop she could find to pick up some provisions. It wasn't anything particularly earth shattering, but given the dire state of our circumstances, she completed her self-appointed task to the best of her ability.

She was successful in obtaining the basic necessities that are the backbone of any celebration which consisted of mini sausage rolls, cocktail sausages, hastily and haphazardly cut egg mayonnaise sandwiches, fizzy juice, some children's confectionaries and a confusin bowl of random crisp flavours mixed together. She h even bullied David and a few other innocent soul assist her in creating and strategically hanging a pie old wallpaper that she had scrawled "Welcome Home" in what I prayed was a brown pen.

"Sonya, you really didn't need to do all this," I smiled, seeing how much effort she had put in.

"Well, it's not every day your best friend, that you never thought you would see again narrowly escapes death AND manages to get us some allies!" she squealed, whilst pulling me in for a hug.

"You really believed I was going to get killed? And you let me go anyway?" I asked, genuinely hurt by this revelation.

"That's neither here nor there," she waved off my battered feelings. "I got you your favourite," she sang to distract me.

"I'm not a child, you can't just divert my attention...oh, lemon and lime lollipops!" I skipped over to the make-shift buffet table.

After shovelling more food than was socially acceptable down my throat, dancing to one of David's shoddy ringtones and getting so many high fives that my palms ached, the adrenaline and sugar rush finally wore off; leaving me in a bit of a downer.

I sat slumped in the corner watching everyone enjoying our very minimalistic soirée. It wasn't much at all, but in the grand scheme of things it was perfect. That is the difference between us and the writers, our life goals are very simple and unmaterialistic compared to their greed and constant one-upmanship. The smiles dancing on everyone's face and the sudden shift in atmosphere was proof that we will prevail, because this was the very essence of being human. Empathy, kindness, compassion, remorse and comradery, are all things that we should possess if we are to excel and continue as a species. The writers had mutated into the opposite of what we should aim to be and were willing to drag us kicking and screaming to the brink of, if not to, obliteration.

My anxiety and the pain in my shoulders from carrying the metaphorical world on them, was beginning to ease off a little as I watched my little gang. My eyes were suddenly heavy and my mouth could barely contain the excessive yawns that were pouring out of me at an alarming rate. At one point I worried I may swallow the room up in one, exhausted gulp. I closed my eyes briefly and snuggled my head into a gap in the wall that I swear was created just for my head.

There was once a time where my dreams were my favourite place in the world to hang out in. Now however, they seemed to be an unwelcoming, harsh minefield of taunts and home truths.

Every time my eyelids came together for their nightly (or sneaky daytime) love affair, my brain came into the party, kicked out all the nice dreams and unlocked the cupboard housing the dark ones, plying them alcohol and recreational drugs. Once they were fuelled and their inhibitions had been lowered, my brain started goading them to act out their full potential. This led them to pick from the evil shelf and re-enact whatever nonsensical situation they could think of. It usually ended with me being killed/betrayed/disappointed and waking up covered in my own sweat.

The party night was no different. I woke up startled as Sarah's knife tip had narrowly escaped my neck and I grappled with my own shirt collar. I gasped to regulate my breathing as I embarrassingly cast a quick look around the room. Thankfully, everyone was passed out from partying and no one witnessed my pathetic self attack.

The nightmares were getting more and more with each nightly visit and it was getting har convince myself each time that there was no hidden meaning in each one.

I stretched my aching body, dragged it up from my place next to the wall and then tip toed towards the bathroom. I was abruptly distracted by the flickering of a blue light with the outline of a slumped body in front of it. The blue flickering light was an incoming video call that showed missed (seventy-nine). The slumped body belonged to David.

"David," I whispered, shaking him lightly.

"Go away," he croaked, without bothering to look up.

"Someone is calling you, are we waiting on a phone call?" I quizzed.

"What?!" his head shot up like an espresso filled meerkat.

His deafening roar was enough to wake the dead, so, naturally the gang all sprung awake like weird little sleeping lemmings.

"Who is it?" I held my breath, waiting on his reply.

"I honestly have no idea, but bloody hell have they been desperate to get hold of us," he tapped to the now missed (eighty-one).

"Is it not our new-found friends?" Someone from the darkness asked.

"No, no, we agreed to remain in contact by Morse Code for now. This number and line wasn't released to anyone that we reached out to. I forgot I even had it, to be truthful, I am a little flummoxed here."

David was looking at me as if I was going to provide much-needed answer meanwhile, whoever it was ntinued to call. I decided to take the lead.

"Move," I ordered David as I shoved him off his and clicked to answer.

The screen was fuzzy and out of focus, like we were seeing through the eyes of, well anyone from this room that was still drunk or hungover. There was someone talking to us, but the voice kept breaking up and the face was hard to make any features out.

"Lauren...I...Sarah...find you...not on your side...I am the enemy...stop you...I hated you...me...you will die...friends too...hospital...Transference...what they are doing is for the greater good...I have friends in high places...I never loved you...you will die by my hands...good luck."

Her face was frozen on the screen, contorted between a scowl and a smirk as her threats beamed out to me in broken pieces. Not as many broken pieces as my shattered heart was now in mind you. I mean, this was not brand new information to me, but to have it said to me straight from her vicious, hate fuelled little mouth was enough to make me die a little inside. I think, deep down, I always prayed that I was wrong about Sarah. That her misplaced hate for me growing up was actually her interpretation of love, that she was just overwhelmed by it all and didn't know how to show it in any other way, except creepy. I also hoped that her actions of late were mere coincidences and that the world was trying its best to paint her as a villain, when she really had nothing to do with it.

The awkward, pity looks that were aimed solely at me, confirmed what I was struggling to accept as reality, what they already knew as gospel, my sister wanted me dead.

I was feeling a close connection to a deity that have never once given the time of day, hoping he wo provide me absolution and accept me into a pea fate. But then I would turn against him in the thought, blaming him for allowing me to go such turmoil. It was as if my feelings were on an all-inclusive holiday on a rollercoaster ride and they were having the time of their lives.

"I know you are deep in the state of misery just now, but you need to come and see this," I was dragged, kicking and screaming by Sonya from wallowing in my self-pity.

David's computer screens were flashing between a plethora of different news channels in all different languages from across the globe. Snippets of my video footage in the hospital were being broadcast concurrently at that very moment.

"Does this mean?" I hesitated.

"It means your coffee date has kept his word, he also isn't slow at going fast!" David looked positively shell shocked.

"Is this really happening? Is everyone seeing this?" I stuttered, slightly in disbelief.

"Yes! I thought we had weeks, months even to wait or, or, to come up with a plan of some kind. But nope, your new buddie has gone for the quick, sharp, get it over with approach," David gasped, incredulously.

Liam was working hard on another keyboard, tap tapping at an impressive rate followed by a lot of exclaiming and head scratching.

"Whatever hacking software they have, is like nothing I've ever seen, they have basically taken over all transmissions! It's being played "live" on television, radio, internet; it has been uploaded onto every website nd shared on every social media outlet. The writers are ing desperately to shut it all down, but for every one ted, another two seem to pop up! No news channel en brave enough to air it, I imagine they are giving chance to do so and if they don't, they will do it "

Once again, we were all huddled round the screens watching the world wake up to the reality around them.

"Are those pictures of us and our names?" I gasped, titling my head at an angle to look at the screen.

"Indeed, it is, they are pre-empting to prevent our demise," David grinned.

"Or, they have just put a bounty on us?" I asked, with suspicion.

"Wow, the paranoia really has you in its clutches. They are announcing us publicly as the whistle blowers. If anything happens to us, the writers will be the first under suspicion and held accountable," he chuckled, a little too patronisingly for my liking.

"Let's not get carried away here, this is not a get out of jail free card. They can and in all likelihood, still will, want us punished for exposing them," Sonya joined in.

"Sweetheart, this is what we have been working towards, all of us," David remained calm and undeterred.

We continued to be glued to the screens for the remainder of the day, watching it all unfold like a badly scripted soap opera. It wasn't until after nine pm that any of the news channels gave up the charade and conceded to air the story as well. They probably realised that by not airing it, they were deemed to be implicating themselves rather than being perceived as taking a stand against false news.

The uncertain sighing got less and less as the story broke around the globe. It's strange how all news channels were the pinnacle of corruption and helped to blindfold the public to reality, yet, here we were, relying on them to dispense the truth and validate all our effo...

Whilst I watched the elation and relief wash ove... group's faces, I couldn't help but feel underwhel... it all and completely, utterly alone. I still had a... out there baying for my blood, our blood that...

257

and her prediction of my death would be unaffected by the outcome. I couldn't go bouncing back into the loving arms of my family like all these guys would be doing with theirs. Sarah would do her dandiest to make sure I was ostracised and no one would miss me or notice when she took me out.

"Are you still thinking about Sarah?" Sonya can read my face from fifty paces.

"Yeah, even if this is all over, even if she doesn't kill me, can you imagine how it feels to know that your best friend and sister will only be satisfied once you have stopped breathing?"

"Best friend?" Sonya raised her eyebrow almost to the back of her neck.

"Shut up, you," I laughed. "You know what I mean."

"I do know what you mean and you're right, I don't know how you feel, honey. I think the only person that could come close to sharing your feelings would be... Abel?" She shrugged.

"No, don't be hitting me with Bible chat. I couldn't cope with it right now."

"Come on, you need to rest that tired, overworked little brain of yours," she took my hand and led me to my designated bed. She tucked me in and lay with me, lightly brushing my cheek with her forefinger like I was her restless toddler.

I fought going to sleep because, well, my dreams didn't fare much better than reality these days. Who ows what was awaiting me to drift off? Let's face it, is moment in time there were no scarier monsters or as than my big sister. Awake I couldn't properly e what she would do to me. Asleep, well that was wn personal cinematic preview of the up and coming film of my life, starring me, playing the part of me, and the devil playing the part of Sarah.

God, I wish I could hate her, but the truth is I just couldn't.

"Good night, Sarah. I still love you," I sniffed. As I closed my eyes together, I was almost blinded by the dampness of the tears that involuntarily poured down my face.

Chapter 35

"It's not my fault, I don't know what happened," David was whispering into the darkness. "Fuck! This is irreparable."

I lay as still as I could. I attempted to slow my breathing in a bid to hear him more clearly. Who was he talking to?

"David? Who are you talking to?" Sonya strode over to him.

"What? Talking to? I was talking to myself. I deleted a file I needed, but I can try and download another one from elsewhere," he replied, with his voice shaking.

"Listen, I've been thinking, if all of this is linked up to bank balances can we not hack into the banks and move the money around so everyone has the same amount of money?" Sony enquired.

"You mean Global Wealth Redistribution?"

"I'll take your word that it's called that. You have the skills to do it; it makes perfect sense, doesn't it? If everyone had the same amount of money, then everyone's child would be a risk. Transference wouldn't be to be used."

"It wouldn't work," he turned away from her.

" totally would."

"No, it wouldn't, I know more about this than you do," David sighed.

"But, why wouldn't it work?" Sonya persisted.

"I have toyed with the idea of Global Redistribution many times, but we need to be mindful that it happened in Russia in the beginning of the nineties. The new democratic government decided to execute a radical privatization program, selling off a lot of assets, mines, factories, companies. However, in their idealistic spirit, they decided to share the wealth. Every citizen got a constant amount of special currency vouchers that could be used to buy shares of these entities on auctions. The idea was good in theory, but absolutely devastating in practice.

"No one knew the real value of these pieces of paper. The country was in deep economic crisis and a lot of people struggled to feed their families. No one knew much about what the companies and entities were worth. So, after short time, most of the people sold or lost the value of their vouchers, whilst a small group accumulated a lot of wealth and got a lot of profit.

"It would be the same with money. People don't have the same capabilities, influence, or connections and knowledge is still an extremely valuable asset. For a short period, everyone would have the same amount of money however; education, background, experience, work ethic, and other factors wouldn't change. Very quickly the wealthy would become wealthy again.

"In fact, the wealthy might even become richer. If you had forewarning that this would happen, the smartest thing to do would be to burn through every bit cash you have. After all, there are things besides mc Stocks/jewels/real estate, etc. Buy as much as y then you have nothing left to take. When the we redistributed you get some of your money h

261

resell or otherwise use the property you bought for monetary gain and you will come out sitting pretty well on top.

"On the other hand, the poorer family that was living wage to wage gets a minimal, momentary boost, but it wouldn't make any real lasting difference to their lives.

"In this hypothetical situation, we would end up in the same spot where we are now; maybe with a slightly different, renewed elite and a few crazy years later, but the same spot nonetheless. The whole exercise would be fruitless." I was almost choking on David's smugness.

"You had to go all super geek on me there?" Sonya laughed.

"Sometimes, simplifying things for you just doesn't help at all, I need to tell you like it is before you will believe that I know what I am talking about."

"But, what if the money…"

"I SAID NO!" David's angry voice echoed round the shelter.

I couldn't see Sonya's face, but I could tell that she was fuming as everyone stirred with a start and cast their glances towards where they were sitting.

"Is everything alright?" Liam queried.

"We're fine. This one thinks Global Wealth Redistribution is the answer to our prayers," David snorted.

"It could be," Liam nodded to Sonya.

"Don't you bloody start," David jumped up and stormed out of the room.

Why was he getting angry over solutions to our present? He had been acting strange since the truth Transference got aired to the world. Maybe it was only getting to him. He had been the one to keep throughout all of this, maybe he is finally stressed like the rest of us I mused.

Sonya had decided to ignore his little outburst and proceeded to google Global Wealth Redistribution armed with a pen and a notepad.

"What's wriggled up his arse?" I yawned.

"I really don't know, but if he doesn't dislodge it soon and get back to being the little geek I know and love...I will not be held accountable for my actions," Sonya boiled.

"Do you want a hand?" I perched myself on the table in front of her.

"Lauren?" Sarah's voice boomed out of the screen behind me, making me squeal like a trampled pig.

"What the hell! Is that Sarah's video message?" I panted.

"Ha, ha, ha, yes, it is. Let's watch it again." Sonya pressed the play button.

"Lauren? It's me, your sister, Sarah. I have been so worried and trying to find you. I think you think I am not on your side or that I am the enemy, but it's not true. I want to help you, stop you getting yourself killed. I know you always thought I hated you, but the truth is you mean the world to me. If you don't let me help you, you will die, your friends too. I knew when you came back from the hospital something terrible was going on. I did some digging and found out about Transference. I finally found the place. What they are doing is shocking, pretending it's for the greater good. I have friends in high places that are going to help expose them. They have been in touch and you can trust them. I just wanted you to know that I never meant to hurt you, I love you much. These bastards will not get to you, remember promise? You will die by my hands, when you hundred and ten years old, we will die togeth living a wonderful happy life. Good luck baby

The video was as clear as day, no interference and no ominous message of hate and threats of death.

"I don't understand. Why would David keep this from me? Why did he show me the other one with half the words missed out?" I asked Sonya, scared.

Everyone in the room had adopted the same look of confusion that I had, this video was literally right at his fingertips, why didn't he show me it? What was going on? Was Sarah *not* connected to Transference after all?

"You had to keep fucking snooping," David's voice appeared back in the room.

We all turned around to see David pointing a gun right at my face; he had an agitated look about him that made him almost unrecognisable.

"I knew it! I knew you would reveal your true self eventually if I kept on pushing you. Lauren only helped you snap sooner," Sonya breezed.

The conversation continued between David and Sonya like there was no one else in the room, all we could do was stand and listen to them as shocking revelations were made.

"When did you find out?" David asked.

"Oh, don't worry, David, your acting skills are second to none darling. I didn't become suspicious until I was double checking the packages the night before posting. I couldn't sleep, and decided to check they were all ready for posting the next morning. They were all blank, every, single, one. I knew it wasn't an accident. You are too good at all this tech crap, so I added it to the that went to Sarah's contact."

You did that on your own? You added the file? t so happened to add it to the one who will bring

u say? Oh, look at you showing your alliance rs oh so suddenly. You honestly think I am

264

this dumb bimbo? I have spent enough time around you to pick up some basic IT skills. You let your guard down around me, I saw how Sarah's contacts name made you recoil every time you picked it up and I knew it meant something."

"Well. What a turn up for the books. My indignation knows no bounds when I think of what you have done, wife. Although, I must admit I am grateful I no longer have to endure our tedium mundane life a second longer."

"That day we met, it was a setup, wasn't it?"

"Of course it was my clueless, beautiful, intrepid little flower. We had long planned that the first trial of Transference was going to be the McNeil girl. The only connections to them that may have caused us issues were you and Lauren. Unfortunately, you were deemed the most susceptible to being manipulated. It took weeks of me hanging about that library until you finally dropped in and the rest as they say, is history. I was your babysitter if you like; we knew if you got too involved you would turn to your "spy" friend for help. You both made this whole thing so easy."

"Why let us film it if there was even a risk of it being leaked?"

"We had to make it look real; there was never an intention of it leaving my grasp. That was a rookie mistake on my part, one that I will suffer terribly for."

"Who is our outside ally? And why have you let them help us?" I demanded.

"That, we don't know," he laughed, angrily. "It's the only thing we cannot figure out."

"So, none of it was real? You never loved me?"

"I am flattered that you thought I would ever lower my intellectual standard for the likes of you. I have a wife in my real life waiting for me; she knew I had to take this mission for the greater good. Please don't allude that you never once questioned us as a couple."

"Yes, as a matter of fact I did. But in my reality, you were punching well above your weight Mr. You may be smart, but you are the embodiment of evil and all it stands for, you and your putrid friends."

"Look at you using big words, at least our time spent together wasn't a complete waste."

"Here's another four for you, dear husband, fuck…you…"

The room was so tense you could chew it up and blow bubbles with it like it was chewing gum. This revelation was the absolute kick in the balls that none of us had seen coming nor deserved.

"It was the perfect cover. Blend in, in plain sight. Lead you all on a merry dance, make you all feel vindicated, significant almost, and distract you enough to let us pave our way of thinking to the vagrants," David sneered.

"Was this all just a game to you?" Liam shouted.

"Kind of, I did need a vacation. I was paid handsomely, and I did have tremendous fun mingling with you mere underprivileged fools. It is laughable how much you have convinced yourselves to just accept trudging through life with very little," David laughed, so hard that he dropped his gun.

I grabbed it, and shakily pointed it at the place where David's heart should be, if he indeed did have one in there.

"You made me believe my sister wanted me dead!" I wept at him.

"That was never my intention; she just popped up and made it so easy to portray her as the enemy. Again, she was merely a distraction to allow us to continue our work in the background. I got sloppy. I let her get too involved in her quest to find you and she has proven to be more than a persistent, little inconvenience."

"This ends now, David," I informed him.

"You aren't going to shoot me, Lauren. You don't have it in you, it is this kind of behaviour that you are fighting against," David replied.

"You're right, I won't shoot you, but she will," I passed the gun to an over eager Sonya.

"Let's just call this our divorce," Sonya smiled, pulling the trigger and shooting David through the heart.

Chapter 36

I submerged myself into the bath for a lot longer than I had planned, in the vain hope that I could wash the last couple of nights from me and stop my skin from crawling. The copious amounts of food presented to me on a shiny trolley lay like an offering to the Gods. It consisted of strawberries, champagne, chocolate, a varied collection of meats, vegetables that were both in and out of season, and cake. Don't get me wrong, in any other situation this would have been a feast fit for a king and I would have gluttonously shovelled it down my throat whilst watching trash television however, food was the farthest thing from my mind.

Sonya was weighing heavily in my thoughts and I wondered if I should just pop round to her room uninvited? I had called her numerous times, but I was always greeted with "I'm fine, stop calling to check up on me," quickly followed by the dialling tone. She was my best friend in the whole world, I knew her better than she knew herself, and I knew she would be enveloped in complete turmoil over creepy David. Still, I also knew her well enough to know not to push her when she was fragile or I would face the wrath of "Crazy Sonya" and that; I did not have the energy.

I hauled myself out of the now cold bath and balanced on the edge, unsure whether to slide back in again out of sheer laziness or head over to the ridiculously colossal bed that I am pretty sure was an amalgamation of three double mattresses. I opted for the latter, begrudgingly padding my way over for a quick glance at the food that had been ordered on my behalf, without my requesting it.

Once I was comfortable in bed, I braved to switch the television on for a glimpse of the uproar our revelations had caused. It was not easy viewing. Every channel was streaming snippets of the video footage with "Breaking News" tap dancing at the bottom of the screens; even the news channels had relented and were jumping on the supposedly shocked bandwagon.

It had all unfolded rather quickly in the shelter. David was dead, and the gang and I were devastated and unsure of what our next steps were. Did the writers know where we were? Was it safe for us to evacuate our new humble home? Were we still targets? The questions were endless, and with each answer, more questions were being conjured.

Once we were positive that David was in fact dead and that his evil spirit wasn't going to jump into one of our bodies to complete his design, we clung together whilst trying to format our own plan. David's hated corpse was causing much distraction, so Liam and some of the stronger members dragged him into a corner and covered him with a blanket. Sonya continued to show no real distress over the fact that she had just shot her husband in stone cold blood. I mean, she was in shoc' about what had transpired, but there just seemed to be great loss for him as an actual person. She had suspicions long before this all kicked off, ha desensitised her? Had it enabled her to separate her emotions and prepare her for the inevitable outcome?

Liam quickly took charge; it came to him with ease to step into his predecessor shoes and try to lead us all to triumph. His eyes were wide in disbelief as he trawled through email after email, decoding and decrypting, sweating profusely as his curious fingers typed and clicked.

"We really should have been paying more attention to David than we had been, I can't believe we trusted him! We literally sat back in here and let him steer our ship right into the rocks," Liam growled.

"Is it all so obvious?" I asked.

"Well, it is now that I know that he is a rat bastard! To the untrained eye, he was every bit our hero as he was making out to be. To our trained eye that wasn't watching what he was doing? We could, and should, have rumbled him a lot sooner than this. I failed at the first lesson, trust no one."

I watched helplessly as Liam repeatedly slammed the palm of his uninjured hand into his forehead. He was truly pissed off at himself for letting us all down.

"Look, do we continue to cry over the spilt milk or do we clean it up and use a fresh cartoon?" I tried my best to sound positive.

It must have worked in some way, because after pursing his lips in deep thought for what felt like an hour, he pulled himself together and started typing equations that to me resembled Hieroglyphics.

We all continued to huddle around him like witness- to a traffic accident, you want to step in, but you you can't help. You want to look away, but you n overwhelming urge to see it out to the end and re everything pans out.

"Ok, so far I can see that he hasn't given our location away to the writers, but that doesn't mean that they weren't privy to this information before we headed up here. I can't guarantee that we are safe here and I also can't guarantee that we are safe on the outside. What I can guarantee however, is that the person you met with the other day, Lauren, is not one of his contacts that he has been communicating with regularly. When they popped up in Morse Code, that surprised and shocked look he had was real. He hadn't been expecting any replies because he thought he had sent out blank packages," Liam smiled.

"So, we can trust him? Can we reach out to him via the Morse Code again?"

"At this moment in time, he is the only option we have to get out of here alive. All the others have been involved this whole time; they were all laughing at us behind our backs, nay to our faces, as we slept. Is everyone comfortable with me sending him a SOS?" He looked around at our dishevelled faces. Slowly but surely, we all nodded yes or similar to authorise Liam to message my fancy luncheon date and pray that it wasn't yet another trap that we had wilfully skipped into.

I wasn't trained in Morse Code, he could have been making arrangements for a date with someone from his dating app for all I blooming knew, but I trusted him. He had a different air about him than David; he seemed to emit a sense of ownership and determination which never once revealed itself from David's un-furrowed brow.

I felt like a kitten vying for his attention. I desperat ly wanted to stick my head under his arm and rub face on his jumper for him to tell me, "There, everything will be ok."

I was highly aware of how disturbing and unnatural it would be to perform such an act, so I gave myself an internal shake and perched beside him in a non-invasive and nonchalant manner.

As I sat beside him working away furiously on the keyboard with one hand, I couldn't help but notice Liam, as if for the first time in my life. He smelt, well, not the best in the given circumstances, but under all the slightly offensive smells lay a subtle hint of Liam-ness. His broad shoulders were stooped over and concealed under a heavy knit jumper however; the outline of his muscles could still be seen to the perverted eye. My eyes roved themselves about and stopped at his face, he had an almost Greek God look about him, if Greek Gods were nerds and his hair teased his face ever so gently. I couldn't actually remember if he had always sported his jet-black tresses, longish and curly, like a teenage heart throb, or if this was what he had to settle with for the time being.

Then, realisation hit me like a freight train, I fancied Liam!

"Shit," I breathed, out loud.

"Is everything ok?" Liam abruptly stopped what he was doing to face me.

"Oh, my God, please don't look at me," I thought to myself whilst blushing within an inch of my life.

"You don't look too good," Liam pointed out, placing the back of his hand onto my forehead.

"Oh, my God, please don't touch me either!" I creamed inwards.

He put a careful hand around my wrist to check my
e. It was beating quicker than high school gossip
and I couldn't do a thing to stop him. His hand
and gentle, and his big brown puppy eyes were

searching into mine for some kind of clue as to why I was on the verge of a cardiac arrest.

This was possibly the first time in my entire life that I started imagining scenes of the ground opening to swallow me into hell or for the writers to throw a grenade into the shelter and kill us all. Either would have been acceptable to me to prevent me from doing something embarrassing.

"Lauren? Lauren, tell me what's wrong," he looked both worried and startled at my inability to speak.

I was frozen to the chair. My mouth remained clamped shut, and all the wriggling, squirming and stuttering in the world was not helping me in my attempt to avoid any further attention. Sonya casually made her way towards us, took one look at me and rolled her eyes so hard that they almost squeaked. She knew full well that I was three drinks away from ripping off my clothes and launching myself on top of him, even though I was as desirable as a limp handshake.

Seeing Sonya dismiss my inappropriately timed and truly inconsequential issue, made me jolt back into the reality of our life or death predicament. This made me jump and topple off the chair into a sexually frustrated mute on the floor.

"I'm ok, I'm ok," I shot up and dusted myself down before sprinting away. I didn't even grace him with as much as a second glance.

"If you're sure, Lauren, I'm always here if you need me," he shouted after me in a sultry voice.

Great, now even his voice was beginning to sound sexy. This had to stop before I ended up being charged with a sexual assault when we escaped this mind wasting, sex dungeon.

I approached Sonya with caution, waiting on tear into me about how pathetic I was being and h had bigger issues than me having the hots for someone. But surprisingly, she didn't. She stared at me in stony silence until a smile finally crept over her face, and she began passionately kissing the back of her hand. I shan't lie; I would have much preferred if she remained in her depressed state and refused to talk to me than have to watch this sad, uncomfortable, one man love act.

"How are you coping?" I sat down beside her and nudged her with my elbow.

"I can't talk about it, or him," she shook her head. "Not until we are out of here and far away at the very least."

"I understand. We need to keep our heads clear."

"Excuse me, ladies," Liam interrupted. "I have sent the SOS to your boyfriend, Lauren, so hopefully we can get some help to get out of here pretty soon," he winked at me.

"He's not my boyfriend! I don't even know the man, plus he's old! He is a friend of a friend," I scowled at the thought of him being my boyfriend and of Liam thinking I had a boyfriend.

"Jeez, Lauren, I was just winding you up because you had a coffee date with him. Sorry, not a date, but a coffee with him. Or you met him, but it wasn't a date. Coffee," the fear for his life caused him to stutter.

"It's ok, we are all a little tense just now," I glanced over at David's blanket grave. "Let me know if you hear anything back from the SOS."

He retreated to his one true love, the computers, leaving Sonya and I together in a comfortable silence. It wasn't the first and it certainly wouldn't be the last time we were drained of all socially acceptable standards communication. Simply just sitting beside each other fficient for us both.

After an age of filthy, tired, contentedness, Liam finally came bounding over to us like an excited toddler that had just found a new disgusting thing to play with.

"They are coming to rescue us! Well, I hope that's their plan anyway. I sent them across our location, and a brief outline of the events that have unfolded," he paused, out of respect for Sonya.

"Go. Tell the others the good news," Sonya half-heartedly ordered.

The immediate cheering was the ultimate give away of how much everyone was desperate for this to end, no matter the outcome. We had all witnessed, heard, and endured so much in our time together that even death was beginning to look like a good escape.

The cheering turned slowly into loud exhaling, which eventually turned into strained silence, and ended in frustrated pacing. If they didn't turn up anytime soon we may very well start turning on each other and there may be nothing left to save.

We humans, in general as a species, do not deal particularly well on the patience front. Mix in a cupful of exhaustion and a sprinkling of fear and we had become a potent mix of chemicals just waiting for the right spark to set us off.

No sooner had our last nerve intertwined with another's last nerve to generate a toxic mix of homicidal thoughts, when we were distracted by pandemonium.

"SOS RESPONSE TEAM!" A shout came from outside the shelter.

"This is it guys, we either get helped to live, helped to die" I stood up and attempted to fix unfixable trousers.

"WE ARE DOWN HERE," I bellowed in darkness.

We were manhandled so quickly that we didn't have a second to consider if this was a good or bad move. The SOS team hurriedly huddled us into waiting vans like we had just been rescued from a great disaster. Well, I suppose we did look and smell like we had been trapped in an upturned rubbish truck for months on end. They loudly briefed us that we were being taken to a top-notch hotel for safe keeping, just until we got cleaned, fed, and basically made to look human again. We weren't told very much else and it was made clear that questions were not tolerated.

Our heroes, until proved otherwise, were dressed all in black, sporting gun holsters and all sorts of fancy gunnery gear. Don't get me wrong, it was obvious that they were some sort of assassins, but they appeared to be more like the type of assassins that are hired to protect the president; suave looking, with a hint of off the scale crazy mixed in.

So, here I was, lying in my hotel bed trying my best to enjoy the expensive room I was holed up in, but failing miserably. The world as we knew it was falling apart with horrific, graphic riots, my best friend has turned into a killer, and my sister was *not* the head of a murderous scheme against the people. Oh, and to top it off, I now also had a crush on someone that I never knew either existed or ever planned to keep in touch with once we had escaped to whatever form of freedom we could salvage. How had my life become so damn complicated?

I had only been sleeping for a couple of hours when hotel phone trilled into life, waking me up grumpier Sarah had even been. I was compos mentis enough se that I was an unattractive pile of disgusting- should never be released into the world. My had rolled up to my neck only to reveal my unkempt body and hairy legs that would make a man recoil in shock. I had slobbered so much that the pillow was physically stuck to my face. I also must have at some point opened a bar of chocolate and thought better of it, because that had been discarded and had melted all over me.

"Such a treat you are," I sniggered to myself as I stretched over for the phone.

"Lauren?" a voice whispered.

"This had better be good. That was the first proper sleep I've had in hundreds and millions of years," I yawned. "Who is this?"

The phone clicked off before I had a chance to probe any further into my anonymous caller. I couldn't place the voice. I knew all of Sarah's voices that she had tormented me with over the years. I also knew that she wouldn't have wasted a chance to annoy me even further than waking me up would have done.

I was aware that the world had descended into chaos and anarchy outside, but for the time being I was still completely and utterly shattered. I was unable to care, so, I rolled straight back over onto my chocolate bar and slipped once again in to joyous slumber.

The mystery caller continued to intermittently wake me up until I gave in and ripped the poor phone line out of the wall socket. I maybe should have been slightly more concerned that the caller not only knew my name and where I was currently residing, but also the fact that the last few calls were merely just a subtle breath. To be honest, I didn't give a tiny rat's ass who or what they wanted from me. I was too caught up in my cocoon bed with no haunting and disturbing dreams to terrorise me. Even if they chose to upgrade their stalking to m intimidation, breaking and entering or even murder

I still truly couldn't have cared less as long as they didn't wake me when they were executing it.

I woke up refreshed and alert, albeit covered in chocolate, sporting self-inflicted, Chinese rope burns round my tender neck, from the phone cord and lay pondering about everything that had happened over the past few days. If there were to be awards handed out for prioritising situations and life altering events, I would most certainly not be a running contender for first prize or even a sympathy prize due to my lack of sense of urgency. After all we had endured, all the trials and tribulations, all the trauma, not to mention the remaining uncertainty that awaited us all in the grand scheme of things, my mind still seemed to wander back to Liam.

In the cold light of day, it was pretty obvious that I had misconstrued my feelings for Liam as anything other than what they were, loneliness mixed in with depression and the small matter of being entombed together. When I tried to think of him now, being a colleague as such and an acquaintance, I felt nothing but embarrassment and I was positive that any advances made by me would have been unsubtlety spurned. The last thing Liam would have needed right now was a slightly unhinged, possible top ten most wanted criminal contender, launching herself onto him akin to an obsessed, boy band mad, teenage girl.

No, I really was glad that I had panicked and didn't do anything rash in the shelter. I can now concentrate on Sarah and Sonya although, not respectively. Sonya was trying her utmost to emulate a woman who had not just had her whole world crumble down on top of her, but she cannot pull the wool over my eyes. I didn't earn the ge of best friend by sporadically liking her social a statuses.

I scraped the melted chocolate from the body parts it had encased, threw my hair up into a ponytail with an elastic band and shoved on the hideous choice of clothes that had been left in the room for me. I could only imagine the clothes had been purchased by a blind man.

"Like I don't have enough issues in my life without wearing stuff like this," I sighed, to the empty room, closing the door behind me.

As I approached Sonya's room, I felt immediately sad for her that she had just lost the love of her life. Killed the love of her life is more accurate, but I shook my head as the image of her finger pulling the trigger flashed before me. We all know now that he genuinely wasn't the love of her life and was just "doing his job", but for the time they were together, until yesterday, he was her whole life. Let's be honest, it probably didn't help that she had lowered her standards immensely to marry David, and yet in his mind, he was the one slumming it with Sonya. He wasn't my cup of tea in any way shape or form as a suitor for my best friend, but he had won Sonya's big, soft heart over and trampled it right into the drain. Poor, Sonya. I just wanted to melt myself onto her skin so she could wear me like a protective cardigan. More like an (incredibly) slightly creepy, over protective, cardigan. In fact, scratch that entirely, the thought of it has just freaked me right out of my own mind. Maybe just a normal hug will suffice.

I lifted my hand to knock the door, but I was quickly distracted by a commotion behind me and craned my neck round for a quick nosey.

"Get fucking off me before I punch that nose of yours and fix the fucking thing," a familiar, stern voice echoed down the corridor.

"Sarah!" I exclaimed.

"Lauren!" she shouted back.

I was giddy with excitement at our reunion and galloped right into her...hand as it slapped me across the cheek.

"I think we need to talk, don't you?" She flared her nostrils in rage.

Chapter 37

Sarah's face looked haggard and weathered, even though she had tried her best to conceal it with numerous layers of stale make-up. I scanned every inch of her features, her stance, her affect or lack of, for any sign of confirmation that she was here out of genuine concern for me and not out to get some voyeuristic kicks.

"I've been looking for you," she almost won an award for pointing out the obvious.

"Erm, understatement of the year, Mrs spy who slapped me," I shot back, rubbing my tingling jawline.

"Well, excuse me for actually giving a crap about you, Lauren. I almost got killed a few times myself you know. Even just now trying to get passed Mr Sleaze Ball and Mr Big Nose," she stuck her tongue out at the appointed bodyguards.

"Behave, Sarah, as if your own friends would harm you," I tutted.

"My what, now? My friends? What the fuck is that supposed to mean?" She looked positively startled.

"Well, these guys here, the guy I met f lunch…you were our mutual friend after all, were not? You sent them video clips for me? Although I admit we thought you oversaw Transference for time."

For the first time in my life I could see that Sarah looked scared, quickly followed by crest fallen. I followed her to a large wooden window frame, both of us perching onto the edge in silence.

"Lauren, I don't know anything about any of these idiots or who they work for. I got a phone call in the middle of the night from a woman I have never spoken to before. She didn't say much, but she gave me the name of this hotel and said you were here and that you were safe, I just had to come."

"So, who the heck has orchestrated all of this? Who is the one behind us being helped?" I thought out loud.

"Why did you think I was involved with Transference?" She asked without looking up.

"You are joking, right? Where shall I begin?" I laughed. "When we finally found the hospital, not too long ago, our surveillance of the place showed you inside the premises talking to someone and may I add, looking very important to them. You knocked Liam down with your car, who just so happens to be one of my gang, when he was trying to get our footage out there to the public. I was then shown video footage of you ominously threating to kill me, Sarah. I have spent so long in hiding, but I was mostly hiding from you."

She looked as if I had leaned across and punched her right in her guts. She barely looked up from the floor as she gulped deep breaths before replying to me.

"I know I have been hard on you over the years, auren, it's just... I love you so much that it scares me the very core. I kept you at arm's length to try and ct myself, you know I am not a feely type of , I didn't know how to handle it, Lauren. When d dad first brought you home with them, this , fragile thing, I knew after that first glance re my missing piece. After hating you as you

282

grew in mum's tummy for so long, it suddenly all made sense when you joined the family. My whole purpose was to love and protect you from all the evil in the world. Ever since that day, I have tried my best to keep you safe. But obviously, I have failed," she sniffed.

I'm not going to try and lie here; inside I was ecstatic to hear this information. I have never witnessed Sarah look so vulnerable, so open, and so human. I always knew deep down that she loved me in her own quirky way, but here she was baring her soul to me and I just wanted to punch her in the arm or pull her hair out, it just felt like a dream.

"I knew straight away that something wasn't right when you were mysteriously admitted into that hospital, and not allowed any visitors. When you came to mum's house after you were discharged, as soon as I saw you it confirmed to me that you were well in over your head with something, and so I started digging about. I'm confused though, I found that hospital about a year ago, without even breaking a sweat, what took you guys so long to find it? Why was it only recently discovered? As for the video I sent... I didn't send anything to you or to anyone else for that matter. I uploaded some videos onto my interthingymawebly account to show you how much I cared for you when I finally found you. I caught the feelings bug and I was scared that I might lose them, so I needed proof for you," she smirked.

"David," I sighed.

"You mean Creepy Dave? What about him?"

"It turns out that David has been playing us t' whole time we have known him, he was working fo' Transference team, and just toying with us to ke distracted. In hindsight, it is kind of obvious now had been sending us on wild goose chases to himself, and his bosses. He oversaw the fin hospital or rather, used all his power to hide it from us. We were at his mercy; he had all the technology, the brains, and the contacts. Even his marriage to Sonya was all a sham, a part of his sick game."

"So, he kept the pictures of me from when I visited the hospital for answers until such a time he could turn you against me? Hacked into my interthingymawebly, and manipulated my videos? I will kill him with my bare hands," she seethed, pacing back and forth in front of me.

"What about Liam?" I pushed, suddenly protective of him.

"I have a few contacts of my own, not as sophisti- cated as this mob, but contacts none the less. I knew you would be with Sonya, who would in turn be with David. Liam was tracked as a close contact who had peculiarly disappeared when you all buggered off. When he resurfaced, I got a call telling me where he was, and I sped all the way down to question him, knocking him down was just a happy accident. After chatting to him at length I thought he didn't know anything of your whereabouts, so, I let him go."

"You didn't put a tracker on him?" I asked.

"Put a tracker on him? What the hell kind of people do you think I rub shoulders with? I thought you were caught up in a hood rat, drug thing with gangsters or something; my contacts are in the Police! I had no idea you were heavily involved in Transference until I saw ɔur ugly mug on my television screen. By the way, m nearly died on her feet when she saw you."

The realisation hit me like a strong gust of wind, that was far more conniving than any of us had given ˡit for. He had managed to not only convince me ster wanted me dead, but almost destroyed me my own mind in the process, all for kicks.

He knew all our weaknesses and he used them against us like a human game of chess. Slowly moving all his pieces to exactly where he needed them to be.

"David's dead," I informed her, despite her not asking of his whereabouts.

"Just as well he's dead. The things I would have done to him wouldn't have been lady like at all, not in the slightest. So, who are these people? And more importantly, what are we going to do?" She whispered.

"I was hoping you would know the answer to that. After Sonya killed David, we changed your status from the enemy to our hero, but I take it that's not the case?"

"Negative, little sister, I got that call and was conflicted whether it was true or not, but then you know what I'm like better than anyone, nosiness got the better of me," she smiled.

Sarah wrapped her fingers into mine, and rested her head onto my shoulder, which made me do a double take at her showing me affection. I snuggled my cheek onto the top of her head, and closed my eyes. It was the most serene and comfortable I had felt in my entire life, and I wished that we could just stay like this forever.

"Sorry to interrupt, but you are both required to come with me," a bald man was talking in front of us; he didn't look sorry.

It was a nice feeling, it felt as if I had come through the storm of life, and nothing was going to ruin my natural high. We followed the bald man with our arms linked together, giddy at being reunited, and me being free from Sarah's oppression. You would be forgiven thinking we were newlywed lesbians.

Sonya and I frequently got mistaken for being ers. Not because we were inappropriate with ea but because we were so comfortable with e and we were terrible for having a lack boundaries. Ok, we were sometimes inappropriate, if you call pulling out each other's wedgies, picking food from our teeth, and checking each other for sweat stains, then yeah, I can totally see now why people would think that.

As if by magic thinking, Sonya was in the room that the bald man had led us to, alongside Liam, and the rest of the gang. The sight of Sarah did cause a few noticeable gasps that triggered Liam to jump up and knock his chair over. Fair enough, she had run over him and left him in a cast.

After I had calmed everyone down, explained everything, and Sarah had been fully exonerated of our accusations against her, we turned our attentions to the bald man. He had remained in the room as we caught up with each other, but he didn't interrupt us or show any interest in executing our demise.

As if on cue, the bald man addressed the room.

"Ladies and gentlemen, now that you have been re-acquainted with each other, can you please be upstanding for the honourable, Lord Angus MacIntosh," he opened the double doors with such ease.

"Thank you, Rupert, let's tone it down a smidgen for the time being, know your audience," he used his hand to gesture Rupert to basically pipe down the amateur dramatics.

The well-groomed man that stood before us, was my lunch date and presumably, in charge of our SOS team. 'is eyes scanned around the room and settled happily on familiar face that was blinking repeatedly back to

, Lauren, I trust you slept well?" He enquired. He lifted her hand, and tried to kiss the back it. ves, I am Sarah, no to the kiss, thanks," she nd back aghast.

"Feisty, like your sister," he chuckled. "Please do be seated," he signalled to the plush seating area.

"I was delighted when you entrusted us to save your lives in addition to revealing your location to us. I was saddened however, to hear about the untimely but completely justified demise of your leader, David," he made a point not to look directly at Sonya.

"On behalf of all of us, thank you for responding so promptly. We were like sitting ducks after the revelation of David's treacherous ways," I too, avoided Sonya's glare.

"Yes, he did indeed play his part awfully well, too well, but that's neither here nor there at present. What is important is what our next move is, I mean, as you can see, we have blown the lid completely off Transference and what they stand for. Now we must deal with the aftermath of not only besmirching "the writers" as they have been so aptly named; but also, the revolting public."

"A bit harsh calling us revolting, you didn't last long hiding your true colours!" Sonya snapped, at Angus.

"Oh, no, not in the slightest am I hiding any feelings of grandeur over anyone, I simply meant revolting, as in, the rebellious rise, you know, mutiny." He looked bemused, at Sonya's outburst.

A shamefaced Sonya was consoled by Liam which made me twitch involuntary for two reasons, 1. I should be consoling her; she is my best friend and 2. I wanted Liam's attention on me, not Sonya. My feelings of jealousy for the both of them were as surprising as th_ were unsettling, I thought I was a better friend potential girlfriend than that.

The room remained silent as the sea of faces patiently for a morsel of good news to come this, something to give us all a little hope. Sensing this, Angus continued.

"There is something noteworthy to share. As far as we can see, David never provided the writers with anyone else's information in this room, except you two," he nodded, to Sonya and I. "For whatever reason that shall remain unknown, he never disclosed any of your names other than a rounded-up number of how many of you there were. I hope that this is of some comfort to you and you take it for what it is, a life jacket, and not an insult to your abilities or importance," he mollified, their slightly dented egos.

It was amazing to watch, and literally feel the air in the room shift from ominous and awaiting impending doom, to joyous at being given a second chance at life. Everyone jumped up and exchanged excessively long hugs and kisses, whilst dancing around the room in such elated glee that it was almost impossible not to smile with them.

"So, that's it? We can all go back to our lives innocuously? Liam stopped, in his tracks.

"It seems so, we have been through every bit of machinery, every file, every piece of communication between David and the writers, and we cannot find any evidence contrary to that. David kept such a tight lead on what was happening behind the scenes. Dripping you all measly pieces of false information that he must have deemed your identities to be irrelevant.

His plans were to never allow any of you out his ⸱ches, not alive at least, anyway."

'What a lovely thought, to have been insignificant ⸱und noise to a bunch of toffs," Liam looked ⸱sulted.

⸱hat it's worth, the extras in the film are just as the main actors," Angus offered. "You can

288

all remain here for as long as you need to or wish. I have no intention of throwing anyone out, especially as it is all a bit chaotic and perilous out there."

Like a stream of sheep, everyone left one by one muttering "thank you" and "good luck" from their bowed, mortified, ship jumping mouths. I was astonished at the pace at which everyone fled the room; you would have thought they had just opened a buffet at a wedding. As Liam proceeded to hot foot it with the rest of them, I felt myself slump into an instant depression at the thought of never seeing him again.

He shuffled nervously towards the door, chewing his bottom lip, and picking lint from his cast that wasn't there whilst avoiding the three of us, four including the bald man, gawking.

"Lauren, I can stay behind if you want me too? Purely in a professional manner to see out whatever plan we devise," he mumbled.

"Yes!" I squeaked, higher than I intended. "Any help would be appreciated," I cleared my throat.

"Jesus, can you both like, get a room or something," Sarah rolled her eyes, she was an expert at doing that.

"We have many rooms here to choose from," Angus joined in on my torture.

Liam looked as though he regretted stopping with every fibre of his soul, and would much have preferred if I had said no or if David had been reincarnated as a cat and scratched his balls off.

"On a serious note, we need to run through our options that are slowly depleting, please do join me in c dining room," Angus headed off in the opposite di tion.

With his hands firm behind his back, Angu with a grace that you didn't often see thes people. He was a confident man, educat

289

patronising, handsome but not attractive if that makes sense. Sonya, Liam and I followed behind in single file taking in the beautiful architectural aspects of the property and the beautiful art pieces that hung elegantly on every wall.

It was the most graceful building I had ever had the pleasure of being in, but it was also confusing. It was a hotel, but Angus treated it like his home, and there were never any visible guests strutting around. There were streams of staff and help in every corner of every room, some busy, and some giving orders to others, but there wasn't any other "normal" people around.

"Do you own this hotel?" I finally asked.

"Why, yes, I do, it is a family structure that has been handed down the MacIntosh line over the years. For four months out of the year it is open to a very select few to fulfil my philanthropy requirements, but for the remainder of the year I like to reside here and connect with my family roots."

I soaked in all the elaborately painted portraits of past and present family members of the clan MacIntosh, all looking rather spiffing in their family tartan looking proud, but humble. I stopped dead in my tracks, causing Liam to crash into the back of me which was the highlight of the past twelve months of my life.

"I recognise her," I gasped out loud.

"Yes, I should imagine you do," Angus double backed to meet me.

"I don't understand, exactly how is it that you know ?" I quizzed.

"That magnificent creature you are so admiring is iant wife on our wedding day.

Her name is Lady Sophie Camillia MacIntosh, the Third, known as Camille to acquaintances, but to friends she much prefers…"

"Cammy," I answered for him.

Chapter 38

I held my breath for as long as I could muster before I passed out in front of all the guests. After months of planning, crying, eating cake, crying and eating more cake, the wedding of the year was about to begin.

Everyone looked so beautiful and carefree in their carefully picked ensembles. The decorations were placed just perfectly so, and the humanist was waiting patiently at the end of the aisle. This was a day I would never have placed a bet on at the local bookmakers as ever happening, it felt so random and rushed, but somehow also felt so right.

Liam looked so handsome in his suit, shuffling nervously as he adjusted his buttonhole for the fifteenth time. He slicked back his hair with trembling hands hoping no one would notice him.

Sonya was all over me like ants at a picnic, checking my dress wasn't tucked into my knickers, and that boob sweat marks were nowhere to be seen. I had rolled antiperspirant under my boobs in a poor attempt to ᵛent stains from happening, but it caused my sweat to of mingle in with it like a paste and it was making ss stick to me. I don't usually wear high heels d was disappointed to learn that heels were a non-negotiable requirement to enable everyone to look roughly the same height in the photographs.

I stood at the start of the aisle and could see every single person in the room turn their heads to admire me walking up to the make shift alter. It must have only been about one hundred feet long, but it may as well have been via a jungle followed by a swim through shark infested waters for all the fear that had struck me. Oh, God, why did I ever say yes to this? There was still ample time to turn around and flee, but Sonya being Sonya sensed that I was getting cold feet and shoved me in front of her so I couldn't escape. Well, I could still escape, I would just have to climb over everyone, and the chairs to do so, but it was completely achievable.

As "Here comes the bride" was played by an arthritic two hundred-year-old man on a piano that was twice his age, I shuffled myself forward, begrudgingly towards the smiling humanist that awaited my presence in front of her. Everyone gasped at the blushing bride that was floating passed them in a vision of unadulterated beauty. As I glided past them, I breathed heavily, and squeezed the last remaining drop of life out of my bouquet.

I stopped abruptly, and took my place that had been rehearsed so many times prior to the actual event, why do people feel the need to do that? I always feel it is unnecessary and ridiculous, but who am I to argue with tradition.

The haunting rendition of "Here comes the bride" finally came to a shaky end, and everyone got themselves comfortable to hear the impending nuptials that they had been summoned here to witness.

"We are gathered here today for the joining of souls… Sonya and David," the humanist bellowed even the deaf pianist got a fright.

Being bridesmaid to your best friend when you are single is not a chore I wish to involve myself in ever again. Sonya took the opportunity to preen and primp me to try and snare me a boyfriend, because and I quote "it would be so romantic". No, it wouldn't be romantic, it wasn't romantic, and I felt like I was up for sale to anyone willing to take me on for a camel and a few bags of grain. Sonya had spent more time and energy into turning me into a faked tanned, high heeled, Barbie doll than she had spent on herself, because apparently a bride always looks beautiful, no matter what.

It's funny how on the day of the wedding I barely gave Liam the time of day, I mean, we worked together in the gang and stuff, but he was never anyone I would have said was my type of boyfriend. He wasn't even supposed to be invited to it, he was there merely as a replacement for David's brother/best man who had been struck down with last minute food poisoning.

David didn't have many friends at all because, well, he was David, and a quirky paranoid loner. Liam had been drafted in with seconds to spare as he was one of only a few male acquaintances that he liked. I couldn't help casting my mind back to that day as we waited on Angus returning from an important call that he had been called to, just as it was revealed that Cammy was his wife.

So, who were the random, long distance family members that had turned up to see David say "I do"? His mum and dad were unable to fulfil their duties as Mother and Father of the groom on the day due to them being koned to France to care for an aunt on her death bed. a had never met them, not once, before or after they t married, and if she ever pushed him on it, he runt about their relationship being complicated, out. I could kick myself at how obvious it was

294

that he was dodgy, the signs were all there that a dead man on a fast horse would have seen them.

Sonya had remained unusually quiet this whole morning, but who could blame her? Her life as she knew it was in tatters, and we were all likely never going to win this fight no matter how hard we tried. Sarah was stuck to me like a mollusc since she decided to embrace having feelings, it was painfully sweet and welcomed, but I wished she would dial it down a notch. As for Liam, now, I wouldn't mind him slithering himself in between me and the chair…I closed my eyes to try and regain some sense of composure.

"I am dreadfully sorry for the terribly timed interruption," Angus flounced back, into the room.

"Is your wife the nurse from the hospital?" Liam asked bluntly.

"That's an awful, crude description of my Cammy, but then I suppose that is all you have known her as," Angus looked offended.

"Liam didn't mean anything by it, Angus, it just threw us off guard a little seeing her up on you wall," I tried to soften the atmosphere.

"Yes, well. My Cammy is many wonderful things in this world, generous, beautiful, and loyal. She had such an infectious laugh, it was impossible to be anything but jubilant around her," he stared at a photograph of her, wistfully. "But, a nurse she is not," he huffed.

"So, what happened?" I pushed.

Angus rose to his feet and headed over to his exquisite selection of worldwide alcohols that were standing like proud soldiers on his credenza. The crystal decan' that looked as though it had taken quite a hammerin' late was being utilised once more as he poured ou neat Whisky's. Rupert dashed across the room a role and very existence was being made redundant, but Angus waved him off and gestured him to leave.

He handed out the glasses to us without waiting to see if we actually wanted one and then nestled himself into an offensively large armchair.

"Approximately three years ago, Cammy and I had been approached, as had all the landed gentry, with the proposition of Transference being introduced into society. You see, PODD had already started to raise its ugly head amongst the higher classes, and they had come up with the premise of Transference to appease the terrified families. Now, you have to understand that, we were never given full disclosure about either process, we were just pooled together and promised a cure."

He downed his drink and continued with his story.

"They sold us this tale of PODD, how it had arrived, suspected from Japan and how it was killing our innocent children. They said they had managed to come up with a cure called Transference and how it could be removed from their little bodies completely.

A few months into the epidemic, they approached us again as a community, pleading for people to come and work in this super hospital they had built. Of course, my Cammy was one of the first to volunteer to work there, anything to help those poor babies find peace. It wasn't until she got there that the true horrors were revealed to her. All the other volunteers were happy to turn a blind eye in the name of the greater good." He stopped, to sneer at the thought.

"She immediately confided in me and begged me to and put a stop to their murdering ways. She sounded n, desperate to leave the institution and tell the what was going on. To prevent this, they kid-
her and have been holding her hostage at the
nowing I couldn't do anything as they would

kill my beloved wife. She is a nurse there, that's what she is paraded as, but only to try and preserve her life.

"We are only allowed to communicate by letters, that is why I knew you would come into my life, Lauren," he smiled, pitifully at me.

"Before they stole her from me forever, she had told me in detail what was really going on and how PODD was in fact created by them. The only reason I have not been exterminated is because I am far too important in our world. I would be missed almost instantly, questions would be asked, and investigations instigated.

"She wrote to me sweet poems and memories of when we were courting, but one day she sent ramblings of how her, Great Aunt Lauren must be looked after in the event of her untimely death. I knew instantaneously that it was code for something, but I couldn't pinpoint exactly what. All I was certain of was that she didn't have a Great Aunt Lauren."

"You took a gamble when you asked for me when we made contact?" I replied.

"Precisely that, my dear, Lauren, I turned up with expectations of it all being part of their game, but my Cammy just knew you were brought to her for a reason."

"But why did David not alert the writers that you had seen the footage?" Sarah jumped in, suddenly interested.

"What could they do? They would never have believed that I would expose them. David had to keep contact with them to a minimum, he obviously thought he was in full control of the situation," Angus dismissed her query.

"Have you heard from them? Or Cammy?" I ask cautiously.

"No. And I won't, I shouldn't think. I h doubts that Cammy is no longer on this mortal that she most likely suffered the worst kind of death, but exposing them is what she would have wanted," he looked devastated. This was the first time he has ever admitted out loud that she was dead.

"There must be something we can do?" Sonya joined in, to progress the conversation.

"About Transference? Have you not been keeping up to date with the latest news correspondence? They have stepped out of the shadows, the charade is over. They are continuing with Transference, and not giving two hoots who knows now. Those that have the power to stop them don't want to. Most of the unfortunates have accepted it and the ones that want to stop it simply do not have the means to," Angus informed us.

"So, exposing them has been utterly pointless? People have been killed, and will continue to be killed, for fuck all?" Sarah asked, as charming as ever.

"I love your passion, your drive and your sense of community spirit, maybe without the profanities though, young lady," Angus raised his glass.

"Life, itself is pointless," Sonya added, poignantly.

"My child, please don't ever think in that way! If you let them convince you that life is meaningless, then they have won. I trust you are feeling a tad jaded after the devastating realisation that your husband was the axis for these repellent happenings?" Angus asked sympathetically.

"I'm coping surprisingly well despite my outbursts reflecting otherwise. Once you have your husband's true olours and intentions laid out to you on a platinum, mond encrusted platter, it's difficult to mourn him se, well, I never really knew him. I have been our whole life together back over and over in my d it angers me how blatantly obvious his manipulation was. Love truly is blind… and deaf… and mentally unbalanced," she grimaced.

We paused in silence to absorb the sounds outside that indicated there was utter carnage and uproar going on. I could swear they were getting closer and closer to us with each passing minute.

Something soft and gentle was hovering above my hand with the delicateness of a butterfly. It hesitated ever so slightly, before resting on top of and curling its way round my fingers in a protective manner; I was relieved when I looked up and saw it was Liam's hand. He didn't utter a word to me, nor did I to him. I rubbed my thumb on the top of his fingers to assure him that his touch was not offensive. A tingle slowly swam its way up from my hand throughout my entire body and settled in my stomach. This in turn made it flip like an inexperienced gymnast trying her best to impress her passive aggressive coach.

"My dear, you, with the sharp tongue who's name escapes me. Out of interest, how did you manage to obtain access into the hospital?" Angus was snapping his fingers at Sarah.

"It's Sarah and I am not a waitress, so stop snapping your fingers at me. I have contacts within the police as I have already explained to Lauren. One of them is quite high up and I asked him to help me get into the hospital. Although, in all likelihood, he is part of Transference as well, hence why he got me in, to allow me to exhaust my searches. I told him that Lauren had been in a crash and that I had found the hospital she had been staying in. He was quite gleeful as he pointed out it was off the rad and that he had more pull than me to get us access was with me the day we visited, we were taken on of the gardens, and advised that although data pro did not allow full disclosure on Lauren, she w

ously a patient that had since been released," she informed us, matter of factly.

"And nothing warranted a full search of the facilities? Nothing looked untoward?" Angus pressed for more information.

"Not in the slightest. I remember thinking I wish I had been in that car crash, because it could have been easily misconstrued as a luxury spa. The staff seemed innocuous enough and were very keen to help me understand that there was nothing sinister about the place. Saying that, I didn't tell my contact the full reason as to why I was looking for it, I just said that I was concerned it was some form of mental institution, and once I had seen it was not, I would let it drop."

"So, your contact fed you a metaphorical bone to shut you up?" Sonya summed it up into an obnoxious, little bow.

"I guess," Sarah shrugged.

"They are without conscience, but they aren't as silly as they appear to be. Every move they play has been carefully considered, there was an underlying reason they entertained you, Sarah. Maybe the cost was getting too expensive for them, you were protecting Lauren, someone would avenge you and they would be avenged so on and so forth. Maybe they assumed it would be in their best interests to just nip your wild imagination in the bud" Angus mused, out loud. "Whatever their reckoning, you were extremely lucky." He scoffed, as a full stop.

We remained in silence with the exception of the ∕ing mob gathering outside, and the crackling of the fire that would have welcomed chest nuts being ⅃ on it. Or marshmallows to the more common of ∼ke me. My hand was getting a little sweaty from ∼nd blanket, but I desperately didn't want him

300

to remove it for fear that I wouldn't ever get a chance feel it again.

"Where else is the PODD disease they have created, being manufactured and stored?" Liam asked Angus.

"Oh, my dear fellow, as far as we were led to believe it is all being done in that one hospital. From creating it and testing it, to selling it, you name it and it gets performed there. It's a closely guarded concoction and operation, nothing in regards to PODD or Transference is permitted to leave the grounds. Deliveries are sanctioned with strict regulations, and are delivered from the hospital direct to the recipient, in any country, by hand. It doesn't leave the designated Transference couriers sight under any circumstances. Why?" He queried.

"It's obvious to me that the only way to stop this madness is to go straight for the belly of the beast. The hospital needs to be destroyed," he informed us.

"What about all the people in there? There must be hundreds that will be killed as well!" Sonya gasped.

"More like close to thousands, the tunnel is as deep as it is long, my learned friend, but that isn't what concerns me. You see, all staff members in there gave up the right to be spared death the moment they accepted their repulsive jobs that only heightened their misplaced, repugnant views of the world. All the other poor souls that are in there, are so against their will, and to be perfectly frank with you, they deserve to be put out of their misery. You saw the tests that are conducted on them, it's beyond barbaric," he spat.

"When you put it like that, then yes, in this instance it would be being cruel to be kind," Sonya agreed.

"My reservations to this proposal are as follow be successful it would need to be a bomb that ca pretty impressive punch to it, I mean, a pretty fashioned wallop. Where on earth could we obtain that kind of weaponry from? And, for it to be effective it would need to be detonated from inside the hospital if we categorically wanted everything to be destroyed," Angus nodded, to himself.

"Gee, your roles and responsibilities for this job should you choose to accept it will include deception, having no feelings, performing mass murder, oh and committing suicide. Basically, becoming a terrorist, let's all beat a path to his chair for the job!" Sonya was now laughing in hysterics.

"Certainly, there was a time when my resources could fulfil such a requirement however, given my reputation as already being the black sheep of the inner circle, I can no longer live up to that standard of achievement. We need to be honest with ourselves here, where will we find someone who has access to that kind of horsepower, and who in their right mind will volunteer for such a mission?" Angus was shaking his head in defeat.

"I'll do it," Sarah stood up.

"You can source us a bomb?" Angus's eyes almost fell out of his head.

"Yes. I will also be the one to take it into the hospital for detonation," she replied.

"But, you will die," Angus urged.

"I know."

Chapter 39

"You promise you won't leave me?" I begged Sarah.

"Cross my heart and hope to die, stick jaggy needles in my eye!" She sang back to me.

Call me naïve, call me deluded or just call me plain dumb, but I had every belief that she would come back for me, and not leave me all alone. She flicked her hair at me before almost inhaling her cigarette to the core, and blew it out like she was putting out birthday candles.

She turned on her heels and sashayed up to the unsuspecting bouncer. I could see she put her hands on her hips so her boobs looked much bigger and she was pouting like a duck. I couldn't hear what was being said between them, and casually looked away in an attempt to make me look not too bothered about her being refused entry. When I rolled my head back, Sarah was nowhere to be seen, and the bouncer was sniggering directly at my face.

I stood out in the cold like an orphaned child, awaiting my big sister to prance out and tell me I too was allowed in, but alas, it never happened. The bouncer had told her that she could get in all she wanted, but I was too young, and with that, I got dumped quicker than tweed coat on a summer's day. As each hour passed I convinced myself of many things like; maybe the was so busy that she couldn't get back out for me, right? Or, even though she had all of our money, she thought I got home safely, and in one piece.

Five hours, twelve taxi kerb crawlers, three attempts to kiss me and one offer of the time of my life later, Sarah came bumbling out of the nightclub and threw up all over the wall.

"You promised you would come back for me," I whined.

"Yes, I did, I also lied, Lauren, get used to it! Life is all about lies and let downs, I am basically giving you a life lesson here," she hiccupped her alcopop breath towards my nose.

Her voice echoed in my brain as I stared out of the window into complete darkness, with nothing to console me except my memories. Sarah had run out of the house to meet her police contact about getting her hands on some ammonium nitrate, and to put an end to Transference hours ago. She had guaranteed me that the plan was fail proof. She would conceal the explosives; get back into the hospital with her contact, plant the bomb and come straight back to me. We would detonate it together and live happily ever after knowing that PODD had been destroyed, thus putting the world back to right again.

I knew that this was just another yarn she had spun me filled with empty promises, and with no regards to our safety as we waited patiently. She wasn't coming back to me, and she wouldn't get two feet close to that hospital again.

"I get that she is your sister and everything, but why o you look up to her so much?" Liam rudely interrupt- my nightclub memory.

"She's my sister. I need her in my life; I can't live ut her!" I replied, hysterically.

304

The thought of Sarah not being on the same earthly plane as me, never seeing her again or hearing her shrill voice was simply sending me spiralling into the mother of all panic attacks.

"Breathe, Lauren, breathe," Liam panted, like we were in a Lamaze class.

The room was spinning, and my chest was clamped as tight as a vice. I stumbled back onto a chaise longue, and gripped the edge for dear life.

"I can't bear to see you like this, Lauren. Its soul wrenching watching her destroy you," Liam looked away.

"You don't understand!" I shouted.

"Well, tell me, because this absurd fascination isn't normal," Liam snapped.

"She's…"

"She's what?" He urged.

"She's the only person on this horrid planet that has ever loved me!" I sobbed.

"That's not strictly true, Lauren, I… I have loved you since I set eyes on you over a year ago. All this time I have ached to hold you and wipe away your tears. I don't care anymore if you reject me, I have to tell you."

I felt a sudden rush of emotion and familiarity in Liam, like I had known him my entire life. My heart swelled up with the rush of realisation that I loved him. The finality of acceptance to how I felt made me feel like I was going to combust. I also became aware of the overflowing tears and snot that was smeared all over my face and I questioned his sanity over loving such a disgraceful looking creature.

"I love you, too," I gushed.

Liam looked into my eyes like he was going to off and take a long swim into them, caressing m softy with the back of his fingers that were stic

305

of his cast. I closed my eyes as I felt his touch and my breathing became more ragged than when I was previously panicking. He pulled me in gently towards him with his other hand that had snaked behind my neck, causing my hairs to stand up like little soldiers.

"I want you," he whispered.

He kissed me lightly, waiting on me indicating that I wanted him to ravish me then and there, which I did want him to do, and I did indicate for him to do so. I reciprocated his advances and kissed him passionately, moaning as he climbed on top of me and thrust himself against me, his hands fondling any part of me that he could reach. I wrapped my legs around him as he slipped his hands inside my shirt, fumbling like a teenager on a drunken night out down the local park.

It may have only lasted a few minutes, but it was the most intense, fulfilling and insatiable sexual experience I had ever encountered.

Before we had time to catch our breath, and I had time to start feeling self-conscious about what had just happened between us, Sonya knocked on the door.

"When love's young dream is finished doing the nasty in there, you might want to come through to the den," she sniggered.

I looked around hastily to see if we had left any evidence of our little tryst, but the only thing that was obvious was Liam's lustful look towards me. He tucked himself in and wiped whatever had come from my nose and eyes onto his face with the back of his hand, throwing me a mock look of disgust.

"You're everything I have ever dreamt of and ," he kissed me again, making my knees wobble.

trust that I don't have to have any furniture de- from that room?" Angus lowered his glasses, ur creased clothing.

306

"So, what's going on?" I evaded his question with expert precision.

"You tell us. Sarah has activated her audio and requested that you be present for her video link," Sonya informed me.

We waited anxiously to see if Sarah had indeed managed to worm her way back into the hospital and I prayed that she would come back to me in one piece.

"Lauren?" Sarah's face jolted me out of my thoughts.

"Sarah! Where are you?" I quizzed.

She was sitting on a floor with her legs crossed, surrounded by white walls, clutching a vial and a set of keys.

"Baby sister, it's time you knew the truth," she took a sharp, deep breath. "You have been right the whole time. You have never been confident enough to trust your judgement, especially when it comes to my involvement. PODD and Transference was, was my idea, my creation, my baby. I decided to use the McNeil's as our prototype family simply because they were your neighbours. I thought I could monitor the whole project, especially you and Sonya and test the waters quite easily. I recruited David to babysit you both."

"Why are you saying all this?" I raged.

"Because it's all true, Lauren, the hospital pictures of me? I was doing my usual weekly check up to make sure everyone was completing their tasks to my satisfaction. I knew where you all were the whole time; it has all been total bullshit, Lauren, from start to finish. Everything you thought about me was placed into your head by us, for us."

"I don't understand, you wanted me to think y were corrupt, then you didn't want that and now yo again?" I cried in disbelief.

"I needed to play on your combined love and fear for me. I needed you scared to keep you safe, and out the way, a necessary distraction, if you will. When David died, I used the timing to make you believe I was innocent again so I could be near you and keep you safe. You have to believe me, Lauren, my intention was never to bring you to any harm or allow anything bad to happen to you."

"I was certain that your story was too suspicious, it didn't seem feasible in the slightest," Angus spat in revulsion. "YOU, are the reason my Cammy is dead and you had the gall to sit in OUR house and act out your little repugnant pantomime!"

"I know, I am the most abhorrent person to ever walk the earth. I will make what I can right. I lost my way in life; I am responsible for so many deaths that I honestly do not have a ball park figure. Me, I caused all this pain and suffering and for what?" She wept.

"Oh, fuck no. You don't get to be upset missy, there is a special place in hell for you," Sonya replied.

"I need to try and right the wrongs I have caused. This isn't the person I want to be, the way I want life to be. You are so pure, and so honest, Lauren; your love is the only constant thing I have ever had. Bonding with you and reconnecting with you made me remember who I used to be, and let me be very clear; I meant every word I said to you."

I truly didn't have anything to say. What could I say? The person I idolised my whole life had tuned out to be the maker of all evil. I surprised myself at how quickly my love had flipped into complete and utter hatred for her and I could no longer hide it.

"Why did you come back into my life? You could stayed away and let me believe you were the enemy, which you are. Why are you pulling my head apart like this… WHY?" I raged.

"When the footage was sent to Angus and he released it to the public, I drafted in a team for damage control. I came back to save you, but everyone else was to be eliminated. Sorry." She hung her head in shame.

"So, there is no bomb? And you aren't in the hospital?" Liam asked robotically.

"No, no, there is a bomb, and I am in the hospital." She pulled back her jacket to reveal explosives that were attached to her, and then spun the camera round to show a clinical looking room.

"I don't understand," I shook my head.

"I obtained the explosives from one of my many secret bunkers, and swanned straight into the hospital with no questions asked. I am in charge around here, no one questions me," she chuckled. "The thing is, only I and three other people are aware of how this building was engineered. We knew we were dipping our toes into the unknown, we never anticipated that the whole process would be accepted as quickly or as submissively as it was. We needed a back-up plan that would allow us to disappear as quickly as we had arrived should the shit all hit the fan."

"But, it hasn't, you can still come out of this smelling of roses, and Transference will be as natural to people as breathing," Liam joined in.

"I appreciate that, but this isn't what I want anymore. I need penance for my sins, PODD needs to be destroyed, and the world can move on. This building h been made with explosives pre-hidden into the w once I push this button it will trigger them all, and everyone and everything in it to a pile of dust. Y caused this, Lauren, you made me realise that be your hero, the person you really have been looking up to your whole life."

She looked heartbroken at the thought of me no longer stuffing her up on a pedestal anymore, I almost felt elated at how the tables had turned, and she was now looking up at me.

There was a definite feeling of smarm radiating from me up here in my ivory tower, and I shan't lie, I got a little buzz out of it. I can only imagine how Sarah has been feeling for years knowing that she has had the fate of the world at her finger tips.

"There will be no trace of anything left, I am ridding the world of the most evil thing that has ever been created," she sighed.

"PODD?" I confirmed.

"No, me. I always told you that your life would end at my hands, little sister, well now my life is ending at yours. I have always loved you, and will continue to into my next life."

"I love you too, Sarah, why don…"

BOOM!

The explosion was so horrifically deafening. My ears were ringing and none of us could take in what we had just witnessed. I didn't see her arms move or any indication that she was planning to follow through on her plan.

My eyes stung with sadness, but also in a strange way of pride. Yes, she had perpetrated the most heinous ~nd despicable acts, but she was also the one to put an ◝ to them.

◝My phone vibrated into life causing me to shriek ⸂arah's name flashed up onto the screen.

⸂lo?" a voice warbled on loud speaker.

⸂ny!" Angus exclaimed, grabbing the phone ⸂king hand.

The End

About the Author

Jan McPeake was originally born and raised in Drum-chapel, Glasgow, however, she has lived in Milngavie, Glasgow, for the past 10 years with her husband and young son.

She has been writing since she was 11 years old, when one of her poems won at a local poetry competition. This opened her eyes and heart to her true calling in life - disappearing into another world between pen and paper.

Although Jan has continued through her life with a career in Account Management, she has never stopped her true passion - writing. She even squeezes in time to bake, much to the delight of her friends and family (not appreciated the same by their expanding waistlines!).

Jan is an advocate for kindness whilst generating support and fundraising for many charities close to her heart.